T0194047

DANGEROUS LEGACY

THE SECOND SON

C. S. ARNOLD

DANGEROUS LEGACY
THE SECOND SON

iUniverse books may be ordered through booksellers or by contacting:

iUniverse
1663 Liberty Drive
Bloomington, IN 47403
www.iuniverse.com
1-800-Authors (1-800-288-4677)

ISBN: 978-1-5320-7011-2 (sc)
ISBN: 978-1-5320-7009-9 (hc)
ISBN: 978-1-5320-7010-5 (e)

Library of Congress Control Number: 2019903423

Print information available on the last page.

iUniverse rev. date: 03/25/2019

To my husband. Through the years he has been my best friend and my inspiration. Without his encouragement and support, I would never have thought I could do this.

ACKNOWLEDGMENTS

Thank you to the editors.
Your comments were a learning experience.

PROLOGUE
1914

C ount Zurowski looked around at those at his table. He was a fortunate man. His countess had given him a son, his heir. Now they were expecting their second child, which would keep the title further away from his brother and the chance he would ever inherit. All was well. The count had a talisman to protect his future. He wasn't superstitious, but it had brought good fortune to the Zurowskis down through the years.

The count sat at one end of the table with the countess at the other end. To his right sat his mother, the dowager countess, along with Józef, his brother, and an unmarried older sister. To his left sat a widowed sister and the village priest and his nephew. The priest's nephew would never have been invited to such a dinner, but he was a visiting relative. The candlelight did nothing to soften the unfortunate features of the young man's face.

"A toast to the countess on her birthday," said the count. He lifted his glass, and they all turned to her. "And in her honor, I will show the jeweled crucifix."

Reverently, he lifted an object from a velvet-lined box. The object seemed to catch fire and glistened, throwing splinters of color on the faces of those at the table. All eyes were on the golden crucifix embedded with jewels and a throbbing carving of the crucified Christ.

Awe and reverence registered on seven of the faces. Greed gleamed in the eyes of the eighth.

The dinner was over. Good nights were said; guests were not returning to their homes that night, so they were shown to their rooms, and the family retired for the evening.

In the morning, the box that held the jeweled crucifix was empty. The talisman was gone.

CHAPTER ONE
1939

———————————— ❧❧ ————————————

S tefan Zurowski was going back home. Back to Domani z Camin, the "House of the Rock," his ancestral home that had bred and housed Zurowskis for centuries. The place was nestled in the Masurian Lake District of Poland, a valley as old as time, with lakes sparkling and clear from as far back as the postglacial age. It was what he loved—the land, the workers in the fields, even the very stones in the edifice.

His university days were past, and he'd been knocking around in Warsaw without much purpose, helping a bit with preparations for the threatening German invasion. But he wanted to help protect their estate and its people, and now his father was summoning him home. This was an unusual call, and his heart soared with the thought that he had been called home to stay.

It was unusual that no one had met him at the train station, but he didn't mind the walk through his beloved countryside. The castle came into view just over a small rise; it was strange that the dogs didn't signal his arrival.

Things weren't right. As he neared, the scene was all wrong. No horses in the distant pastures, no workers in the fields, and it was too quiet.

Bodies became visible as he approached the drawbridge. Workers whom he had known lay slaughtered, limbs twisted at all angles. It was clear they had fallen from blows by bayonets and machetes.

A shadow crossed the door's threshold and then materialized into flesh. Instinctively, Stefan defended himself with a nearby rock. He felt the man's skull crush beneath the blow.

Stefan entered the house and took in the ravaged scene left by the marauders—torn tapestries, slashed paintings. He gripped the doorjamb as the scene in the study at Domani z Camin blurred before his eyes. The shock hit him in the pit of this stomach taking his breath.

Blinking his eyes and breathing deeply, he forced the room back into its normal proportions. The dark paneling and the heavy furniture had always been the same in this room. Only the two figures slumped over the desk weren't as usual; the contrast was jarring.

Konrad, his older brother, rested his head on the desk, his neck at a fatally twisted angle. Blood pooled like a halo around his dark blond hair, but it was beginning to congeal, black and thick.

His father, Count Zurowski, had been seated beside Konrad at the desk, and his head was propped on his limp arm, which was draped over a small pile of books. A tiny rivulet of blood trickled from a wound close to his temple and down the bound edges of the thin volumes and puddled on the clean white pages of the open estate ledger. Stefan stood transfixed at the sight of his father's face; he thought he saw the count's eyelids flutter. Then the faded gray eyes opened; they looked nearly white now, as though the color was draining out. He was looking straight at Stefan. His mouth moved soundlessly.

Stefan crossed the room and knelt by the desk, his ear close to his father's mouth.

"Stefan, find Frederic." Frederic had been the count's estate business manager since before Stefan was born. The count may have made all the decisions, but it was Frederic who executed them. "He will tell you why I sent for you to come home." His voice was a whisper. A thin trickle of blood oozed from the corner of his slack mouth. "Stefan, Frederic went to"—a weak cough interrupted his labored message, but the word came through clearly "--Danzig. You must hurry."

These were the last words Count Zurowski spoke to Stefan, his son, or to anyone else on this earth.

In a panic, he took the stairs to the nursery. Lena, his stepmother, had been shot, and tiny Hanna lay beneath her. They were both beyond his help. Lena had died in the nursery, her body protecting the baby. He had covered their bodies with blankets from the crib.

Anne, his sister. He must find Anne. He staggered down the stairs and out onto the terraced gardens. Anne lay on the ground, rose petals stuck to her naked body with her own blood. Treads from heavy boots marked her white skin, black sketches, rain-diluted, and streaked. That she had been raped was obvious. Stefan covered her with his jacket as he knelt beside her. He held her against him, tears streaming down his face. She was still beautiful in death.

He must bury Anne; he couldn't leave her to the elements. He went to the stables where the tools were kept—the horses were gone. He picked up a heavy spade.

A soldier appeared, and Stefan stepped quickly back inside the doorway. The man approached the stables, and Stefan raised his spade. As the soldier entered, Stefan came up behind him and smashed the heavy end of the tool into his skull.

There would be no time to bury his family, not even Anne. He could hear the rumble of vehicles in the distance. So he could not be spotted, he ran back into the castle and escaped through a window farthest away from the oncoming patrol. They would see their dead comrades and be on the lookout for the one who had killed them. His coat still covered Anne. They'd notice that. He must be gone. The count had said to hurry.

And Stefan Zurowski went to search for Frederic.

For past generations, Zurowski sons had carefully obeyed the orders of their fathers; tradition was strong and even more binding in death.

It was not out of any affection for his father that Stefan felt obligated to find Frederic, but the sense of responsibility was heavy upon him. His family was destroyed, his house and lands were out of his control, and he was the last living Zurowski of the royal House of Zurowski. He was now Count Zurowski.

Anne's blood clung to his shirt. He wretched violently, vomit erupting from deep within him. He straightened, panting, and held his face up to the cool dampness of the air.

Dazed, he began his journey from his ancestral home in northeast Poland toward the west. Stefan knew that the fastest way would be through Warsaw. The horses were gone; he would again be on foot.

Without noting his footsteps, he made the familiar trip from his village to Warsaw and was not conscious of the little puffs of dust his shoes kicked up as he walked in the dry, rutted road. Neither did he feel the warmth of the morning sun on his shoulders.

Sadness rode on his back as he put more distance between him and his home. Why did they have to kill his entire family and household staff? They could have confiscated what they wanted without the murderous rage that was evident. Whether they had been part of the group of soldiers being mustered for Poland's defense or a rogue unit on its own, Stefan might never know.

He began to feel like an exile, never again to roam the hills or sail and fish in the myriad lakes born in postglacial antiquity. He plodded on until his thoughts changed from where he had been to where he had to go: to Warsaw and then on to Danzig.

When he had left Warsaw for Domani z Camin, the main thoroughfare and all smaller ones leading in and out of the city had been crowded. Columns of marching soldiers used the roads, side by side with peasants riding in wooden carts or walking with long, determined strides. Cars shared the highways with pedestrians. They were one in purpose. Warsaw, their capital, must be defended because Hitler was determined to take their country.

Some people, especially the elderly, were on the same roads but traveling away from Warsaw. To them, the most important task was the defense of the villages and their lands.

He remembered when he and Konrad had agreed that the land must be defended. He had wanted to stay at Domani z Camin, his family estate, but he could not.

It was May 1939, and he was graduated from the university in Warsaw, and he had gone back home. All the years he was away, he looked forward to returning home to stay. It was not enough to be home only at holidays.

Frederic had met him at the front entrance and embraced him. "Stefan, so good to have you home."

"Where is everyone?" Stefan asked as he looked around.

"Countess Zurowski, the baby, and Anne are visiting the Janinskis this morning but will be home by lunch. Anne will be sorry she was not here when you arrived," Frederic said.

"I'm looking forward to seeing her." Stefan smiled suddenly as he thought how her eyes would shine, and she would run to meet him. She must be sixteen now.

"Your father asked that you come to the study when you arrived. Konrad is with him." He led the way down a corridor that was wide and dim. The high ceilings kept the temperature cool. It had been warm in Warsaw; the forecast was for a long, dry summer.

The study was paneled with intricately carved dark wood—smoke from thousands of candles over the centuries had seasoned and darkened the wood. Now the study was lit by electricity, but even much of that light was absorbed by the dark wood, heavy folds of draperies, and massive furniture.

Cheerful rays of light emanated from the lamps but disappeared into the deep red of the upholstered chairs.

"What is the news from Warsaw, Stefan?" asked Count Zurowski. There was no pretense of being glad to see his son.

"Is the army mobilizing?" Konrad asked.

Stefan showed no emotion as he answered his father and older brother. "There is nothing definite. The rumors are becoming more frequent and serious. The armies aren't mobilized yet, but there is a lot being done secretly."

"Are you working for Poland in these underground operations?" the count asked pointedly.

Stefan hedged. "Sir, I've not had much time, but I'm involved slightly."

"Stefan has received honors from the university, and I imagine his studies took a great deal of his time." It was Frederic, again, as always, the cushion between the count and his second son.

"Yes," the count nodded absently, without a word of congratulations.

"You received honors, Stefan?" Konrad extended his hand in a friendly overture. "Good for you. Now that you are back, we will find something for you to do. Perhaps we can plan a defense for Domani z Camin in case of future attack."

Stefan was about to agree when the count waved away the suggestion as if it were no more than prattle.

The count was past seventy, but his tall, straight figure still commanded respect. His eyes were steel blue and sharp.

"No, Konrad. Now that Stefan is finished at the university, he will probably wish to return to Warsaw and become more involved with war defense preparations." The count made such involvement sound distasteful. "Soon, something will come about, I'm sure."

"But, Father, shouldn't Domani z Camin be protected as well as Warsaw?" Konrad exclaimed.

"My son, it will be. Surely, we can continue to protect our land, even with Stefan gone."

Stefan felt the sharp edge in the count's words, cutting his remaining ties to the place he loved. He had been home fifteen minutes and was being forced to leave.

"The count is right, Konrad. I can help Domani z Camin by working in Warsaw," Stefan said. He would not let either know how deep the thrust had gone.

Stefan's spirit cried out to stay, to walk through the fields, and to greet his neighbors and the workers of the fields. The air was different here, exhilarating, reviving. His body brought his soaring spirit into subjection.

"The train leaves our village in twenty minutes, and I can just make the station." Stefan walked from the study with Frederic at his back.

"I'll drive you, Stefan," Frederic offered. He put his cap on his head and opened the front door.

Stefan's luggage was still in the large entrance hall. Stefan and Frederic carried it to the car.

"I'm sorry, Stefan." Frederic's words sounded painful. He had been apologizing to Stefan for his family since Stefan was a boy. "There is nothing more I can do."

"I know, I know." He laid his hand on the older man's shoulder. "You have done your best."

They didn't exchange any more words until Stefan was on the train. From the open window in his compartment, Stefan could see that Frederic's face suddenly looked crumpled with age.

"Take care of yourself, Stefan. Write to us of the news from Warsaw," Frederic called as the train pulled away. "Don't forget that God will take care of you. Trust him."

Frederic had been Stefan's spiritual mentor, discipling him in the ways of the Lord. Frederic had led Stefan into the knowledge that Jesus Christ could be his intimate friend, a direct contact to a loving heavenly Father. Frederic and Stefan attended a small protestant Bible study when it was possible, where they found deeper understanding in the Holy Bible. This was another secret that the two shared. Frederic would have been dismissed had the count known. He would have considered it to be a weakening influence. Stefan knew that he could not have survived over the years without his walk with the Lord. Now his faith was what held him together.

Stefan forced a smile and waved. He couldn't trust his voice. He was leaving his beloved Domani z Camin—he'd been asked to leave his home! He had not even seen Anne, but Frederic would explain to her.

When he'd gotten back to Warsaw, he'd rented a flat on Czacki Street, not too far from the Church of the Holy Spirit. That had been May, nearly four months ago. An eternity, really.

Things were different now. He was leaving Domani z Camin again, but there was no train journey this time. All trains had been militarized; they carried soldiers into Warsaw, but there was not even room for all of them.

As Stefan stumbled past a railway station in a village halfway to Warsaw, he saw a group of old men gathered around a wireless. The pain and sorrow of the ages was creased in their faces.

Bewildered. Stefan stopped and looked at them. Were they feeling his loss at Domani z Camin? No, they could not have heard of that yet. But the time would come when they'd learn of the ravage at Domani z Camin, and they would mourn the loss.

"It has happened," an aged peasant whispered sadly. He wiped his dry, cracked hand across the front of his soiled shirt.

"What?" Stefan asked. He had not heard the man clearly; his brain was numbed from the scene he had left at his home.

"Hitler is bombing Danzig and Warsaw! And there was not even a declaration of war!" The man shook his head angrily and walked slowly toward an old woman. She seemed anxious and nervously clutched at a scarf tied around her gray head.

Stefan felt detached. The horror of war had started for Poland, and he could not feel anything. His heart had already been torn out as he had stumbled through the devastation at Domani z Camin.

By the time he got to Warsaw, it had rained. Black smoke rose from the city like a funeral pyre. The Nazi artillery and aerial bombs had lit the blaze in their first attack. The acrid odor from the fire bit into his nostrils and stung his eyes as he approached the city. The Warsaw that he knew, where he had worked to help with fortifications when his father's summons had come, was gone.

The attack had come on September 1, 1939. Funny, Stefan thought, September 1 was also his birthday. Strange that he would recall his birth date now, but he would have given the twenty-five years of his life to have spared Warsaw this.

Before he had left Warsaw for his home at the end of August, there had been rumors that the Nazis were very close to doing something. Stefan knew that his father had been more concerned with the raiding attacks of the Russians on the east. They weren't getting the publicity that Hitler was enjoying, but their advances were real. It was the Red Army that had devastated Zurowski Castle, the Domani z Camin, and murdered family and servants, although the news had mentioned that they were becoming Poland's ally.

Cautiously entering the ravaged city, Stefan felt rather than saw the destruction of familiar landmarks. At night, it would be dangerously easy to lose one's way amid the uncharted ruins of the streets.

He went to where he calculated Jerusalem Street to be at the center of the city and found two towers of twisted metal that proved to him that he knew where he was. These towers, rising like blackened skeletons toward the smoke-darkened sky, were all that was left of the once luxurious railroad station. When he had left Warsaw, the station was crowded with foreigners, waiting for special trains to take them to safety. Transportation to Danzig likely would be difficult, and he would have to walk the 260 kilometers from Warsaw to his destination. His aloneness stabbed him like a cold steel blade.

Stefan found the Aleje Ujazdowskie. He had loved to walk along this boulevard graced with trees and beautiful buildings as it stretched from the Belvedere Palace at one end to the heart of the city at the other. Streets leading to the boulevard were now cluttered with burning rubble.

The American embassy had been owned by friends of his father, the Czartoryskis. It was now gutted by flames. Although blackened by fire, the shield of the United States of America, fastened to the side of the house that faced the boulevard, was clearly visible from the street. The eagle on the United States shield looked on in fierceness at the devastation wrought upon another country that proudly displayed the eagle as its own symbol.

The Citadel was gone; so was the Bristol Hotel. The new modern apartment buildings had also been leveled. Stefan remembered attending a dance at the Blue Palace, the home of Count Zamoski. Its architectural splendor, as well as its exquisite interior furnishings, was reduced to a mass of smoking ruins by Nazi Germany.

Surely some buildings had been saved. Stefan searched out the section of town where he knew there were many churches. It would comfort him to see them.

They were gone! His heart sank.

He had loved the baroque Dominican Church since he was a boy. He remembered peeking into the heavy front doors and watching the white-robed friars pushing mops over the black and white tiles of the floor. It always brought to mind live pieces on a giant chessboard.

One Easter he had gone with Frederic to a special Mass at the Church of the Holy Spirit. Stefan had liked the stark simplicity of the black and white tiles of the Dominican Church, so the carvings and gilded monuments of the Church of the Holy Spirit had seemed frivolous and gay. Outside, the streets were sloping from Freta Street gently to the Vistula River, where they used to pass the Church of the Nuns of the Holy Sacrament. Now there were just fragments of building materials. Nothing was left of the red-roofed convent that had been alongside that church. He could recall vividly the black-clothed nuns going in and out. Only lifeless, blackened stone and wood remained.

It was nearing twilight. Stefan felt an aversion to spending the night in this shapeless, unfamiliar place. His flat had been on the second floor of the apartment building; now only the ravaged ruins of the ground floor remained.

On the outskirts of town, as he went north and a little west toward Danzig, Stefan encountered a peasant. The old man was riding in a heavy wooden cart drawn by a horse.

"Sir, may I have a ride?" Stefan asked. He climbed aboard when the man nodded his assent.

As Stefan lay back in the cart, resting his head on the rough side boards, he was glad for the old car tires that had been put on its wheels. This was the only innovation to the cart from when this old man's father had used it, but the rubber helped cushion the bumps.

Even more weary from his emotions of the day than the long trek he had made on foot from his home in the valley northeast of Warsaw, he fell asleep. This sleep was deep and dreamless—an escape from the horror of his present reality.

The trip by cart took most of the next two days. Stefan learned that the old peasant with gnarled hands had lost everything but his horse and the cart. Stefan supposed that was why the man had refused his offer to drive the cart. Holding onto the reins must have helped him keep a grasp on reality. The old man said his name was Kacper, but other than that, they said very little to one another.

Stefan was left with the clothes on his back and an empty title. As the second son of Count Zurowski, he had never expected to inherit the ancient castle and lands of his family. Now, he would not allow anything to keep him from regaining his inheritance when this conflict was over. The catastrophe that had made him Count Zurowski had only postponed his claiming the things that gave the title substance.

He did have something to do. The dying request of his father that he go to Danzig and find Frederic gave him a purpose. Stefan's mother had died giving him life, and after his father had ordered that a nurse be found for the tiny boy, Count Zurowski rarely gave Stefan any notice. It was through

Frederic that Stefan received his monthly allowance and any instructions his father had for him.

Count Zurowski considered only his first son and heir as necessary to him. Stefan's older brother was given the name Konrad Piast Zurowski, the same name his father bore and his father before him. It was a time-honored name handed down through the Zurowski family since 1226. It was their claim to royalty.

Stefan had been more than a little surprised when Frederic had been instructed to enroll him in the same university in Warsaw from which his brother Konrad had graduated. Even more unexpected was that his father had specifically chosen his course of study. His studies would give him knowledge of forestry, lumbering, and the management of the business procedures of such large industries.

It was true that some of their wealth came from their forests, but mainly it was their agricultural product. Never had Stefan been included in any family business. Now he had hope.

He had waited for some explanation as to why he was to be educated thus, but none was forthcoming. He enjoyed the next few years of school, but not one word did he hear from his father except through Frederic. Occasionally, there was a short, stiff note from his stepmother, but his father's second wife, Lena, only had time for the two daughters she had borne the count. Anne was now sixteen, and there was a newborn infant, tiny Hanna.

The letters he longed for were from Anne, his beautiful stepsister. She crowded the pages full of people, little drawings, and incidents from home that helped to dispel his loneliness. He was born to Zurowski Castle and the land. He felt alien anywhere else. The friends he had made at the university could not touch his deep need. His sister supplied the lifeblood from home. His underlying strength came from his faith.

He jerked upright, bringing himself into the present. He didn't want to think of Anne. He could not remember her without being tormented by the picture of her mangled body and pale blonde hair making a pillow for her still, white face. He didn't want to think of Lena and tiny Hanna—Hanna, who would never have a chance to really live.

It was dusk, and Malbork Castle came into view. The dimness of twilight added to the feeling he had of going back into the Middle Ages. Stefan knew that passing through those gates would be like stepping back in time—far back to a time before this present loss.

The castle had been built beside the Nogat River. He knew that water barriers had served as important defenses for castles of this time period. The brick walls and the round brick gateways capped by steep conical roofs were reflected in the water. The buildings behind the walls were mirrored as dark shapes. These black images had swallowed up the details of the structures that had been so carefully erected by the thirteenth-century builders.

The reflections didn't show the arches and the small single windows in the walls. The black building in the water did not boast the short, square towers with window groupings and modest spires. The reflected castle was primitive German Romanesque, devoid of the beginnings of Gothic ancestry shown on its counterpart above.

The peasant driver turned the horse onto the lane leading toward the castle itself.

Stefan panicked. He could not go to the castle. Zurowski Castle was almost the twin of Malbork. In his mind, he was walking through the courtyard at Domani z Camin. He could see the knight's hall with the arch-braced roof. Scenes of the horror he had experienced so recently involving his own family flashed before his eyes. He felt his own helplessness and bereavement mingled with the cry of outrage from his ancestors. The burning pain intensified with the realization of his irreplaceable loss. Not only his roots but those of his forefathers had been twisted and torn from the rich Polish soil. The raw nerves lay exposed to the elements.

He didn't even notice the gash in his leg caused by a metal support as he jumped from the wagon. In blind hysteria, he ran and ran. Fleeing the intolerable acts of the present, he was driven even harder by the death scream of his past.

Stefan knew the peasant had watched him lunge from the cart and heard his cry of fear. He knew the agony he felt as he stared at Malbork Castle could be read in his face.

Darkness was falling fast. Stefan watched as the old peasant and his horse headed for the safety of the castle walls of Malbork.

Gone! It was all swept away. The sight of Malbork Castle disgorged his suppressed memories. A torrent of emotion tore through his body.

Faster, faster. Now the sound of his running feet became a pounding in his head. The blood pulsated in his brain until the throbbing threatened to explode his skull.

Stefan collapsed, facedown, and stretched full length on the bare earth, his body racked with sobs. The loose soil from the road caked with the sweat on his face. The fine hairs of his nostrils became coated with dust as his starving lungs sucked greedily for air. He prayed desperately for strength.

He grieved deeply. Waves of sorrow washed over him—regret for his family, for Poland. He was sorry for beautiful Anne. With tender, helpless pity, he mourned for Anne, Lena, and little Hanna.

Drained of emotion, Stefan never knew when he fell asleep. He slept on the bare ground, a man of dust against the dust of earth. All material elements had been stripped away. His cover was an overhanging tree branch, and then the closest thing was a dome of night's cloth held in place by shiny pins of light.

Stefan felt the warmth of the fingers of the morning sun as they slipped through the overhanging branches onto his cold body.

He awoke and slowly got up. He rested his hands on the small of his back as he gently stretched his chest upward. His body was stiff. There was a dull throb in his head, and his eyes burned. His swollen lips had cracked, and he felt their roughness with his tongue. The blood had dried from the gash on his leg.

The river was invitingly near. Kneeling on the bank, he cupped his hands and splashed water over his face and neck. The cool water caused bumps to prickle over his face and neck. He took out his handkerchief and wiped his face while he scanned the road in the direction he would take.

If he walked fast, he should reach Danzig by nightfall. He tucked in his shirt and tightened his belt. There was nothing he could do about the pangs in his stomach, reminding him of his hunger. He had eaten sparingly of the bread and cheese the old man had offered him along the way. His sack of provisions had been adequate for one but not two.

The terrain ahead was flat and broad. The tree under which he had slept was the only one in sight. As he began walking north toward Danzig, he thought dispassionately of the night before. His capacity for feeling emotion had died, leaving him empty.

It was true that Malbork Castle looked like their own Zurowski Castle—and with good reason. Both had been built in the thirteenth century. The bridge at Domani z Camin that spanned the moat was still in use and was the only entrance to the complex. The courtyard, smooth and level, rolled gently back to the main entrance to the castle and then to the large entrance hall, the wide stairs, the echoing great hall, and the four separate wings that had housed so many Zurowskis for so many decades. Whether the family was large or small, there were always empty rooms and space to spare. Domani z Camin, house of the rock, had been expected to last forever. Perhaps it would last for all eternity, but it no longer housed Zurowskis.

It was more than the similar style of architecture that bound Malbork Castle with Domani z Camin. Stefan mulled over the histories of both as he walked toward Danzig—and Frederic.

The early enemies of the Polish were the Prussians. The German Knights of the Teutonic Order had been invited by Konrad, Piast Duke of Mazowsze, to help the Knights of the Teutonic Order undertake missionary work among the Prussians on the northeastern borders of Poland. How was Poland to know she was inviting in a group that was to become a far greater threat than the Prussians? The Knights of the Teutonic Order lived and headquartered in Malbork Castle. Stefan remembered Frederic telling him the history—that the Teutonic knights settled and extended their authority along the Baltic Coast. Later, the Teutonic knights merged with an aggressive missionary order called the Knights of the Sword.

The ascendancy of the Zurowski family began with their part in the Polish-Lithuanian victory over the combined forces of the German knights at Grunwald. When, in defeat, the grand master of the Teutonic Order himself surrendered and paid homage to the king of Poland, the king honored a few of the valiant warriors; Konrad Zurowski was one of the most zealous patriots.

The king of Poland bestowed upon him a captured estate, and Konrad Zurowski took the name of the king to add to his own: the first Count Konrad Piast Zurowski came into being. Generation after generation of descendants gave the revered name Piast to the firstborn son.

Stefan knew that from the Battle of Grunwald on, the Teutonic Order survived only as a weak religious organization. He loved to hear this story of when his family had earned their land. Ever since, it had been theirs to tend and love, and each successive generation had done this to varying degrees.

The part of the story he loved best might have been only a legend, but when he was a lad, he'd begged Frederic over and over to tell it to him again. It was a story of knights, wars, and a priceless treasure.

Frederic loved the story too and told it to Stefan many times in hushed, mysterious tones. Again, in his mind Stefan pictured Frederic's face as he would begin to tell the much-loved tale. He never seemed to hurry, yet his efficient movements accomplished everything he undertook, on time and well.

The simple chore of polishing the lenses in his round steel-rimmed glasses was performed as thoroughly as the year-end estate reports for the count. With his soft white handkerchief, he methodically cleaned each lens in a careful circular motion until the glass sparkled. When he put his spectacles back on, his high, scholarly forehead would crease as though he were reaching back into his thoughts for the age-old remembrance. A smile would come on his face, accompanied by a twinkle in his eye.

"Once upon a time, it was the time of the Reformation." The story always began the same way, although the content varied a little with each telling.

As Stefan walked to Danzig, he relived the words of the story. It was a safe subject to dwell upon as he made his way to the city.

The characters in the story were always the same, too. There would be Albrecht of Ansback, the last grand master of the German Knights of the Teutonic Order, the then-current Count Zurowski, and an old priest of the Teutonic Order.

The grand master disbanded the order and made their possessions and lands into a hereditary fief for his own family. The old priest within the order had a little band of followers who bravely opposed the grand master. But the priest's handful of friends were killed, and he was forced to flee for his life. In doing so, the priest found refuge at Domani z Camin, Count Zurowski's castle. The count was a very brave and devout Catholic.

For months the grand master searched the forests and watched the castle, but he was finally forced to admit defeat and abandon the hunt.

The priest was a very old man and soon died. He was buried in the Zurowski family plot, but before his death, he gave to the count a jeweled crucifix. Worth a king's ransom, the crucifix had been brought into Poland by the first Teutonic Knights as a sign of authority from the pope himself. Stefan loved the story. Frederic's vivid description of the jeweled crucifix was burned into his brain. A look of love and reverence would cover Frederic's face, and the detailed account of how the cross looked never varied.

The crucifix, he had said, was eight inches tall. The golden cross was outlined in intricate gold filigree. The figure of the crucified Christ was skillfully carved from warm, glowing ivory and mounted on the face of the cross. Each thorn, amid emerald leaves encircling the crown on his head, was a black pearl, and the wounds on his body were rubies. The blood drops from the wounds were tiny rubies. The back of the crucifix was encrusted with precious jewels, and the edges of the cross were set with rubies matching the blood drops on the ivory figure.

On his deathbed, the priest said that he wished to atone for the wrong the knights had done to Poland. He wanted the count, as a descendant of the patriot Zurowski at Grunwald, to have the crucifix for the wrongs perpetrated against the Polish people. The priest's anger was hot against the grand master for abandoning religious endeavors. His final reason for giving the count the valuable crucifix was that the Polish gentry were strongly against the Protestant influence making itself felt at the time, threatening a schism.

Once, when Stefan was ten years old, he had drawn a picture of the crucifix, carefully painting in the colors of the jewels. It was to be a Christmas present for his father.

Stefan burst with eagerness to give his gift to the count; he was sure that he had found a way to gain his father's favor. It was true that his father never said anything about the crucifix, but the count was a busy man. He never had time for Stefan.

Christmas Eve was a lovely winter's day, and Stefan was the first to see the evening star. The sighting of the star signaled the beginning of their traditional wigilia supper on Christmas Eve, and then gathering around the decorated tree and exchanging of gifts. Stefan was certain this would be the day when his father finally noticed him. The memory of the story of the crucifix would soften the count, and he would think fondly of the one reminding him of the legend of the family treasure. His hands trembled as he extended his gift to the count. A nervous smile tugged at the corners of his mouth.

The count noted his younger son's excited behavior as he carefully removed the wrapping and opened the gift. The blood drained from the count's face and his lips were drawn into a tight, hard line. His cold eyes shot splinters of ice in Stefan's direction.

"You wicked, ungrateful boy! How dare you mock me! Never, never give me a"—his mouth twisted— "*gift* again."

Stefan felt his father's wide hand hard across the side of his face. The blow struck his heart like a dagger.

So, at the age of ten, Stefan completely lost his father. It was on that Christmas Eve that the count died in Stefan's mind. This was the only way the boy could bear the hurt. Never was the story of the crucifix mentioned again by either Frederic or Stefan. A part of his childhood was extinguished.

Frederic was there. He comforted Stefan as best he could and became the go-between for father and son. The count never again found an occasion for conversation with Stefan. It was Frederic, always, as a father substitute.

After so many years of silence, Stefan felt no bitterness. His faith had allowed him to experience forgiveness for his father when he turned his life over to God. The man had been dead these many years. Only his shadow had been at Domani z Camin directing, urging, manipulating.

It was more than obedience and curiosity that made Stefan want to see Frederic. In this time of personal crisis, he was drawn to him. Now in Poland's trouble, Stefan felt a renewed kinship to him. The feeling lay dormant, but now it surfaced, urging him on.

The first part of Danzig that Stefan saw lay in ruins. But he had reached his saturation point. The horror no longer registered on his senses. Pungent odors met his nostrils and tears sprang to his eyes. The response was purely physical; no emotion was involved.

He saw a building that a bomb had hit squarely, leaving only two walls that met in a corner on the north side. He couldn't recall the identity of this building. Stefan sat down and leaned his back against the cold bricks. He had reached Danzig, but daylight was almost gone, and it would be dangerous to try to find his way in the dark. There were no familiar landmarks in the maze of brick and splintered beams. He had about two hundred zloty in his pocket, but there was no place to buy food tonight. He might be dead in the morning; if not, he would look for Frederic and try to find a place to buy food.

He went to sleep. The dream came in gently at first. His whole family was gathered around a Christmas tree, and his father was smiling at him, thanking him for the lovely picture he had drawn for him. Stefan could feel warmth from his father's glow of pleasure.

Then, one by one, the faces of the people changed, appearing as he had seen them in death. The holiday scene changed into a nightmare. He relived finding them, one by one.

Again, he came upon Anne. The harsh cry of anguish brought him wide awake. He had checked the stables and realized that most of the outside servants were gone, along with the horses. Then, walking back to the house through the garden, he had found her.

Sweet little Anne, with the pale-golden hair and angelic face. Visions of his sister's mangled body rent his thoughts. Her face had been left untouched, leaving her looking like a broken Dresden doll. Raped and beaten; blood pooled around her and her torn clothing. A soldier had dragged her onto the formal terraces behind the main house where he violated her and stamped out her life with his heavy boots.

Stefan had found her discarded body among the rose garden. It had rained that morning at Domani z Camin. Drops of rain clung to the white petals of the rose lying beside her head; there were drops of rain on her cheek. Tears had blurred his eyes, and the white rose and her cheek became one. Her body and the rose bushes around her had been trampled by steel-studded boots, and only her face and the full-bloomed rose beside her remained undamaged.

His face was damp with sweat. The cool night breeze dried it, but the visions didn't disappear with the beads of perspiration. The ache in his head was worse, his eyes burned, and his throat was dry. He huddled against the wall for warmth and didn't doze off again until nearly dawn.

CHAPTER TWO

───────────────⬥───────────────

F rederic had been searching for Stefan. Józef Zurowski, the count's brother, had gone to a great deal of trouble to send for him. Frederic would take care of the details if he could find Stefan.

The *Baltic Queen* left port tonight, and if Stefan wasn't on it, then the entire ship's voyage would be in vain. He had only one day left to search again for Stefan. So much could go wrong. He knew if Stefan had gotten the message, he would have gone home, and once there, the count would have sent him to Danzig post haste. Frederic waited there with signed documents for the count's attorney and last-minute loose ends that needed attention.

Frederic had to assume that Stefan had the message and was on his way to Danzig. He would not even entertain the possibility that he could have become a war casualty.

If Frederic found Stefan, it might be for the last time. He may, in fact, have seen him for the last time anyway. The war was escalating. New reports of the areas hit came in every hour. Warsaw had been hit as hard as Danzig. Stefan would have to come straight through the city.

The German attack on the Westerplatte had been thorough too. Enemy flags flew from several high places to signal mastery. An oil depot was still in flames. A crane standing against the horizon was like an arm extended in a plea for help.

Frederic filed away his fears, straightened his shoulders, and quietly left the house. Threads of light were just beginning to show in the sky, like white ravels on a black coat. He would need to search for Stefan during every available minute of daylight.

Too, Stefan would have news of Domani z Camin. Concern for the ones he had left behind had been causing Frederic much unrest.

He stood on the front steps of the tall, narrow house and thoughtfully rubbed his palms together. He had searched for Stefan in the queue lines at food shops, before and after the bombing. He searched the cafes too. If Stefan were in Danzig, he would have to eat. In these past few days, it was necessary to stand in long lines to buy food. If you got there early enough and so weren't too far back in the line, you would be able to buy enough to keep you alive for one more day.

Frederic knew his sister Kasia had been storing up food for months in fear of the rumors. Still, the milk and eggs would not keep for an extended time, and on some days, he watched her leave early to be toward the front of the line. On this day, Frederic's faith wavered a little, but he knew that Kasia had prayed for Stefan's safety, and she told him they had a sign.

"If our house had been destroyed, then Stefan would not have had a place to come when he arrived in Danzig," she reasoned. "God takes care of his own little ones."

Kasia's husband had been dead for many years, and they'd had no children. He had left her a small income, but when Frederic asked her to move back into the house where they had grown up as children, she sold her own home. She stayed in their home while he was working at Domani z Camin, and he came home on vacations and holidays.

When Frederic brought little Stefan home on holidays with him, he watched her encircle him with eager arms, accepting him as she would have one of her own.

No, nothing could happen to Stefan. He was just beginning to have a future. Frederic would find him, and they would have that last day together before Stefan departed from Poland.

Frederic turned his steps to the southern part of Danzig. He had not found Stefan in any of the food lines, so maybe he had not been in Danzig long. Stefan would have entered from the south, so Frederic would begin his search there today. The buildings in that part of the city were skeletons of their former selves, and there would not be too many places for someone to find shelter.

About a block from where he stood, Frederic saw something huddled in the corner, where two brick walls met and made an angle. It might be a bundle of rags, or it might be a person. As he got closer, he could make out a pale face and wheat-shock hair profiled against the rough red of the brick. Then he knew who it was, and he began to run as quickly as he could through the dangerous ground cover of broken bricks, glass, and splintered beams.

He knelt beside the sleeping figure and put his hand on his shoulder.

"Stefan." It was a statement.

He watched Stefan come awake. Shakily, Stefan stood up, and as they embraced, their tears mingled.

A welcoming light sparked in Frederic's eyes, bringing animation to his worry-worn countenance. Straightening his shoulders, he looked like Pilgrim standing tall after his encounter at the Wicket Gate. His burden of the count's message for Stefan had become heavier each day as he sought him in vain. That was over!

"Stefan, how did you find things at Domani z Camin?

"Gone, Frederic, they're all gone! I couldn't even bury Anne." He tried to share the burden of the images he carried, but he couldn't speak. He held tightly to Frederic.

"Come, Stefan. Kasia will be waiting for us."

Under Frederic's cheek, Stefan had felt hot, and his eyes were a little glassy. Frederic felt Stefan's tall frame tremble, and he struggled to help Stefan along. He walked closely to keep the taller man balanced.

By the time they entered Kasia's well-scrubbed kitchen, Stefan was again steady on his feet. Frederic could tell that the cool morning air had braced him and taken some of the flush from his face.

"Stefan, come in, come in. We've been waiting for you!" Kasia greeted him as though there had been no question that he would come.

"Kasia, it's good to be here; good to see you. You knew Frederic would find me." He smiled fondly at her beaming face and hugged her hard.

"No, Stefan, I knew that God would guide Frederic to you. I've been saying prayers for you."

"Ah, Kasia, you don't know how badly I've needed them."

"You can talk later. You will want to wash up, and then both of you can have some breakfast. I was able to get fresh eggs, milk, and some fruit. Another miracle, eh?"

They ate in silence.

"Kasia, I do feel better. Breakfast was very welcome. If I could have some medicine, I think I'd be on my way to good health."

Frederic watched Stefan pick at the fruit on the table and drink more coffee. The scene could have been so natural if it weren't for the task before him.

With his forefinger, Frederic carefully outlined the squares on the blue-and-white checkered tablecloth. Then as the words he wanted to say came together in his mind, he clasped his hands in front of him on the table and looked at Stefan.

"How much did your father tell you when he sent you here?"

"His dying words were 'find Frederic.' Nothing else. I don't think he was even aware of Konrad beside him at the desk."

There were so many questions that Frederic wanted to ask. *How did it all happen? How did they die?* But he had seen the closed look come over Stefan's face. He was familiar with the expression. Even as a little boy, Stefan could not be coaxed to tell a secret he wanted to keep. The hurt had been locked away.

"Stefan, we didn't hear of any bombing west of Warsaw. We thought surely that Domani z Camin would have escaped," Frederic said.

"There wasn't any bombing at home. An invading patrol of the Red Army attacked before I arrived. Just shortly before, I assumed. They had left only two guards, and I was well able to take care of them."

"Everyone was killed? The servants?" Stefan had answered his questions, but there was still so much he had not heard.

"The family is dead. Some of the servants, those in the house, were dead. I had thought perhaps the others had escaped, but it's more likely they were marched to concentration camps. Most of our servants were Jewish. Poor devils would be better off dead." Stefan turned to face Frederic. "There's nothing for us to go back for. The Russian soldiers have posted a government seal on the front door, claiming Domani z Camin as property under the protection of the Russian Army. The warning is explicit: Trespassers will be shot. It's over, Frederic. Generations of Zurowskis living at Domani z Camin has come to an end. I barely had time to get away before the rest of the patrol returned."

Stefan's words rang with unaccustomed authority. Frederic was reminded of the count. He had not noticed the resemblance before. Fleshed out, Stefan would have the look of his father, and all would have recognized it.

"Frederic, tell me now why my father sent me to you. It was the only thing he spoke of as he lay dying."

Frederic looked at Stefan, the man, but in his mind, he was seeing Stefan, the boy. The child had given Frederic's life real meaning with his eager questions, always concerning Domani z Camin, the crops, the tenants.

"Stefan, do you remember the story I told you when you were quite small about the Teutonic Knights and a runaway priest hiding at Domani z Camin?" Frederic began.

"Yes. But what has that to do with now?"

Frederic ignored the question. "Do you remember the part of the story about the jeweled crucifix?"

"Yes, yes, but what of it?" he demanded.

"It's true, Stefan, all of it."

"True?" he echoed blankly. "But it was just a story you heard from the village priest. It was never spoken of at Domani z Camin."

"No, it was never mentioned at the castle," agreed Frederic. "The priest and the treasure are facts."

"But, Frederic, why did I not know?"

"Because before you were born, a few months even before I came to Domani z Camin, the crucifix was stolen."

"Who took it?"

"Ah, Stefan, that is the question that haunted the count for years. The piece is priceless, but there is a legend attached to it that your family believed. The good fortune of the House of Zurowski was assured as long as the jeweled crucifix was in its possession."

"Surely my father didn't believe that! He was hardly superstitious."

"No, not at first. But things began to happen. Let me start at the beginning, on the night the crucifix was stolen. It's fresh in my mind because the count told me the story only recently, when it became necessary." Frederic took a deep breath and then continued.

"It was a family tradition to show the crucifix on special occasions. There was a small dinner party on that night for your mother. It was her birthday, and the count had chosen to show the crucifix in her honor. It was then they also announced they were expecting a second child. That was you, Stefan." Frederic looked at Stefan, who sat very still in his chair. "There were eight in attendance. The count and the countess, of course; the count's two sisters, your aunts; the old countess, your grandmother; and your uncle Józef, your father's younger brother. Also, present were the priest and his young nephew, who was visiting from Krakow."

"But, Frederic, who took the crucifix?"

"That is what each asked. They also asked what would happen if it weren't found."

"And what did happen?" Stefan asked.

"The next morning when the jeweled crucifix was discovered missing, it was not the only thing gone. The priest and his nephew had spent the night in the castle, and the nephew had disappeared."

"So, the priest's nephew took it?"

"So, it was believed at the time. And then unrest started in the household. Józef had always been too ambitious as the second son, and he never had enough to occupy his time. He had been planning to leave for a long time, and he did leave Domani z Camin and Poland that very week. When he left, your grandmother went half mad with grief. Józef had always been her favorite."

"I don't remember her," Stefan interrupted.

"No, she died when you were about two years old. The count blamed all tragedies on the loss of the jeweled crucifix: the loss of his brother, the death of his beloved wife when you were born, and the death of his own mother while you were so young. He forbade any further mention of the crucifix. Consequently, no one ever spoke of it again after that night when it was stolen."

"Was the priest who told you the story the one who was at the dinner party?" Stefan asked.

"Yes, but we had only been discussing legends of this locale, and he told the treasure story as such. I only learned last week that he was actually present at that party," Frederic said, readjusting his glasses carefully.

"Frederic, this is very interesting, but why was my father so intent that I learn these facts now?" Stefan's voice was tinged with impatience.

"Your father finally found out where the crucifix was only a few years ago. Józef had it in America."

"America!" Stefan exclaimed.

Frederic nodded. "Yes, when Józef left Poland, he immigrated to the United States of America. It was known he took a young servant named Jacobson, but it was not known that he had taken the crucifix."

"But how did Father find out?"

"Stefan, that is the point to this situation. Józef wrote your father four years ago and told him that he had the crucifix. He offered to return it under certain conditions."

"What conditions?"

"You must remember, Stefan, that the jeweled crucifix is a powerful bargaining tool. The loss of it had warped the count's thinking. He would agree to anything to get it back. It meant security to him."

"The conditions, Frederic—what were they?"

"You." Frederic examined the bewilderment and hurt on Stefan's face, but when he didn't respond, Frederic continued. "You were to be educated as your brother, Konrad, had been. Then you would be sent to your Uncle Józef in America to become your uncle's heir, and Józef would send the jeweled crucifix to the count. The agreement was made up and signed."

"I was to be given no choice?"

"No. Your father said you were being honored to be the one to restore the treasure to its rightful home. The count said it was your duty to go. It was a matter of the Zurowski family honor."

"Exiled to restore honor!" Stefan's short laugh sounded bitter to Frederic. "Now what? The count is dead."

"But the agreement stands. The jeweled crucifix arrived in Danzig aboard the *Baltic Queen* just before the bombing. It leaves tonight, and you are supposed to be on it to return to your uncle Józef."

"But my father is dead. The crucifix is no longer important to him."

"Your uncle sent the crucifix in good faith. He's expecting you. I must arrange for you to secretly board the *Baltic Queen*. Patrols guard the docks, but tonight a few sailors are to board the ship."

"Frederic, do you have the crucifix?"

"Yes." He left the room and quickly returned with a wooden box, black with age. "Stefan, as the new Count Zurowski, the treasure is yours."

Frederic opened the case. It was a moment of awe. It was exquisitely crafted in gold and jewels. The small Christ figure of ivory seemed to throb with life.

"Ah, Frederic," Stefan said on a breath. "It's magnificent. No wonder my father mourned its loss. No doubt he would have complied with any of Uncle Józef's conditions. He probably felt he was getting off lightly by losing only me."

To Frederic, Stefan's words didn't sound bitter, just matter-of-fact. Frederic did not disclaim them.

"I must, of course, go to America. Frederic, I will return the crucifix to my uncle in exchange for my freedom. This should be honorable for all with the name of Zurowski."

"Now that you have truly decided to go, we've much to do. I want you to go to the docks and familiarize yourself with the area. There are arrangements that I could make only after you arrived here in Danzig."

Frederic took the small case containing the crucifix and returned it to its hiding place. Then he left the house quickly.

CHAPTER THREE

$\sim$3⅗$\sim$

S tefan stood on the wharf and concentrated on the ghost of a shadow on the wet horizon. As if by strength of will, he made the vague shadow take the form of a ship. Squinting his eyes, he could make out another incoming vessel.

Ah, good. The harbor would be busy tonight, and no one would notice just another seaman. Scanning the vessels already harbored, he noted an oil tanker, two freighters, and even the rare sight of a floating grain elevator in the area where the *Baltic Queen* was docked. The *Baltic Queen* had held Stefan's attention for the past hour. Hardly ever was a passenger liner seen in the harbor, and even this passenger-freighter now anchored some distance out was unusual. Frederic had said the ship had been out there for several days, and there were numerous rumors about it around the docks. There was new activity as the tugs started making their way out to the *Queen*. Maybe the vessel would really be brought in. Maybe all he had heard was true.

The morning sun was bright but gathering clouds would bring premature evening with a promise of a dark, murky night. The nighttime would be shrouded in shadow, and men who walked could not be identified.

His own future was covered by a similarly dark veil. Only the first step was dimly lit by a small spot of light, and he was being urged to take it. The next step would plunge him into total darkness. Ignorance of the truth added to the blackness. How much of what he had been told could he believe?

He did know, however, what he had to look back upon. His home, his family, and his friends were gone. They had been suddenly and horribly destroyed. As he had fled his village, the ground seemed to crumble behind him. There was no path back. He was caught! He had no place to return, but the future that opened to him was an unknown quantity. Only one choice was honorable. As the sole survivor of his family in their home country, he must travel to his father's brother in America. To uphold the honor of his family, he must fulfill the agreement between his father and uncle. There was nothing left here for him now—only memories that raged through his subconscious in dreams of anger and horror. The family honor was the only thing the Russian army could not take from him. It was an intangible that even Hitler could not blow out of existence. He would return.

His father had made the agreement for him; his father's death gave Stefan an almost sacred obligation to honor this agreement. Curiosity pricked him too, that his uncle, whom he had never seen, would go to such great lengths to get him to America.

Zurowski lands would be too tempting for the invading army to pass over. Huge fields filled with grain, heavy and ready for harvest, were indeed a prize to an army greedily conquering land to extend their western borders. Swallowing up the present crop, they would look forward to making the land produce as abundantly for them.

Zurowski family lands had been mercifully saved from the partitioning of Poland in 1772. And when Prussia, Austria, and Russia had bullied their way into Poland, claiming huge slices of the land as their own, Domani z Camin had been ignored.

The three countries had been intent only on the large pieces of cake, so the crumbs were left. In the late seventeenth century, Domani z Camin land was only a crumb compared to the neighboring estates. The old, inoffensive count living at Domani z Camin at the time was considered eccentric and allowed to live in peace on his many acres of tangled growth and dense, thick forests.

With the restoring of Poland to an independent republic in 1918, the Count Zurowski of that time took fierce pride in the land again. Perhaps his imagination had caught fire from the cry of freedom on the lips of every Polish patriot. Their motherland could be partitioned out of existence, but the living, vital thing that was Poland would live on in the hearts of its people. When their country was restored to them, the Polish government, which had lain dormant just beneath the surface of the people's captivity, sprang to life.

Zurowski land had flourished with the passing years. The now-cleared virgin land produced, as though in celebration of being set free. The forests were abundant with pine, spruce, and larch. The beginning of the exportation of agricultural products elevated the importance of Domani z Camin even more. Having emerged as one of the leading exporters in their province, the castle and its surrounding hundreds of rich, tillable acres sat like a fat little lamb before a hungry lion. This was certainly not the time spoken of when the lion would merely lay down by the lamb.

Stefan Zurowski was brought rudely out of his thoughts by the sharp jab of an elbow in his side from someone on the edge of a passing crowd.

Although much of Danzig was destroyed, the wharf was intact, but it was crowded, like the entire coastal city. Refugees poured into this free city as a place of safety away from towns fast falling to the Nazi bombing and infantry. True, there was no physical safety here, but the Germans still had not taken complete control of the city. No citizens were allowed to leave Danzig by way of the ships in the harbor. It was a matter of time. Germany wanted Danzig, the Corridor, and Silesia.

This might be just a start.

As Stefan started back toward the house, he noticed that the rain falling on charred and glowing timbers caused steam to rise. The odor of things smoldering lingered in the air.

A little lad sat in what likely had been the bedroom of his home. Clothes, dirty and ragged, hung on his bony shoulders, and he squatted on thin, spindly legs beside the bed frame. The burned frame stood there, uncovered and obscene.

Stefan walked toward the boy, but his eyes widened in fear, and he ran away, whimpering.

"No, wait ..." Stefan called to him and held out his hand, palm up, in supplication.

The small lad didn't stop.

He knew how alone the boy felt. Very early this morning, he had awakened to a hand gently shaking his shoulder. His first reaction had been to pull away and run.

Frederic had told Stefan only part of the reason the count had wanted him in Danzig, but surely there were more details. The only clear thing that he had learned was that he was to go to his uncle Józef in America. The question of why, however, burned in his mind. What was the real reason his uncle wanted him badly enough to give up a treasure he had once stolen?

Frederic had said that the *Baltic Queen* was leaving tonight and that Stefan was supposed to be on it. It would be dangerous to attempt to board the *Queen*, but Frederic was now making final arrangements for Stefan to do just that.

Only Frederic and Kasia had expected Stefan, and no one else was to be enlisted to help him until the last minute.

Never had Count Zurowski entrusted a task to his second son. It was totally out of character; therefore, Stefan was sure he was to go because he was thought to be expendable. Perhaps it was his brother, Konrad, whom Uncle Józef had wanted, and his father planned to double-cross him. Just a twisted version of Jacob and Esau.

Stefan quickened his steps as he approached Frederic's house. As he walked onto the wooden porch, Frederic opened the door. His expression was grim.

Stefan wondered if something had gone wrong. "What is it, Frederic? Were you not able to complete the arrangements?"

"Yes, yes, they're made. I've changed only one small part of our plan but only as a precautionary measure. I'm glad that you haven't been contacted by any of your friends."

"Do you expect trouble?"

"Not really. It's just that a priest's body was found near a warehouse by the wharf."

"Surely that shouldn't be so unusual. Bodies will continue to be found for many days, and some will never be recovered," Stefan reasoned.

"But this priest was murdered! He bled to death from severe knife wounds before he was found. It happened this morning."

"Saints help us!" pleaded Kasia. "Is there not death enough with this bombing!" She dabbed at the tears in her eyes with a corner of her large white apron.

Stefan slipped his arm around her shoulders. "Why should this affect us?" he asked Frederic.

Frederic took off his glasses and rubbed each lens in a deliberate, circular motion. He answered thoughtfully.

"I don't know, Stefan. I really don't know. Your father said something to me about Józef's diocese in America requesting a priest be sent from Poland. The count said passage had been arranged for the priest on the *Baltic Queen*. He didn't mention it further since we weren't asked to help out in those arrangements."

"Frederic, do you think the murdered priest was the one to go to America?" Kasia asked in horror.

Frederic nodded. "It's a good possibility." He looked at Stefan. "The priest was found in the area where you will go to board the *Queen*. And there was something else."

"What was that?" Stefan felt a shiver of expectancy.

"A suitcase. An empty suitcase was found near the body. There was not one scrap of paper or identification found on the body. The rosary was gone, as was the ring from his hand."

"Could it have just been robbery?" wondered Stefan.

"That is, of course, the most likely conclusion." Frederic put his glasses back on and abruptly turned to his sister. "Kasia, are we going to send Stefan to America hungry?" His eyes softened as he looked at her.

"Hungry! No, no indeed!" She threw up her hands. Her face relaxed in anticipation of a familiar role. "Supper is ready. Come, come."

She linked arms with each man and led them into her kitchen. A mood of vacation settled with them at the table. She served them her special chicken soup with its rich cream sauce and parsley. The smell of fresh, homemade rye bread was familiar and good.

Kasia was again doing for Frederic and Stefan as she had done when they left Domani z Camin to visit the small house in Danzig. Goodbyes could wait.

Stefan felt Frederic's hand upon his shoulder. He startled.

The three of them had been sitting in the small parlor, and he must have dozed. His head throbbed.

The light had faded, and darkness came in the windows. Kasia had placed a small candelabra on the little round table between the faded rose armchairs before she retired.

"It's time, Stefan. We must now hurry." Frederic brought out a sea bag and the dark clothes of a seaman.

As Stefan dressed in the unfamiliar clothes, his home ties seemed more severed than ever. It was all so unreal. He could not think clearly for the pain behind his burning eyes. Surely if he could clear his mind, he would not go. Maybe if he stayed, there was something he could do to help defend Poland.

Frederic handed him the heavy wool coat last. Stefan held it by the collar and flung it over his shoulder.

"No, Stefan, you will have to wear it at all times. It's part of your identification. Don't take it off until you are on board the *Baltic Queen*. This is one reason why." He pulled up the thick woolen collar, revealing a design embroidered in a gold-colored floss. It was the Zurowski coat-of-arms: a crucifix on a medieval shield. "Kasia worked the stitching on the coat, and it will be your ticket to board the *Queen*. This was arranged to be the sign of identification by the *Queen's* captain."

As Stefan buttoned the double-breasted coat, he noticed the front panel was extra thick and stiff. Then he knew.

"The crucifix?" he asked.

"Yes. Kasia altered the coat as a hiding place. She secured the seams just this morning while you were out. The small box is in the sea bag, but now it contains a small wooden plaque with a simple proverb."

"Frederic, I can see why my father trusted you for so long."

"Stefan, I learned much from your father too. He had many excellent qualities."

"I'm glad that you think so."

"One last thing I want to give you—just by the best of fortune is this possible." Frederic's eyes gleamed with satisfaction. He opened another black box that was on the table beside the candles. The candlelight struck the objects inside and reflected prismed firelight. Small flames appeared to be burning within the box.

"The Zurowski jewels!" Stefan said, breathing in sharply. "But how?"

"Your father sent them with me to be cleaned in Danzig by an old retired craftsman living here. His house was bombed, and I had thought the old man and the jewels were lost. Then he showed up while you slept. He is a man of great honor." Frederic handed the box to Stefan.

"Great honor, yes."

With awe, Stefan picked up a square-cut diamond ring surrounded by tiny sapphires. A delicate scroll worked its way around the gold of the band. The bride of every firstborn Zurowski son had been married with this ring.

"Your brother, Konrad, would have been married in three months' time," Frederic said.

"Why did I not know?"

"It was to be announced at an engagement party at Domani z Camin, in the tradition of your family. You truly come from one of the great families of Poland, Stefan."

"There was never a place for me in that family, Frederic. A castle of one hundred rooms or more but no accommodation for the second son."

"It was true, Stefan, but it was your family's loss."

"Thank you, Frederic. And thank you for making my life bearable."

These were the first words of this kind that had ever passed between the two. In the current personal and national devastation, such words could be said without embarrassment.

"There was no time to devise a clever hiding place for the jewels, but Kasia did find an acceptable one. The bottom of the sea bag now has extra padding and a double lining."

Frederic removed the dark clothes, socks, shoes, and shaving gear from the bag. He then placed the small flat chest containing the jewels, including the bridal ring, which would have gone to Konrad's bride, into the bottom of the bag. Then he placed a thick board, padded with material and cut to fit, over the box. The spaces around the box had been stuffed adequately so the outline of the box could not be seen. Glue around the edges of the false bottom secured it from falling.

The crucifix could not be away from him for an instant, but he would have to take a chance with the jewelry.

Frederic, also dressed in dark colors, led the way from the house to the warehouse down by the wharf. Stefan had to clutch the back of Frederic's sweater so as not to lose him in the blackness. The tiny penlight offered enough light to keep them from falling over debris, but it was small enough as to not attract the attention of a patrol.

Their destination was a large warehouse, where thirty-five sailors waited to be taken aboard the *Baltic Queen*. An armed guard was posted at the front.

Frederic led the way to a small door at the back of the warehouse. From his pocket he pulled a key and fitted it smoothly into the lock. The door swung noiselessly inward. Stefan felt the roughness of Frederic's sweater as he stepped around him and into the mustiness of the building.

Just before the door closed, Stefan heard Frederick repeat a passage from Psalm 91 in whispered tones: "Thou shall not be afraid for the terror by night; nor for the arrow that flieth by day; Nor for the pestilence that walketh in darkness; Nor for the destruction that wasteth at noonday."

He felt a stirring of air as the door closed soundlessly behind him. There was a gentle click as the key was turned and the lock caught. No other word was spoken.

Then Frederic was gone. Stefan was alone. His dizziness was increasing in the stifling warmth of the building, and he lay his face against the coolness of the metal door. He was beginning to chill, even in the woolen jacket.

But there was not much time. Adjusting the rope handles of his sea bag to a more comfortable position on his shoulder, he freed his hands to feel the rough wooden boxes that were stacked on either side of where he stood, creating a path in the pitch-dark. He knew he would be able to feel his way to the front and would not lose his way. It was a good plan.

He had five minutes to work his way to the front before Frederic's hired comrades made disturbance enough to draw off the guards. While the commotion was holding the guards' attention, a sailor with another key would unlock the door in the back of their own room. He would then pull Stefan into the group as he left the room, locking the door again from the other side. These sailors, all Americans, had been employed by his uncle and were part of the crew for the *Queen*. They had been there to fit into any plans Frederic and the count might have to devise because of the complication of the invading Nazis.

Józef had understood that these were politically uneasy times. His worse fears were realized, but Hitler's bombs had spared the seaport.

Stefan heard a noise that could have come only from a high explosive; then he heard the sound of feet running away from the building and the softer sounds of other feet, moving to open the door that separated him from the American sailors.

The door opened, and Stefan felt himself jerked into a dimly lit room. He was aware of the backs of the sailors as they made a screen for the one man who had pulled him through and then had left by the same door.

A cup of coffee was pushed into his hand, and the room resumed its usual appearance. No one could have seen that any exchange had occurred. Only a short time later, the guards opened the door and shouted instructions. "The *Queen* is ready for the rest of its crew. Quickly. Single file."

As the sailors boarded the *Queen*, the captain flipped up the jacket collar of each man. There must be no mistake.

The *Baltic Queen* was moving out to sea, and Stefan was with the other members on deck. The night wind cooled his burning face.

The captain was moving toward him, smiling, with his hand extended. Stefan stepped forward, held out his hand, and collapsed at the captain's feet.

CHAPTER FOUR

S tefan heard the captain give directions: "Quickly. Let's get this man to sick bay!"

Stefan was aware of being carried. The motion did nothing to help the dizziness that threatened his consciousness.

He became aware of a cold compress on his forehead, and a trickle of water filled his ear. He could not open his eyes. A cloud hung above his mind, threatening to descend, bringing thoughtless oblivion. Still, he could make out what the voices above him were saying.

Captain Joyce's voice was harsh with concern. "Doctor, what's wrong with him?"

"As far as I've been able to determine, I would say he has contracted the plague."

"The plague? Dear God, will he die?"

"It's hard to say." The doctor pressed gently on the glands in Stefan's neck.

"Well, he has to live. He is our 'cargo,' our whole reason for coming to this dangerous port. I've never lost a cargo off any of my ships. I don't intend for this young man to spoil my record! Besides, Józef Zurowski would skin me alive."

The American captain's words belied his true feelings. When he undertook this peculiar assignment, he had done so because it intrigued him. It sounded like an exciting way to have an adventure and make a lot of money. And what a lot of money old Zurowski had spent on this trip! He must have really had a burr in the seat of his bell-bottoms to have organized such an expedition, especially with Hitler on the rampage in this part of the world.

Captain Joyce pulled at his ear, as he usually did when he was thoughtful, and looked at the sick man's face. The bone structure was good. The stamp of aristocracy was there, even in repose. There was a resemblance to Józef Zurowski, but this face looked young and vulnerable.

"Where do you think the blasted lad picked up the plague?"

The doctor observed the captain's bushy black brows drawn together into a fierce scowl and the harshness in his voice as it intensified, but he was not fooled. He knew that the more the captain felt sympathy, the harsher his comments would become.

"There have been reports of several outbreaks of the plague in Danzig. And in Warsaw there were even more. According to our information, this man would have traveled through Warsaw to get here. He could have contracted it there."

"What'll this mean to our crew?" the captain asked.

"Well, he will, of course, have to be quarantined. The thirty-five sailors that he came on board with are the only ones we will have to keep a watch on. He was with them such a short time that there should be no danger."

"Do you have the proper medical supplies to treat this type of condition?" the captain asked, clearly anxious.

"Yes. I made certain of that before we left New York. There was the threat of bombing in Poland before we left. I knew that with the unsanitary conditions caused by bombing, we should be prepared."

"I should've known that we could count on you." It was as close as anyone would have come to referring to the doctor's past.

The captain knew that as a young married man, Dr. Gayjikian had lived in Fumes, Armenia, and he, his wife, and their three small boys had been forced to flee with many others before the Turks. The Gayjikian family fled for safety to the small fortified city of Zeitoon in autumn. They had lived there until peace was brought about the next spring. During those long months, Dr. Gayjikian had watched sickness take his boys and, finally, his wife.

Stefan moaned. He wanted to ask for water, but he couldn't open his mouth; he just listened to the words around him.

"Is he in pain?" Captain Joyce asked.

"His fever is very high. I've given him an injection that will take effect soon. He will then be more comfortable. That is what we must battle—the fever. It goes so high."

"Will he live?" the captain asked.

"He is young, and that is in his favor. But does he have a will to live? That is what we don't know. What has he seen? The memories he holds in his subconscious, if they are bad, could be a greater threat to his life than the raging fever." The doctor spoke with feeling.

"There's no way to know what he has in his mind," Captain Joyce said. "I don't suppose he'll be able to talk soon."

"No. And if he does, we wouldn't know what was delirium and what was fact."

"I wonder what horror there was in Warsaw and the villages to the east. Danzig was bad enough, and we saw only the coast. What's in this boy's mind?" The captain looked closely at the young man's face, as though some clue might remain. "Doctor, I'll not come back until the quarantine is lifted, but I expect a report every morning." Then he added, "There's a priest on board if one is needed." He went out and closed the door behind him.

The door had been closed softly, but the click of the lock was magnified in Stefan's fevered brain. The two disembodied voices had wondered what he had seen. But he had tried to keep back those thoughts. He didn't want to remember, but their continued musings had tripped his memory, and he had no will to fight the scenes that poured into his mind.

Like a film running backward, the scenes took form in his mind. The last thing he remembered seeing was the captain's face. There was kindness in the roughness of the uneven features. Then he felt the warmth of Kasia's kitchen; he felt Frederic's hand on his shoulder again as he slept in the burned-out brick building. He remembered Frederic's prayer for his safety before he left.

Back he traveled to Malbork Castle; he saw clearly the wrinkled face and hands of the peasant driver that had driven the cart from Warsaw. Back, back. He didn't want to remember it all; but he was too weak to fend it off.

He had approached Domani z Camin quietly, just before noon. There had been one guard out front to watch the castle. He had felt no anger at the guard but saw him at first as only an obstacle to his entering the house.

Bodies of his family were inside the house. They had been shot. His father and his brother had been working in the study and both were slumped over the desk that was covered with the estate ledger and stacks of paper.

The once-important work was now merely pillowing for their heads. Only his father was still alive when he reached home but only momentarily.

The scene in the nursery flashed in his mind. His stepmother had been shot as she had used her body to shield the baby. Falling, then, across the infant, she became the instrument of the baby's death.

Not all of the servants were accounted for. The castle had been sacked. Valuable tapestries and paintings had been slashed into ribbons from the vicious bayonets.

He had checked the stables and realized that most of the outside servants were gone, along with the horses. Then, walking back to the house through the garden, he had found her. Sweet little Anne, with the pale-golden hair and angelic face.

He moaned and twisted on the narrow cot.

Stefan had found her discarded body among the rose garden. From that time, Stefan was not sure what he had done. He remembered escaping out of a window when he heard the sound of the soldiers returning. He remembered thinking how their boots would make muddy tracks on the slate floor of the entrance hall. One pair of boots would be stained with blood.

Anne's face burned before him. His father's dying words— "Find Frederic"—followed him as he ran.

The pounding of the words became one with the throb in his head; gradually, both subsided.

He felt the air on his forehead and then another cold compress. As the cold cloth covered his eyes, a pool of blackness seemed to edge around him, promising freedom from the pain. His last thought was of the jeweled crucifix. He must live to return it. He was not free to die yet; there was the honor of his family to uphold.

The Atlantic was choppy, but the waves weren't excessively high. Captain Joyce was in his cabin, going over the course they had plotted for home. There was a knock at his door.

"Come in," he barked sharply.

"Sir?" The young officer from the communications area stood with a worried frown on his face. Joyce could see the fine beads of perspiration on the man's upper lip.

The captain gave his full attention. "What is it?"

"A message, sir. A passenger liner, the *Asthenia*, traveling from Belfast to

Montreal has been hit by a German U-boat. All ships in the immediate area are requested to help rescue survivors."

"Did the message indicate how many passengers?"

The young man seemed to control the stress in his voice. "More than a thousand, sir. Many are American women and children returning home." He handed the captain a piece of paper with the *Asthenia's* coordinates.

The captain glanced at the paper. "Thank you. Radio that we will assist. We should be in their area in forty-five minutes. I'll give orders for a course change. We'll make a wide detour."

Captain Joyce dismissed the young officer and gave the order that sent them to the aid of the *Asthenia*. The war was spreading. Joyce had felt a relief when they'd sailed from the port of Danzig; now he realized danger lurked in the water as well as on the land.

The port of Danzig had not been destroyed, but for days the German guns bombarded Fort Westerplatte on the outskirts of the city. The German battleship *Schleswig-Holstein* fired its eleven-inch guns point-blank into the fortress. The noise of fierce land and air assaults ripped the heavens and played havoc with the nerves of his crew.

As they approached the position of the *Asthenia*, he saw she was settling down by the stern. She looked like a broken model of a once-seaworthy vessel. The U-boat had come upon her suddenly, and the crew had been taken unaware.

The crew of the *Baltic Queen* worked together to rescue 127 survivors. As they were brought aboard, they were wrapped in warmed blankets and taken to a section of the ship temporarily assigned to them.

They couldn't be taken to sick bay because of the quarantine, but none rescued were badly injured, just frightened and shivering. After Dr. Gayjikian examined their cuts and bruises, he ordered hot soup for them and then bed. The ship would be crowded the rest of the way home.

Other ships were in the area and had nearly completed the rescue operation. When the torpedo hit the ship, many had been injured. They had been picked up first. Some were killed. Some would never be found. The horror of the war on the European continent was bleeding into the Atlantic Ocean.

The *Baltic Queen* plowed steadily once more toward New York. The rest of the voyage homeward was uneventful, and so was the condition of the man in sick bay.

The captain leaned against the rail and watched the sunrise. It never failed to fascinate him. As the sun rose from the black of the sea, it was like a gold offering of sacrifice sent up from a buried Atlantis. He would like to have added a prayer of his own for the man below and send it to the heavens on this fiery disk. He snorted at his own fanciful idea and turned to go to his cabin. They would be in port in another day or so, and there was paperwork to get in order. He must also write a letter to Mr. Zurowski.

"Come in," he answered the knock on his door. "Dr. Gayjikian, come in. What's the report today?"

"He is conscious." Both men smiled their relief.

"And what did the young man have to say after so long a silence?"

"He asked for his coat and sea bag. I opened the locker where we had stowed them across from his cot, and he seemed satisfied. He thanked me."

"That's a little strange, but I don't care much how he acts, as long as he's going to be all right."

"Yes, his fever broke about three o'clock this morning, and then he was awake at dawn. When he saw that his belongings were safe, he asked for something to eat."

"Now that's more like it," the captain said. "Asking for food is a good sign. Day after tomorrow, Doctor, we arrive in New York. Will he be able to leave the ship?"

"He can't walk off, of course, but there is no reason why he can't leave the ship. He does not have to be kept under quarantine any longer."

"I need to talk to him before we dock. I have instructions as to the next part of his journey." The captain pulled at his ear.

"Oh, he won't be up to any traveling for a few weeks," the doctor added hurriedly.

"My part is to get him to New York and introduced to the old man's lawyer. From then on, it'll be someone else's responsibility to move him when he's able. Don't look so worried, Doc; they'll take good care of your patient. The lawyer is also an old friend of the family and will care for him until he can send him on. He'll meet us."

The day seemed much brighter, and Joyce smiled broadly as he returned to his paperwork. He suspected that the doctor had worried, possibly as much as he had, about the young man in their charge. The burden of the Polish passenger's illness had weighed heavily upon him. Now he felt light and looked forward to their talk this afternoon.

The scent of antiseptics was reassuring, and the feel of the cool sheets was comforting. Stefan opened his eyes for the second time that day. Earlier that morning, he'd awakened and finally put a face to the voice he'd heard from time to time. The doctor's face was no surprise; there was patience and confidence there.

After eating the thin gruel he'd been offered, he slept. Now he felt clear-headed; the cobwebs of black memories had been blown away.

Captain Joyce introduced himself and settled in the chair beside Stefan's bed.

"Stefan, it's great to hear that you're better."

"Thank you, Captain. I was very surprised to learn that I was unconscious for so long." His accent was pleasing and his English very precise.

"No doubt that was a surprise. Dr. Gayjikian says that I mustn't tire you, so I'll tell you what you must know as briefly as possible." He glanced at the doctor standing at the other side of the bed. He was checking his patient's pulse. "Your uncle Józef hired me, along with my crew, to take the *Baltic Queen* to the port of Danzig. I know nothing of the arrangements that got you into Danzig."

"Truthfully, Captain"—Stefan's voice was low and weak— "I know very little of them myself."

"The important thing is that you were there, and we got you here. We'll be in New York in less than forty-eight hours."

"It was a short journey," Stefan said and smiled feebly.

"Mr. Vincent Ludlow will board us in New York, and you'll go with him. He is Józef Zurowski's lawyer and has further instructions for you."

Stefan looked at Dr. Gayjikian. "Will I be able to go?"

"We'll have an ambulance waiting for you. You'll need about a month to get enough strength to continue your journey."

"My uncle does not live in New York, then?"

"No," answered the captain. "Although Józef Zurowski has business interests in New York, his home is in Minnesota."

"Minnesota," repeated Stefan. "I've never heard of that place."

"It's a beautiful state. I know you'll like it."

"Captain," interrupted the doctor, "my patient must rest now."

The captain nodded and stood.

Stefan's eyes closed as the two men left the room, and he slipped off into a light sleep.

The harbor was crowded. It was a couple hours before the captain finished his ship duties and was able to see the lawyer who was to meet Stefan.

"Mr. Ludlow?" The captain came forward, extending his hand. "I'm sorry to keep you waiting, but the business of getting clearance was more of a chore today. You may have heard that we had 127 survivors of the *Asthenia* on board."

"Very commendable and courageous of you, Captain. Józef Zurowski will be pleased that you could aid in the rescue effort with his ship." His speech had the clipped tones of a native New Yorker. "I was perfectly content to wait."

The lawyer didn't look in the least put out. As a matter of fact, he looked like nothing this world could produce would ruffle his calm demeanor. Not one hair on his head was out of place. In his youth, his hair had been black; now silver streaks, like wings, gave it a striking appearance. His charcoal suit had neat black pinstripes, and a gray bowler rested on the chair beside him.

"Mr. Ludlow, Stefan Zurowski has been ill. He contracted the plague in Poland. He's recovering, but Dr. Gayjikian says that he'll need at least a month's rest to regain his strength."

"I'm sorry to hear that. But I don't think that a month's delay in Józef Zurowski's plans will make too much difference. I will contact him immediately and inform him."

"He will need an ambulance," the captain told Ludlow.

"Captain Joyce, if you would be so kind as to have him carried to my limousine on a stretcher, we will manage nicely."

"Have you talked to our doctor?"

"Yes, Captain, as a matter of fact, Dr. Gayjikian already has spoken to me of Stefan's illness. I took the liberty of calling a local physician, who will be waiting for us at my house when we arrive."

This arrangement gave Mr. Ludlow a little more stature in the captain's eyes. *Maybe this marble statue does have a soul*, he thought.

Captain Joyce gave the order for Stefan Zurowski to be carried to the long black car that waited. He watched as his men carefully placed Stefan's coat and gear next to him on the stretcher, and the captain felt a little pang of regret. He would like to have known this quiet fellow better. He wished there had been a chance to talk to Stefan about the war in Poland.

Ludlow spoke to the physician at his house after he'd examined Stefan, and the physician concurred that Stefan needed a long period of rest. He scheduled a visit every day to check on the invalid's progress.

After a week of bed rest, Stefan was able to have dinner with his host in the sitting room that adjoined his bedroom.

Ludlow's wife had left him years ago, and except for a maid and a butler, he lived alone in his spacious apartment. He was not unhappy with the idea of a houseguest.

He could not waste time, though. Józef Zurowski would expect his nephew just as soon as possible. Besides, there were several things for which Stefan needed to be prepared. He would have a couple weeks to give Stefan the information, and that would leave a week for the young man to digest it.

The maid served their dinner quietly. The lamb chops were broiled just as he'd ordered them, and the potatoes were well buttered and sprinkled with parsley. The peas with tiny white onions were delicious and added color. Vincent Ludlow liked his meals as well organized as his life.

The coffee had been served, and Ludlow now looked across the table at Stefan. Stefan's color was returning, and he was showing signs of restlessness. He was recuperating faster than the doctor had expected. Ludlow could no longer put off the discussion Józef had requested.

"Stefan, you will be going to Minnesota," Ludlow said.

"Minnesota. That's the state Captain Joyce mentioned."

"Had you heard of it?"

"No." Stefan looked at Mr. Ludlow. He didn't offer any help.

Ludlow was surprised. Stefan's father was supposed to have briefed his son on the points that he was to explain further. "Didn't your father—the count—talk to you about the arrangements?"

"My father is dead." Stefan offered nothing further.

"We heard nothing of this. I will, of course, inform Josef as soon as possible."

"No one knew. A patrol from the Red Army marched on Domani z Camin and killed my entire family while I was on my way there. My father's dying words sent me to Danzig to find Frederic."

"Yes, I was told of Frederic. What did he tell you?"

"Frederic didn't know much of the arrangement between my father and my uncle. He was only ordered to go to Danzig to deliver some final papers and make plans for me to meet the ship. Then, when the bombing started, all this became very hazardous."

"Stefan, did you wonder how it would be arranged for you to stay in this country?"

"No." He didn't tell Ludlow that he didn't plan to stay. That was for him to tell his uncle Józef.

"You did know that refugees aren't being allowed to come to this country at this time, correct?"

"Yes. Frederic was very concerned for my safety." Stefan felt sorry for Mr. Ludlow. He didn't seem to be very comfortable.

"Do you know why you're allowed to stay?"

"No." Stefan showed no interest.

"It's because you are officially married to a United States citizen." Ludlow realized Stefan spoke fluent English, but he stressed each word carefully.

"But how can that be? I'm not married. I don't know anyone here in America; I've never been here before."

"You were married by proxy."

"Proxy? I don't understand."

"There was a ceremony in the church and a substitute played your part, so to speak. Currently, marriage by proxy is becoming much more common with the parting of sweethearts in the war."

"But wouldn't I have to give my consent?" demanded Stefan.

"Yes, and we thought you had. We have the signed document."

"My father must have signed it."

Ludlow nodded slowly. "Yes, that could be how it happened."

"Tell me, Mr. Ludlow, did the bride sign her own name?" His voice was heavy with sarcasm, his accent suddenly thick.

"Why, of course, Stefan. She signed of her own free will. She is an adult."

"Who is she, if I may ask?" He was shaken and felt trapped. He had settled in his mind to buy his freedom with the crucifix and return to Poland. But how did one buy freedom from one's wife? Could there be an annulment? Would the church conscious a divorce?

"The young lady is the stepdaughter of your uncle. Her name is Sophia Milewski, or I should say Sophia Zurowski now. A most respectable girl, I can tell you."

"Thank you, Mr. Ludlow."

"No doubt your father was forced to sign for you because you were away, and he was pressed for time. It is, Stefan, the only way I could legally arrange for you to stay in this country now. Things must be kept legal; it's a matter of Zurowski family honor."

"Yes, Mr. Ludlow, honor. I won't back down from an agreement made by my father, the late Count Zurowski. After all, I'm now Count Zurowski, and I'm honorable."

Vincent felt a new respect for the young man across from him. The fact that Stefan was Count Zurowski, a Polish nobleman, didn't impress him as much as the strict code by which he was abiding. The young man had been betrayed by his family, yet he would uphold the word of Zurowski.

"Now, Mr. Ludlow, how is it planned that I get to my uncle's?"

Ludlow once more felt solid ground under his feet, and he could proceed with authority. "A driver has been secured. You will travel by automobile all the way."

"No, Mr. Ludlow, I will make my own arrangements from now on. Please get me a map. Maybe I can take a train? Perhaps a bus? Can you furnish transportation schedules? I will get to my destination my own way."

"Yes, of course, but, Stefan—"

"Mr. Ludlow, please be so kind as to remember that you are employed by my uncle. It would not be in his best interests for you to oppose me. I'll need money. I gave my Polish zloty to Frederic before I left. I won't need clothes; I'll use what I brought in my sea bag." He was up and standing by the door that led to his bedroom. "One other thing, Mr. Ludlow—you may tell my uncle anything you wish, but tell him after I've gone, not before." He walked through the bedroom door and shut it very softly behind him.

Vincent Ludlow had misjudged this man. He did this so rarely that it left him with a strange, unsettled feeling. There was no use in complaining to Józef Zurowski that his nephew refused to obey orders. The old man would just laugh and applaud.

He got up from the table and nearly stumbled from the room. Under his breath, he recounted the things that he had been asked to get. "Bus schedule, train schedule, map, and money. Five hundred dollars should be enough."

CHAPTER FIVE

The long limbs of the spruce swept down and touched the soft dust of the ground, making a perfect hideaway for the young, slim girl concealed in the tepee space around the trunk of the tree. Sophia's thin figure was clad in dusty green corduroy trousers and jacket that blended in with the surroundings. A long scarf was around her neck, warding off the cold. Her hiding place in the tall tree, several feet from the winding path, was near the edge of the forest.

Feeling safe, she could study the stranger coming up the lane with no fear of detection. From a distance, he gave the appearance of a walking scarecrow. His clothes were dark blue and hung loosely on his hungry-looking frame. As he came closer, she could see that his belt had been pulled tight, gathering his trousers around his waist. His thick straight hair, the color of pale straw, was noticeably well brushed. Such healthy hair looked out of place above his pale, drawn face.

As he drew parallel to the tall evergreen, he turned his face in the direction where Sophia hid. Instinctively, she drew back and caught her breath. Then, feeling secure in the safety of shielding pine branches, she took the opportunity to study the face turned to her.

Suffering was stamped on the young man's face, but there were lines of determination around his mouth. The sharp cheekbones emphasized the hollows in his face. The facial bone structure was very good; fleshed out, it would be an arrestingly handsome face.

Viewing him from the shadow of her tree, his face seemed to be planes and angles. The chin was slightly square, with a small vertical cleft. The cleft was only a small indentation, as though hiding the fact that a face so severe should find relief in the form of a dimple.

The eyes were what held her attention. His brows were straight, like slashes on his white face, and his dark lashes framed eyes the color of a stormy day.

Watching the man continue up the dirt road, Sophia no longer thought of him as looking like a scarecrow. The erect figure walked with a firm, strong step, even while carrying a canvas bag. This stranger was not just wandering the countryside; purpose was exposed in his every move. If he stayed on this road, he would be headed for Józef Zurowski's mansion, Forest House.

Stepping from her hiding place, Sophia continued to watch the figure curiously. To her right, where the rolling hill ended in a tree-covered knoll, she saw a sudden glint of the sun on something metal. A sharp crack broke the stillness. Quickly looking back to the lane, she saw that the stranger had fallen. The man lay very still.

Panic seized her. Her first thought was to run; she turned her back on the man, but she could not leave her stranger. If someone at the house didn't want him there, then he was no threat to her. Her enemies were at Forest House. If he were alive, he not only needed help physically, but he also should be warned to go away.

There was a knot of fear in her chest as Sophia saw how still the man lay.

She started slowly up the path, casting fearful glances at the place where she had seen the sun glint on the gun barrel. With the thought that the gunman might still be there, she wanted to hide again in the protection of the tree, but she fought to overcome her fear and ran to the stranger.

Gently, she turned him over. She felt sick at the sight of his blood coloring his neck and soaking through the front of his heavy woolen jacket. She swallowed hard. His face was relaxed, and the lines of stress were gone, leaving him looking young and vulnerable. Tentatively, she brushed back a lock of his hair that had fallen over his closed eyes. She tried to decide what she should do. He needed help immediately. But someone had tried to kill him, so she dared not summon help from Forest House.

Old Lew would help. She would go get him. He could use his donkey to carry the injured man. But first, she had to try to stop the bleeding a little, or he wouldn't last until she got back with help. Once she decided to help him, her actions came naturally.

She took off her boots and then pulled off the heavy white socks she wore. She placed her socks over the wound, fashioning a thick bandage. The wound was on the left side of his chest, below his collarbone. She pulled off her long neck scarf and arranged it under his left arm and up around the right side of his neck. Using the collar of his coat as protection between his neck and the woolen muffler, she then pulled the scarf as tightly as she could. Next, she jerked off her heavy corduroy jacket and covered the man's chest.

Having done all she could, she ran toward the woods and took a small footpath visible only as one approached the edge of the dense forest. As her feet moved over the familiar path, she prayed that Lew was in his little house and that he could get back to the man in time.

It was late afternoon, so Lew should be in his cabin. During the mornings, he checked his traps and gathered roots and herbs. He had told her that he had just about enough stored to keep him this winter. Everyone said he was a worthless old man, but he had been kind to Sophia ever since they had moved into the Zurowski family mansion. When he was younger, he'd worked in her father's lumber operation. She was counting on Lew now.

Arriving at the cabin, she found the small old man chopping wood to add to the cords neatly stacked in the clearing behind his little house. The wind ruffled the thin white hair encircling his balding head as he worked. He leaned against the ax handle, watching her as he waited for her to catch her breath. His blue eyes narrowed as she told him what had happened.

He put on his woolen hat and got her an old coat of his to wear from the cabin and headed for the weathered shed that served as a stable for his donkey, Nellie. Fastening a rope to Nellie's halter, he led the donkey to the wagon and hitched her to it. As Sophia climbed up into the wagon, Lew threw a blanket to her. He mounted the animal, and they hurried off in the direction of the injured man.

Sophia felt great relief. She pulled the coat tightly around her and huddled down to escape the wind. There was nothing else she could do except to help Lew put the injured man into the wagon.

Lew arranged the wool blanket he had brought around the figure of the man.

"Sophia, hold the man's head in your lap to cushion it." Concern showed in Lew's face. "He is very weak, but he is alive. Child, you saved his life. They will be proud of you up at Forest House."

"No," she said fiercely, "they must not know. He was shot by someone at the house, and if we take him there, then whoever it was will have another chance—an easier one with him as helpless as he is."

"Sophia, don't let your imagination run wild. No doubt it was a hunter. This must have been an accident. Who is this boy, anyway?"

"I don't know who he is, but please don't take him to Forest House. Someone will kill him. You know what they did to my brother, Jan. Please, oh please, take him to your little house with you. You can take care of him, as well as Dr. Janda." Her speech had started slowly, but she was rapidly building up to hysterics. He could tell her protest was caused by real fear.

Lew and Sophia got the unconscious man into the wagon. Sophia climbed in to sit beside the man, but Lew eased the man against her and then rearranged the blanket around both of them. He kept the donkey's pace at a slow walk to avoid reopening the man's wound, but he noticed that Sophia was beginning to shake uncontrollably. The sun was nearly down, and the temperature was falling rapidly.

As he guided Nellie carefully back down the footpath to his cabin, Lew considered what he had heard about Sophia. She had been thought of as "strange" ever since Jan's death. Jan was her twin, and they'd had a special closeness. Sophia had not recovered from her loss. At least, that was the report he had heard from Jacobson at Forest House and from the townspeople.

Sophia had been found in shock at the scene of Jan's death, screaming that Jan had been murdered. There had been an investigation, but the ruling had been accidental death. It had occurred at last year's dozynk, the harvest festival.

Józef Zurowski was a Polish immigrant who zealously celebrated the customs of his mother country, where he had lived in his youth. It was on a warm Sunday in late August when all the people who worked for Zurowski—nearly the entire population of Dark Forest, Minnesota— gathered to give thanks and celebrate the age-old Polish custom of dozynk. The ancient custom was intended for workers in the fields to give thanks, but that was a fact that Józef ignored. Hired hands from the farms, his lumber operations, and his mines, along with their families, made up a great number of merrymakers at the celebration.

It had become an annual local holiday over the past twenty years, when the empire of Józef Zurowski provided the town's lifeblood, and the people gladly celebrated. A parade formed on the courthouse lawn in the center of town, and everyone walked gaily to the Zurowski mansion to the music of the fiddle and the bass viol. Most of the town's citizens were also Polish immigrants.

The dozynk began like those in past years. That year, however, Sophia, and two other young girls were chosen from their neighbors to head the procession in colorful Polish costumes. Carrying large wreaths made of the harvested wheat, intertwined with poppies and bachelor buttons, they proudly started from the town square on the five-mile walk to their destination: the party at Forest House, Józef Zurowski's mansion. The fruits of the orchard—plums, pears, and apples—were fastened to the wreaths with red, blue, and purple ribbons. Sophia led the parade with the other girls, clad in bright, vivid clothes. Jan was there, laughing and happy, playing the fiddle.

Everyone was happy. Mostly young people made up the group for the five-mile hike, with the older ones following on bicycles or in their cars. Some rode mules. But everyone came. The mood was carefree and high-spirited.

Józef greeted the people, as his ancestors in Poland had greeted the peasants who worked their lands, in the age-old custom. Inviting the guests into his home, he bade them be seated at long tables generously laden with food. The aroma of roasted meats, coffee cakes, and poppy-seed breads welcomed the visitors, who were ravenous from their hike. Huge platters of golden ears of corn, ruby-red beets, asparagus, and carrots with various sauces made of sweet or sour cream spoke of marvelous cooking in the best Polish tradition. Honey wine was in abundant supply, and the black coffee flowed freely.

After hours of feasting, the children played games, and the young people danced. One of the highlights of the festival for the children was the baking of the dziad, the beggar's cake. Jan was here and there, teasing the children and being attentive to all the girls, but he too had always loved to help with the dziad.

Josef employed Manka, a Polish cook, familiar with the food preparations for their celebrations. The cake was baked outdoors, barbecue-style. She used oak rods about the size of rolling pins, wide at the bottom and narrow at the top, and with a hole in them large enough to fit on the spit. The rods were wrapped with buttered paper and fastened securely by a string. After supporting the ends of the rods with tripods, Manka placed trays under the rods for dripping batter. When the rods were very hot from the blazing fire, Jan turned the rods while Manka poured on the batter with a large spoon. As the first layer browned, another layer was added until all the batter was used, even the batter that had dripped in the trays. Jan rolled his eyes at the children and licked his lips.

The youngsters watched in amazement as the cake baked and took the form of a lumpy spool of thread. When it cooled, they watched Manka frost it with icing flavored with the juice from maraschino cherries. More than one cake was baked at one time, and all the people lined up to receive their pieces as Manka and her serving girls cut from the top. Each slice looked like an uneven oxcart wheel.

After they ate the dziad, the people with very small children went home, but the remaining group was still large. Sophia and Jan entertained many of the young people their own age in active games. The hour was past midnight, and the roaring bonfire was the only light in that area.

In the firelight, Jan's face glowed. Sophia watched her brother proudly. He was a favorite with the young people, and he had just finished a dance with Frannie, a sweet girl who was the daughter of a close friend of their stepmother. Sophia walked around the fire to where he stood, leaning against a tree. He caught sight of her coming toward him and smiled as he stepped away from the tree.

In the darkness, Sophia couldn't be absolutely sure of what she saw. There was a blur of light and black, and then an ax fell from the tree and struck Jan, knocking him to the ground.

Sophia's screams drew everyone's attention to Jan's still form on the ground, and the young people made way for Dr. Janda, who kneeled next to Jan and examined the boy. Then he instructed someone to cover Jan's lifeless body with a blanket.

Lew had watched Sophia accept Jan's death even before Dr. Janda pulled the blanket over the boy's face. He had watched her shiver uncontrollably and heard her screams rend the night air. One minute, Sophia was whole; the next minute, half of her being was torn away.

Old Lew watched as someone carried the body of the young man into the house, followed closely by Dr. Janda and old Father Polzak.

Father Polzak accompanied the family to the closest bedroom with Jan's body. Dr. Janda led Sophia, still crying loudly that someone had murdered Jan, to her room. She was wildly accusing an unknown assailant of dropping the ax from the tree onto the boy's head. Her dark eyes, wide in horror, were the only color in her chalk-white face.

Dr. Janda kept Sophia sedated until after Jan's funeral.

Lew knew that Sophia's insistence that it was murder had been read at the hearing on Jan's death, but it made no difference on the ruling.

The report read that the ax had been lodged high in the tree after a throwing contest and had presumably worked itself loose. Jan had leaned against the tree, and that action had been enough to dislodge the ax and allow the tool to fall. The ax flipped, with the handle extending up in the air and causing the heavy head of the ax to strike the fatal blow.

Lew had seen the happenings that night, but he had not attended the festival. Rumor had it that Sophia disappeared after the festival and didn't return until every trace of the celebration had been swept away. Lew had seen the girl only briefly since Jan's accident, but it was obvious by her appearance that she had not improved.

He suspected that the corduroys she now wore had belonged to Jan, and the jacket she'd used to cover the wounded man had belonged to her brother too. Her hands, clutching the blanket around the man, were reddened, and her fingernails were broken and dirty. The hair Lew remembered as falling in soft, loose waves was not just windblown but tangled from neglect.

Finally reaching his cabin, they supported the unconscious man between them and got him onto the cot inside. Lew set about to redress the wound, which had begun to bleed again. When he finished, he realized that the girl had disappeared without saying another word to him.

"Oh, well," he said aloud, "it's best that he not be moved again for a while. But I'll have to tell Józef Zurowski soon about this accident on his land."

Certain that the young man was alive and in good hands, Sophia quietly left the cabin and ran swiftly into the woods. She thought she knew where the shot had come from. The glint from the gun barrel had come from the direction of an old deer stand, which had been built years ago in a tree. She and Jan had used it for a tree house when they were children.

When she got to the tree, she saw that she had been right. The spent cartridge, clean and new, lay in plain view. She dropped it in her pocket.

Another thought gave her a sinking feeling—no one knew the stranger would be on the trail, so maybe the shot had been intended for her. With fatal intuition, she knew she was right. Yes, the shot had been directed at her.

She just didn't know why.

There was nothing she could do. She wiped the tears from her eyes and started for the house. The big house would be well lighted, and surely it was nearing suppertime.

Józef patiently tolerated her odd behavior, but he had bluntly said that even a dog can be trained to be on time for meals. To Józef, suppertime was a family occasion, and no one dared miss this meal.

As she burst in through the front door, the chandelier hanging high above the wooden parquet floor of the entrance shed its light mercilessly on the girl. She stood exposed to the eyes of every member of the family as they had gathered in the front hall to enter the dining room together.

Dirty, disheveled, and pale from her recent ordeal, she contrasted cruelly with the cleanliness and correctness of her family.

There were guests for dinner. Dr. Janda and his wife and their son, Stanislas, who was recently graduated from medical school, were at Forest House. Father Polzak was there with Father Vladek, the newly arrived priest from Poland.

"Oh, Sophia." A look of disgust marred the perfection of the makeup on her mother's face. "You are more of a mess than usual. Where have you been? And what have you been up to?"

Sophia knew the questions required no answer. She turned from her mother to search Józef's face.

His eyes were hard on her, but there was pain in them. "Sophia, we will wait five minutes while you wash your face and hands, but you won't have time to change." The words were spoken as though to a rebellious child and held the threat of punishment.

As she ran lightly up the stairs to the bathroom adjoining her room, their voices floated up.

"Really, Dr. Janda, there must be something you can do. She's a disgrace to us all."

"Mrs. Zurowski, I'm as concerned with Sophia as you, but I assure you that there's nothing more I can do. By now she should've recovered; there's nothing physically wrong with her. Jan's accident was such a great shock."

"Stanislas, perhaps you've read something about such cases as Sophia's. Being recently graduated from medical school, maybe you've come across some new theory," Marie Zurowski asked the handsome young man.

"That is very flattering, Mrs. Zurowski, but in my opinion, which greatly lacks experience, her mind will heal itself of the shock. When it does, her brain will simply notify all responses to begin functioning normally, which is what Dad said."

They were all seated when Sophia entered, still dressed in the corduroys and flannel shirt. Washing the dirt streaks from her face only added to her pallor. She had missed the azkaski that Antek, the butler, had served in the living room, but these delectable bits were not needed to stimulate her appetite. She felt faint from hunger.

The steaming heat was as welcome as the flavor of the rich borscht with cream. She could take comfort from the warmth of the soup against the chill of the members of her family. The soup things were cleared and the pike au gratin was served, generously buttered and toasted brown. Józef was proud of the fish caught from their own lakes.

"May I congratulate you, madame, on this most excellent pike?" Father Vladek was being very charming to Marie Zurowski.

"Jan and I used to spend many hours fishing for the pike," Sophia said, directing her remarks to no one in particular. No one responded.

Sophia watched Józef's face as he assessed Vladek. Józef had agreed to request a future replacement from Poland for Father Polzak, but she wondered if Józef was viewing Vladek as the best candidate.

Sophia listened to Józef add his thanks for the compliment to Marie.

"We're quite proud of our pstrage lub szczupak au gratin here at Forest House. Manka, our cook, brought along an old family recipe book when she came to this country many years ago. It's been to our advantage. Is it not so?"

"You are indeed quite fortunate in your cook, sir. The baked sauerkraut and yellow peas are better than any I've had in Poland for a long while."

"Thank you," Józef acknowledged the compliment with a slight nod of his head.

Józef Zurowski sat at the head of the table dominating the room, and smoothly led the conversation from topic to topic. The political situation in Europe was by far their most vital concern. Hitler's destruction of much of Poland dealt a blow felt even by the Polish living in America.

Józef's voice grated unpleasantly. "The papers were full of the news of Warsaw's surrender to Germany this week." Józef subscribed to the *Wall Street Journal* and other key newspapers around the country. "I read that the high officials of the Polish and German governments met on the outskirts of Warsaw and arranged for the terms of surrender. The meeting actually took place in a bus."

"Why do you suppose they met in such a spot?" Marie asked curiously.

"Safety, madame," answered Father Vladek. "Safety for the German official, in particular." There was a glint in his blue eyes.

"Perhaps safety," snorted Józef in derision. "Could just be that their artillery bombardment destroyed everything else in the city!"

"Warsaw was such a beautiful place," mourned Mrs. Milewski. "The Aleje Ujazdowskie lined with stately buildings, swaying trees ..." The old woman's eyes misted. Mrs. Milewski was the mother of Marie's first husband.

"The reports we had in Danzig regarding Warsaw were disheartening, madame. All you spoke of was hit, and it was mutilated beyond recognition." Father Vladek's tone was matter-of-fact.

"The Polish people fought even after all odds were against them. Germany reported surrounding Warsaw nearly ten days before the actual surrender," Józef said, trying to console Mrs. Milewski.

Sophia felt sorry for her grandmother. News of the destruction of her home country had to make her heart ache. Sophia knew of heartache.

Her mind kept wandering from the table conversation to the injured man lying on a cot in Lew's cabin. Somehow, she knew that the stranger knew of heartache, too.

"It's America's loss that the flow of Polish immigrants has been stopped. But it's Poland's gain," Father Vladek commented.

"But you're here, Father Vladek, which is proof that some will escape," Józef said. "And I know of one more who made it."

Sophia watched all eyes turn in Józef's direction. His last comment had a different tone to it and their attention intensified.

Sophia knew that Józef didn't make such statements without reason.

"Józef, who would that be?" Marie asked. "Who is it, dear? Are we acquainted with him?"

"No, but soon you'll be well acquainted. As a matter of fact, I've never seen him either. He's my nephew, Stefan Zurowski, and I expect him to arrive at Forest House this week." His tone was pleasantly conversational.

"But should we not go meet him?" Mrs. Milewski asked.

"We shouldn't. He will show up when he's ready." Pride was evident in his voice.

"I saw him." Sophia said the words out loud before she could stop herself. She arose from her seat and stood behind her chair. She needed the chair as a barrier between her and those looking at her.

"Really, my dear, since when have you taken an interest in those around you?" Marie asked.

"I'm sorry, Mother, perhaps I didn't see him. There was a stranger walking up our road today. He wore old clothes."

"Then certainly he wouldn't be Józef's nephew. There is at least one beggar at our door every day."

Sophia had heard a sharp intake of breath when she announced that she had seen Stefan but couldn't tell from whom it had come. It was important now that they all think she was mistaken.

"No doubt you're right, Mother. My mind does wander."

"Sophia, go to your room, please," her stepfather ordered. "You look as though you need the rest. Your mother will have Manka send you up a tray later."

So, her stepfather wanted her out of the way too. She looked at him and knew he believed her. A look of understanding passed between them.

As she passed his chair, she laid her hand on his arm. "Thank you, Father."

She forced herself to walk slowly from the room, listening for any comments Józef might make on the stranger. But when she heard them leave the dinner table, Sophia fled up the stairs as though she were being chased.

Sophia knew that Mrs. Milewski brought memories back to Józef of his own grandmother long ago who had been concerned for the people living on the estate of Domani z Camin. She had taken food and medicine to the sick and knitted scarves and mittens for the children of the peasants who worked for them. Like Józef's grandmother, Mrs. Milewski was concerned for the poor in their town.

Marie paid very little attention to the mother of her first husband, Peter Milewski, after he died. She had moved up in social status from the widow of a banker of modest means in Dark Forest to the wife of Minnesota's most prominent citizen and head of the Zurowski empire. In Minnesota, Józef was thought of as the lumber baron. Once they married, Marie had instantly relinquished the rearing of her children to the nurse and governess, while she played the role of a grand lady full time.

If Józef wanted her dead husband's niece and nephew, Maurice and Monica, to live with them, well, that was all right. Goodness knows there was more than enough room to accommodate them without crowding her, and it gave her the chance to appear charitable in the eyes of their townspeople. And as long as Peter Milewski's mother had enough yarn to knit that endless parade of mittens, hats, and scarves, she would demand nothing more. She knew that Mrs. Milewski reminded Józef of his grandmother. If Józef wanted to assume all the obligations that her first husband had borne, she would accept them. Peter Milewski had gladly taken care of his mother and his dead brother's children, Maurice and Monica.

She was careful to keep the household running smoothly and to maintain an atmosphere in which Józef would be happy to bring his friends. He was just a simple man, unsophisticated, with a talent for making money.

In the nearly twenty-six years that he had been in this country, he had built an empire based on logging and iron ore mines. He'd come from a wealthy family in Poland, and his reasons for leaving his home had only been guessed at so far by his friends and business associates. It was a subject that no one dared to bring up. Józef would discuss logging and mining and the years that he had built his businesses in America, but not one word of his life before immigrating to the United States would he mention.

However, it was common knowledge that Józef had a great deal of money when he came to the United States, and wise investments and hard work had snowballed his fortune. He loved his land, his mines, and his ships, but not his money. Family was of consuming importance to Józef Zurowski.

Marie knew that Józef had woken up when he was past fifty to find that he was alone. He'd married her because she had been the wife of his friend Peter Milewski, whom he had known since they were newly arrived in America. Peter had died leaving Marie and a set of very young twins, Sophia and Jan. Peter had also been supporting his mother, Mrs. Milewski. By taking them all in, Józef had acquired a family, and he was still not too old to have a son of his own. He wanted blood of his blood.

After he and Marie had been married five years, it became obvious that they would have no children together. He had written to his brother, Count Zurowski, at Domani z Camin, to ask for his second son.

It was a hard request for him to make, but he had a powerful bargaining tool.

CHAPTER SIX

Sophia had just finished eating the food from the tray Manka had brought up, and she poured herself another cup of tea. She had heard the guests leave. Now there was a knock at her door.

"Yes?" She stood up from the chair and walked toward the door with the teacup in her hand.

She opened the door. It was Maurice.

When her uncle, Filip Milewski and his wife had been killed in an automobile accident, Sofia's knew that her father, Peter Milewski, had given a home to Maurice and Monica and Peter's mother. When her own father, Peter Milewski, died, Josef married her mother, and they all moved into Forest House.

"Ah, cousin, how are you now?" Maurice closed the door behind him and walked deliberately close to her.

She was filled with loathing and shame. The head so close above her own was well kept—the black hair was combed back from a neat, center part. His dinner attire was spotless and his cologne heavy and sweet. She closed her eyes and remembered his hands. So restless. His long fingers were tapered but straight, to the point of looking stiff. His flawless, manicured appearance effectively covered up his sickness to nearly everyone. But she knew. Jan had known.

Maurice held a lock of her hair between two of his stiff white fingers.

She took a sip of tea noisily and carelessly let a trickle escape from her lips and spot her corduroy shirt.

He stepped back as though he had been slapped. "Sophia, for goodness' sake! Must you always be so untidy?"

She forced her eyes to meet his. She hoped her expression was innocent.

No longer could Jan protect her from their cousin Maurice, but she had discovered a way to keep him from touching her with those terrible, searching hands that had so many times sent her fleeing in terror.

She had been eleven years old and her cousin Maurice had just celebrated his eighteenth birthday. He had caught her in her room after his birthday party. She stood before him in her new white dress. It was ruffled; the sleeves were puffy, and the bodice was snug.

"Come here, Sophia." His voice had been soft. She hadn't moved.

"You are growing right before my eyes, little Sophia. I must see how much you have grown." His words became ugly.

But when he started rearranging the folds of her dress and continued mumbling under his breath, she became terrified. As she turned and fled, the sash of her dress tore off in his hand.

His laughter had followed her.

Her mother had found her in her room. She had taken off the party dress and with her scissors was cutting it into small pieces. Marie was so angry that Sophia was afraid to tell her about Maurice. Instinctively, she knew that she wouldn't be believed.

From then on, she was careful to keep away from Maurice, but she could feel his eyes always upon her. Finally, unable to bear it any longer, she told Jan.

Jan had laughed and told her that Maurice was just a sissy. "I hate his goody-goody manners and his clean white shirts," he had said.

She'd heard Marie say many times, "Jan, why can't you be more like your cousin Maurice? He keeps so clean."

The twins were always together—Sophia for protection, and Jan because he liked having a follower wherever he led.

She had mourned Jan's death, but when the normal grief had begun to subside, she realized that she was now without a champion. She had discovered by now that Maurice sought out no girlfriends his own age. Those white hands would reach out for her, and he would laugh at her fears.

"Uncle Józef won't wait very patiently, Sophia. But he did say he hoped that you had found time to have your bath. I do say, cousin, that I quite agree with him. I think you've worn that same corduroy shirt for a week." He left her suddenly.

The shirt she had on was nearly as repulsive to her as it was to Maurice, but she preferred it to him. She wondered how much longer she would need to pretend that she was deranged over Jan's death.

Sophia had accidentally discovered a new defense. Everyone knew that she thought someone was responsible for Jan's death, but she couldn't be sure. Her hysterics and grief-ravaged appearance had caused a look of distaste on Maurice's face. *I think this will keep him away from me.*

As the water filled the bathtub, she thought of what she had hoped would be her salvation.

It was a year ago now, but that afternoon was still fresh in her mind. It was a few months after Jan's funeral, and she was listless from the tranquilizers Dr. Janda had given her. He had ordered her to take a nap each afternoon. On that day, Manka had insisted on bringing her lunch on a tray and had waited while Sophia ate. Then Manka smoothed Sophia's blankets, gathered up the tray, and left the room.

Soon afterward, Józef had tapped lightly on the door and had come into her room.

He pulled a straight-backed chair near her bed and sat down. He took her limp hand in his own. His eyes were intense, and Sophia had a feeling that he was not there to inquire about her health.

"Sophia ..." he began hesitantly, "we are all hurt by Jan's death. We can truly sympathize with you."

A large tear escaped from the wounded expression in her brown eyes. "Thank you, Father." Her voice was steady, and there were no further tears.

"I've loved you and Jan since you came to Forest House with your mother. I'm also fond of Monica and Maurice and your grandmother. You know that, don't you, Sophia?" Józef looked at her for understanding.

"You've been very good to me," she assured him.

"I hope you can understand what I'm going to say." He took a deep breath. "Although I love Maurice like a son, he isn't a blood relation. I have no son of my own." He hesitated. When she nodded her understanding, and he said, "I must have an heir!"

He stood up and paced back and forth. Hurriedly, he told her of his nephew in Poland, of the jeweled crucifix. Then, abruptly, he came to the point.

"Sophia, it's arranged that my brother will send his second son here to Forest House next year as my successor. But, Sophia, marriage is the only legal way he can stay here at this time. Will you marry my nephew, Stefan Zurowski?"

He stopped pacing and sat down again in the chair by her bedside.

The proposal didn't surprise Sophia. The shock was in the fact that a father would sell his son.

"His father is willing to 'trade' him for a crucifix?" she asked. Pity went out to the unknown son.

Józef waved her question away impatiently. "You under estimate the crucifix and my brother. The deed is done, Sophia. Vincent Ludlow is at Forest House with the necessary forms for a proxy marriage. It's urgent, dear, or I wouldn't have approached you." He was torn between the need for haste and the need not to scare this wounded girl. "Will you marry him?" he asked again.

"When?" she asked.

"This afternoon at the church. Ludlow will stand in for Stefan, and no one except Father Polzak will know. For Stefan's safety and the security of the crucifix, it must be kept secret."

Sophia's features were flat, and she looked beyond Józef to the corner of the room. "Yes, Father, I will marry him."

Józef breathed a loud sigh of relief. "You won't be sorry, Sophia. Stefan will inherit all I have, and you'll be his wife."

"I love Forest House," she said simply. "I love you, too, Father."

He stood ill at ease. He had expected that he'd need to break down her excuses one by one. It was anticlimactic.

"Thank you, my dear. I'll send Helka to help you dress; you still look weak. I will tell your mother that Dr. Janda wants to see you in his office, and that I must go to town anyway. Vincent Ludlow and I do have an appointment with my lawyers in Dark Forest later today to draw up a new will."

"I'll be ready quickly," she assured him.

The intervening months since that day a year ago had passed quickly until now it no longer seemed real. She didn't remember what she'd chosen to wear for the ceremony. It was true that she loved Józef and Forest House, and suddenly she had seen this unknown Stefan Zurowski as a replacement for Jan.

She thought Józef had been a little surprised that she had agreed so readily to the marriage, but he apparently was so relieved that he'd made no comment.

When she had signed the papers, she hadn't thought about the demands of a husband upon a wife. She just wanted someone else to stand between her and Maurice. She was so tired of wearing Jan's clothes, and she longed to be able to give her hands and hair the proper care.

Now, she slipped into a soft green-wool dress and brushed her hair until it shone like bronze. She had not taken so much trouble with her appearance since Jan's death. Carefully, she transferred the shell casing from her trousers to the pocket of the dress.

But she was sure that the stranger on the road had been Stefan. As she recalled, there was something about him that had reminded her of Józef. On the path leading to Lew's cabin, he had whispered a few words. She had recognized the words as Polish.

She walked down the carpeted stairs, opened a door to the left of the entrance hall, and entered the library. Her family was there, waiting for her. The scene looked peaceful and domestic.

"My dear, you do look much better." Józef smiled kindly at her.

"Yes, one would think that sometimes our dear Sophia pretends just a little." It was Monica, Maurice's sister.

Sophia had seen a panther sunning itself on a ledge once and been reminded of her cousin Monica. Her black hair, green eyes, and languid movements made her irresistible to her admirers. But danger lurked. The almond-shaped eyes in her oval face gave her a delicate beauty, hiding the claws buried just below the surface.

"Do you think our little miss has been fooling us all?" Maurice asked his sister as his eyes searched Sophia's face.

"Now, you two, lay off. Dr. Janda said that there was nothing wrong with Sophia," Józef admonished.

"It's just a matter of time." Marie made a token effort of support in her daughter's defense. "I do hope she proves him right soon. Many more appearances like tonight, and she'll make us the laughingstock of the town."

"That is quite enough from all of you," Józef told them. "Stefan Zurowski has indeed arrived from Poland and is on his way here. And I want to tell you all why he has come. I owe you that much."

Sophia watched all eyes fasten on Józef. Even little Mrs. Milewski looked alert, and the click of her knitting needles stopped.

"I've made a will naming Stefan Zurowski, my only blood relative"—he looked pointedly at Marie— "as my sole heir."

"But, Uncle Józef, how is he able to get here now?" Maurice asked, putting a voice to the question that lingered in all their minds.

"How he got here is a thing of the past. And why he's to be allowed to stay is an accomplished fact."

"Score a victory for clever Uncle Józef!" Monica cheered softly.

Józef smiled.

"So, he's coming to Forest House. How *is* he to be allowed to stay?" Marie demanded.

Sophia glanced nervously at her mother because she knew the answer would focus attention on her. She drew farther back into her wingback chair.

"Because, my dear, our Sophia was married to Stefan by proxy last year."

The silence was broken by a shrill laugh from Monica. "But, dear Uncle Józef, why little Sophia? She has never had a boyfriend and nearly faints if a man looks at her."

"She willingly agreed to the arrangement."

"But surely, Uncle—"

"Monica, it's done," he said decisively. "Marriages have been arranged for centuries in the old country. If it sounds new to you, it's because you are so young. They'll adjust. And there will be sons to carry on the Zurowski name."

"Sons!" Monica laughed. "Children? *I* would be much more likely to produce an heir!"

"That is probably true, Monica"—he kept his tone even and smiled as he spoke— "but with Sophia, we can all be sure that it will be a legitimate one."

Monica's face flushed an unbecoming red. She turned her back angrily and looked into the fire in the stone fireplace.

"Józef, there is no need to be rude and insulting," Marie said.

Józef ignored his wife's comment. "Now, family, as I was saying, Sophia is married to my nephew. And we all now are awaiting the bridegroom."

Józef had fooled them all.

Sophia felt Maurice looking at her and felt ill at ease, even with a roomful of people.

Antek knocked discreetly at the door and entered, carrying a silver tray. The firelight caught the glitter of the red liquid and sparkled against the crystal glasses.

Józef ceremoniously served the wine. "A toast, family. I've ordered a toast to our bride."

"Why not?" agreed Monica. "It's all in the family."

Józef slipped his arm around Sophia's shoulders and kissed her on the cheek. "To our bride."

Maurice nodded. "Here, here! But we'll get even with her for keeping such a secret."

Sophia's throat tightened. Maurice presumably had spoken in jest, but she recognized it for the threat it was.

They all drank the wine, and the occasion was over.

"I do love weddings, though," Mrs. Milewski said sorrowfully. "It's too bad that we missed out on a chance to have one."

Marie always looked surprised when her ex-mother-in-law spoke. "It's a little after the fact, Mother," she scoffed.

"Yes," Józef agreed, "we can't have a wedding. But we do want to plan for a party as soon as he arrives."

"Oh, wonderful!" Mrs. Milewski clapped her small hands.

"It's very kind of you, matka, to think of a welcoming party," Józef said.

Mrs. Milewski smiled at his use of the Polish word for *mother*.

It was late when they bid each other good night and started to their rooms.

"Can you stay a few minutes, Sophia? I would like to talk with you." Józef sat by the fire as the others walked to the door.

Sophia kept her head averted. She studied the flowers in the brass bowl that reflected softly in the polished surface of the library table. She knew her mother was waiting for her at the door.

"More secrets, Józef?" mocked Marie.

"Perhaps, my dear."

Sophia sat in the chair across from her stepfather and gazed into the fire. He seemed to be in no hurry to talk.

She could relax here. This had always been one of her favorite rooms. The massive desk in front of the wall of bookshelves—one could spend hours browsing and reading from this library. The furniture was comfortable, and the entire atmosphere was inviting.

She would have felt entirely at ease if it hadn't been for the injured man lying in Lew's cabin. Her husband! She might be a widow before the night was out. She wondered how Józef would react when she told him of his injured nephew.

"You look more relaxed than you have in a long time, my dear. You are feeling better, aren't you?

Sophia loved Józef and felt a twinge of guilt at her deception. But it couldn't be helped. And her deception really had not hurt anyone but herself.

"Dr. Janda said that perhaps a shock would bring you back to your old self." He studied her closely as he continued. "Did you have a shock this morning?"

"Yes."

"Did you see the man who is your husband? Is my nephew here?"

"Yes, I think so."

"But where is he now? Surely there is no reason why he wouldn't come to the house. Ludlow said that Stefan had said he would arrive when he chose and in his own way. But why would he not come straight here once he arrived in Dark Forest?"

"Father, he tried."

"Tried? Then … where is he?"

She stood up and put her hand on the mantel, looking at the picture above the fireplace. It was of Józef Zurowski when he was younger. And down in Lew's tiny house lay a man on a cot with the same look.

"Well, Sophia, what has happened?"

She turned and looked at him. "He was shot as he walked up the lane to Forest House."

"Shot?" Józef was bewildered.

"Yes, and I was afraid to have him brought up to the house. I went to Lew and helped him take Stefan to his cabin. That's where he is now."

"You still think that Jan was murdered, don't you?"

"Maybe." She looked away briefly. "But I was not willing to take the chance with Stefan."

"How is he?"

"I don't know. We stopped the bleeding, but Lew said he shouldn't be moved."

"I'll send Dr. Janda there first thing in the morning. Stefan had been very ill while sailing here, so he was weakened to begin with."

Sophia paled. "I didn't know. At the time, I thought that someone at the house was shooting at him, and I didn't think I should bring him here so whoever it was would have another chance."

"Oh, Sophia, how could you think that? No one here knew he was coming except you and me."

"I thought maybe they were aiming at me," Sophia said, "but Lew said no doubt it was a hunting accident. The shot came from the direction of the old deer stand in the tree. I went there and found a shell casing." She took the empty shell casing from her pocket and handed it to him.

"Why would anyone shoot at you, my dear?" He examined the casing and added, "Yes, a deer rifle could reach that far. So, you no longer believe someone was shooting at Stefan?"

"No. I don't."

"Good." He stood up and stretched his hand toward her. "Come, Sophia, let me walk you to your room, and you get a good night's rest. You've had a hard day."

She clasped his hand. There was strength there, and she pressed his hand against her cheek. "You are right. It's been a long day. But everything will be all right now."

They walked up the stairs together. No need for him to worry.

As they passed the drapery in the hall at the head of the stairs, Sophia caught the scent of cologne, heavy and sweet. She knew it was not a draft that caused the curtain to move slightly.

She squeezed Józef's hand. What if he hadn't been with her?

She locked the door of her room behind her and heard Józef go back down the stairs. She knew that he would waste no time in going down the hill to the cabin in the woods.

Soon, she heard the sound of the Jeep's motor and the snarl of gears as it roared away from the house.

Sophia lay in the bed and listened to the quiet.

Then there was a soft footstep outside her door. She held her breath as she saw the doorknob turn. She heard a soft chuckle and then nothing.

It was a while before she was able to fall asleep.

CHAPTER SEVEN

⋙⋘

It was unusual for the family to eat breakfast together, but the following morning each arrived in the small dining room at about the same time. It was obvious that the announcement of the night before had affected them all.

Józef was more animated and alive than he had been for years. Sophia knew that Marie was puzzled by her husband's actions. Sophia had kept Józef's secret—kept the secret from all of them. Józef had made plans during the night that included everyone. The whole place soon would be an upheaval of activity.

"Maurice," Józef began, "with my nephew expected here, I don't want to leave at this time. You will take some signed contracts for me to Vincent Ludlow in New York. You will wait there until the man in the government office looks over the contracts and returns them to Ludlow. That will take about three weeks." He then looked at Monica. "You may go with him, if you wish."

"Why, Uncle Józef, you're trying to get rid of me. You know how you usually object to my going to the wicked big city."

"Nothing of the sort, Monica. There'll be a crew of carpenters here today—coming this morning, in fact—and you know you would hate the noise and inconvenience."

"What are the carpenters going to do?" Marie asked.

"I'm having them redo the second floor of the right wing for Stefan and Sophia." He looked at his wife as if she should have known.

"Oh," she said, "then I think I'll go to New York with Maurice and Monica. Vincent is always a very entertaining host."

Józef didn't rise to the bait. "Suit yourself, Marie. I'm sure Sophia can choose the colors and fabrics she wants without any help. Can't you, dear?"

"I'll try."

"There will be plenty of samples to choose from. The people bringing them will assist you if you need them. That is part of what we're paying them for."

Marie seemed to reconsider. "Perhaps I should stay here …"

"Nonsense, my dear, you'd just be bored. Go and have a good time. As soon as you get back, you can start the plans for the party. Maybe while you are in New York, you can find something to make the party an extra success. It isn't every day that you introduce a count."

"Count?" Marie looked shocked.

"Did I not mention? My nephew is Count Stefan Zurowski of Domani z Camin. I'm sure you can find enough information in a New York library to satisfy even your curiosity. You've often longed to know more of my family; here is your opportunity to find out at last." He stood up abruptly and walked over to Sophia. "Countess, will you accompany me to the library? I want to show you the plans for the new wing."

Sophia and Józef smiled at each other.

Józef's mother-in-law exclaimed, "Countess Sophia. What a wonderful sound it has. How very nice for our poor little girl."

Józef closed the library door behind them and turned to Sophia. "Stefan is alive. Dr. Janda looked at him last night and agreed with Lew that he shouldn't be moved."

So, her stepfather hadn't waited until this morning to get Dr. Janda. The young man clearly was important to him. "I'm so glad." Sophia didn't know how worried she had been until she heard that Stefan had survived the night.

"Dr. Janda says that it will be at least a week before he can be up, but he said Stefan couldn't have a better nurse than old Lew."

Sophia smiled. She had been right to take Stefan to the old man.

"I don't want the others to know there's been an accident," Józef said. "I want my nephew walking into this house, not being carried."

"Is he conscious this morning?"

"Yes, but he could talk very little. He did tell me of my brother's death. Stefan's older brother, Konrad, was also killed, which is why Stefan now has the title of Count."

"Did he notice anything before he was shot?"

"No. He didn't see the glint off the rifle barrel that you saw. It was a sorry greeting for a newcomer to our country."

He opened the desk drawer angrily and drew out a roll of drawings. He spread the blueprints on top of the desk and pulled an extra chair close for Sophia. "This is the floor plan of the second floor of the right wing." He pointed with the sharpened end of his pencil.

They had their heads together over the drawings and didn't hear the family leave the house. The engine of the powerful car was quiet as it rolled out of the driveway and down the narrow lane to the main highway.

Antek knocked on the library door and entered at the sound of Józef's voice.

"Sir, the building superintendent is here, asking for you." Antek's voice was carefully modulated, but he was not stoic enough to suppress the gleam of curiosity in his dark eyes. Still, he stood straight, correct, waiting for a reply.

"Show him in, Antek." He smiled warmly at Sophia.

The renovation of the entire right wing started in earnest. The architect had drawn up the plans a year earlier, after Stefan had left the university and the exchange agreement with Józef's brother had been put in place, and after the proxy wedding.

The partitions were taken down, and the space created became two huge bedrooms with a connecting door. Each bedroom had its own dressing room and bath. The room on the other side of the partition, running the entire length of the sleeping area, was a huge rectangle that was turned into a spacious sitting room. The rich, gleaming wooden beams visually lowered the ceiling, giving the room a cozy appearance despite its size.

Sophia watched every day as the new wing took shape. Upon entering the sitting room from the hall, one saw a stone fireplace to the left. The hearth's surface was of black slate, as was the mantel.

Sophia chose a thick, luxurious carpet of rich burgundy and cream colors for the sitting room. The deep-red background provided a contrast for the pale cream designs outlined in black. A pair of burgundy wingback chairs sat before the fireplace with an oval beige fur area rug between them. Completing the seating arrangements around the fireplace were matching sofas with plush and comfortable cushions of cream velvet. The draperies at the windows were heavy burgundy velvet, tied back with thick gold ropes to reveal delicate golden sheers.

A tea table stood against the wall beside a small glass-front corner cabinet that displayed a collection of exquisite china cups and saucers. The tea service on the table was a special gift from Józef. He'd had it especially crafted with the Zurowski coat of arms on each piece—the crucifix on a medieval shield.

At the other end of the sitting room, an ebony grand piano stood waiting. Sophia walked to the piano and ran her hand lightly over the smoothness of the wood. She had not played since Jan's death.

In the gold-frame mirror behind the piano, she saw her reflection. There was more color in her cheeks, and she admitted to her reflection that she looked almost alive again. She placed two tall tapers in the silver candlesticks on the piano and looked around. Two comfortable chairs with ottomans were tastefully arranged in this area of the room, with a floor cabinet radio within easy reach. An oval library table held an imported Chinese bowl. The chess board on it was made of teak. The chess pieces were carved ivory.

The wall hanging added a few more strong colors to the room, blending and contrasting with the reds and creams.

Sophia walked into her bedroom and inspected the finishing touches the decorators had made before they left. She had chosen Wedgewood blue for the carpet, and there were darker blue accents in the room. The spread on the wide bed was ivory, bordered with a Chinese print of birds and exotic flowers. Light-blue draperies were embroidered with the same birds and flowers in shades of darker blues. Heavy red ropes held back the draperies.

A small writing desk and a chaize lounge of gray silk were against the wall with the connecting door, leading to the room that would be Stefan's.

Sophia made herself walk toward the door, and she put her hand on the knob. Cold fear knotted in her stomach. When she had agreed to marry this man, she hadn't realized that someday he would appear—that he would actually take form and substance.

"Stop being silly," she said aloud as she opened the door.

A figure stood in the middle of the room, and she jumped.

"Oh, Sophia, I didn't mean to startle you." Józef held out his hand and smiled. "I didn't know anyone was up here. I came to inspect the work now that the crew is gone. They've done a fine job, and it hasn't been but a little more than two weeks."

"Yes, Father. They've done well. I didn't know how to choose for a man, and of course I don't know what Stefan would like at all."

Józef's expression suddenly looked serious. "Sophia, you will be happy.

Don't worry. Just see how you've improved over these past few days. Dr. Janda said it would happen, and now it has. You're almost like your old self."

"Yes. It's restful to have my mind busy with the new room alterations. Do you like this room?" She looked around uncertainly.

It was a masculine and comfortable room with rich browns and heavy furniture. A leather chair and ottoman sat beside a round three-legged table that held a tall brass reading lamp. Above the head of the bed, a forest scene added deep greens and the gold of sunlight. The spread on his bed was bold—gold and brown stripes.

"Neither of us knows Stefan, but he couldn't help but like this room. You have hidden talents, my dear."

"Thank you, kind sir," She curtsied slightly and laughed gaily.

"I'm going to the cabin to see our patient today. Lew sent word that he thinks Stefan will be able to come here in a couple of days. Why don't you join us after lunch? I want to talk to him some before you arrive. There's much that I want to ask. But you need to meet him as soon as possible."

"I'm married to a man that I've seen once. And he's never seen me! Father, it's a little frightening."

"If you can, come to the cabin soon after lunch." He pressed her hand and left the room.

Sophia was in her old room, combing her hair. It had just begun to snow, and she watched the big flakes cling momentarily to the windowpane before they melted. She loved the snow and was eager for her walk, even though she was hesitant about going to Lew's cabin. At least she wouldn't have to be afraid of meeting Maurice. She had relaxed while he was away. If only he never returned!

Pulling the hood of her green woolen coat over her bright hair, she went out to the flagstone terrace. She loved the feel of the wet snowflakes and lifted her face to the sky. If only she weren't so uncertain of her reception at her destination.

She slipped into the woods and started on the path to the cabin. When she and Jan were children, Lew had taught them to walk silently in the woods. He'd said they'd be more likely to be accepted as part of nature and would be able to see the animals. Now it was natural for her to walk quietly on the forest paths.

She heard a sound. At first, she thought it was a deer breaking in the undergrowth. Instinctively, she dodged behind a tree. Then, slowly, she looked around the tree.

About seventy yards away was a figure on a horse. His face was hidden from her, so she couldn't be positive of his identity, but he looked like the new priest, Father Vladek. It was plain to see that he was puzzled, but she could not say what it was that kept her from calling out. He bent his head thoughtfully for several minutes. Then he must have decided which way he wanted to go. He pulled his knitted cap closer around his ears against the snow and urged his horse on up the path, climbing to the right.

That trail led deep into the forest. There wasn't anything to see, except for an old logger's cabin. There was nothing else in that direction but miles of unbroken forest. Maybe he really did like exploring.

The priest had made an unusual request of Józef. He'd asked permission to ride on their land because he said that he liked to keep in good physical condition. Józef had given him permission and told him that although not many people rode horses in this region of the country, there were a few saddle horses at Forest House's stable. The heavily wooded countryside didn't allow for the wide-open expanses that made horseback riding so popular. Father Vladek had thanked him and said he would find an adequate place to ride.

Sophia watched him part the low-hanging branches before he proceeded. *He hasn't chosen a very agreeable trail,* she thought. *If that's really Father Vladek, it's odd that a priest so recently come from Poland is so interested in our North Woods. Perhaps I should tell Józef. A person could easily get lost, especially in a snowstorm.*

As she walked toward the cabin, thoughts of the priest and the man Jan had seen deep in the forest fled to the back of her mind. She dreaded the meeting in the small house.

The cabin was in view. She didn't go to the door but walked around to steal a glance in the side window. The window was open a little, and conversation came out on the cold air. Józef was bringing Stefan up-to-date on the war.

"The launch by Germany was ineffective since it missed the railroad bridge over the Firth of Forth. Normal service was uninterrupted. The explosion was actually on the center pier on Inch Garvie Island," said Józef forcefully.

"But the significance of that raid is that the war has spread to Scotland,"

Stefan quickly pointed out. "Poland was just the beginning. It will spread worldwide!"

"Perhaps, Stefan. Perhaps it will," agreed Józef. "Our U.S. Senate has repealed the Embargo Act."

"What does that mean, Uncle Józef?" Stefan questioned.

"Basically, this means the belligerent countries can now only buy from the United States if they pay cash and if they carry supplies in their own ships," explained Józef.

"That would block Germany from buying from America," Stefan concluded.

Józef said, "You're right; you have a quick mind."

Sophia positioned herself to hear their conversation more clearly.

"There are those in the Senate who are working for the repeal of our Neutrality Law," continued Józef.

"Would this then allow Allies to order aircraft from American firms?"

"Yes," Józef said quickly. "I know for a fact that there are millions of dollars' worth of orders sitting at the ready. They will go into effect the very day this Neutrality Law is repealed."

Sophia knew that her stepfather supplied much of the needed materials.

Józef seemed to hesitate but then plunged ahead. "Stefan, I need you here with me. We can work for the defeat of the enemies of Poland with the means at our disposal—our mines, factories, mills!"

"I could do so little in Warsaw," Stefan confessed, remembering. "And all our efforts combined were useless."

Outside the window, Sophia moved slightly. The men were so absorbed in their conversation that they took no notice.

"Uncle Józef, I came here with the idea of buying back what I thought of as my 'freedom' by returning the jeweled crucifix to you."

"I don't want the crucifix!" Józef broke in abruptly. "I want you here as my heir, working with me!"

Stefan ignored the outburst. "If I had known that I had been given a wife to keep me in this country, I might not have come at all."

"Then perhaps it's fortunate that you didn't know of the conditions of the arrangements before you came to the United States. I want you here, Stefan. There is nothing for you to go back to. Land is here—Zurowski land—that will be yours when I die. We Poles are individualistic, Stefan. Our loyalty is to people, to family, not only to country."

Sophia was impressed by the ardor in her uncle's voice.

"The lack of regimentation in Polish political life is probably what has led to most of Poland's troubles," Józef said. "Regimentation seemed necessary in central and eastern Europe, but we Poles could never stomach it. This was tragic in the old country. But here, Stefan, here in America, individuality is the stuff of heroes, the stuff of dreams." He finished emphatically, "Besides, Stefan, Germany now has the Corridor and Warsaw and Danzig."

Stefan winced as if from a physical blow. "And I had to leave before I could bury my family! What will become of Frederic and Kasia!" It was a painful cry, not a question.

Through the window, Sophia could see the pain registered on the faces of both men.

"You're right, Uncle," Stefan said. "There is nothing to go back to at this time. And now I have a wife."

"It's too bad. I'm sorry about that, Stefan!"

Sorry about that! The words screamed at Sophia. No doubt her uncle was sympathizing with Stefan over this necessity. But as a man of honor, perhaps Stefan would not toss her aside. Did the loyalty he felt toward the Zurowski honor extend to an unchosen wife?

A sob escaped her, and she sank to her knees in the slushy snow. Quiet cries tore from her throat in agony. She only now realized how much she had counted on Stefan as more than simply protection from Maurice. She had wanted a friend.

"I'm sorry about that, Stefan, and I wish that you had known about it before you arrived. Sophia is very young, but she is a good girl."

"I left no love behind, Uncle Józef. It makes no difference to me."

Sophia got up and started running, her feet tripping over roots and rocks. She stumbled, her hood was thrown back, and pine needles and leaves caught in her hair. She fell, and her coat became covered with icy mud. The cold moisture mixed with her scalding tears. She pushed herself up and ran all the way back to the house; her breath came in great gasps.

Her vision was blurred, and she groped with stiff hands at the rail leading onto the wide veranda at the house. She ran into the arms of a waiting figure.

"You're back." Sophia said. It sounded like a fatal admission.

"Dear Sophia, did you miss me so very much?" The syrupy voice acted like a dash of cold water in her face. The heavy cologne choked her. She hiccupped loudly and opened her eyes, sniffing noisily.

She knew her face was swollen and dirty, and she didn't try to hide it from him. He dropped his arms quickly.

"It seems like your improvement was only temporary. You are your sloppy self again, I see. Too bad; you were always such an appealing child."

She escaped into the house to the sound of his laughter. In the privacy of her own room, she flung herself on the bed and stared at the ceiling. Her tears were gone. She had wished many times that she could confide in her stepfather, but she could not. He would no longer see her as an innocent girl. She couldn't bear the thought. And would he completely believe her? Maurice had always been his bookkeeper, a trusted confidant in financial matters.

She had been feeling sorry for herself. She had been romanticizing. Of course, a man who had a wife forced upon him could not expect to feel grateful. *A man who was given a mad wife would naturally rebel*, she thought wryly.

So, she would accept that. This encounter with Maurice helped her come to a decision. Stefan needed her so that he could stay in America. She needed him as protection against Maurice. It was an equitable trade. At least she could bathe regularly and dress again in a civilized way. It was not much to build a life on, but she could have some peace of mind.

There was that shot in the woods too. Someone had killed Jan. She was sure of that now. They were also trying to kill her. Was it Maurice? Would he go that far? It was hard to believe that he would commit murder. But who else could it have been? Who else had wanted Jan out of the way? Was someone in this house her enemy?

Strangely, she thought of the man again that Jan had seen in the woods a year ago.

CHAPTER EIGHT

The man dismounted stiffly from his horse and looked around. This was the spot marked on the map, but there didn't seem to be anyone here. He cursed under his breath. He didn't like working with foreigners; you could never really trust them. They were inferior.

He walked toward the weathered-looking shack. He thought he saw a movement, but maybe it was just a shadow on the window. His boots made shallow echoes on the wooden porch. Surprisingly, the door didn't make any sound as he carefully swung it inward.

"It's time you show up." The words were spoken in faltering English; the tone was accusatory. "You have not been in hurry to come here."

The man who had spoken stepped from the corner. He was built like a squat brick. The skin on his face was splotched red and deeply seamed. The nose was wide, and hair growing from his nostrils curled upward. Straggly hairs from the protruding ridges that served as brows could have been untidy stitches binding swollen lacerations. Mercifully, a thick black beard covered the lower half of his face. He looked to be in his fifties, but already his hair was completely white. The contrast was startling. His eyes bore accusingly into the face of the newcomer.

The man didn't flinch at the foreigner's words. The man was young, but his face would always be ageless. No prolonged emotion was ever allowed to show on his face long enough to leave an impression. Tracks weren't left on stone. His face would remain unlined. His voice was staccato.

"You've been here for a year; don't let it affect your mind. Don't push me, Stash. We tolerate you because we need you. Have you learned anything?"

"The passenger from the *Baltic Queen* did arrive," Stash said defiantly.

"Are you sure? I didn't see him. At the house they didn't think he had arrived yet."

"I saw him with my own eyes!" Stash retorted.

"Where was that?" The question was quick.

"I shot him!"

"You fool! He may be the only one who knows where it is."

"Well, I was not shooting at him anyway. I was aiming at the red-haired girl, but I slipped, and my rifle went off. It was accident." His gravelly voice was defensive. He scratched nervously at the mats of hair on the backs of his thick hands.

"Is he dead?"

"I don't know. I hurt my ankle when I fell and couldn't get back up into the tree to see."

"You're a fool! I wonder that they think you are useful to us at all." His voice was coldly mocking.

"Remember that I can identify it. You would hate to deliver the wrong thing," Stash taunted him.

The younger man just looked at him. "Why did you want to kill the girl?"

"She may know that I'm up here in the woods."

"How?"

"Her brother saw me. He may have told her," Stash explained.

"So, it was you who killed him?" Things were getting out of hand. These blind, bloody foreigners.

"Sure! But no one knew."

"Did no one suspect?"

"Yeah, his sister did. But she went berserk after his death, and no one believed her. After several months, I thought it was safe to stage another accident. She wanders around by herself a lot. No one is with her, now that her brother is out of the way."

"But are you sure he would have had time to tell her?" It was important. They had not arranged for Stash to hide out in this godforsaken country so long for nothing.

"No, I'm not sure. How can I be? I was just going to play it safe."

"Listen and listen good." His voice was hard. "Stay out of sight. It's possible that you may be recognized. And no one must know that you are here." He sneered. "Your face is hard to forget."

"Oh, I stay up here in this logging shack almost all the time. No one comes up here except an old man on a donkey who runs his traps in winter down the hill from here by the creek."

"Stay clear of the old man. And I will keep my ears open for any mention of a stranger seen in the woods."

"If I get a chance to make it look like accident, I will take care of the girl."

"Just make sure that there can be no question that it was accidental. We don't want things messed up now. We are so close to the end." The younger man opened the door and started back out.

Stash followed him. "When are you coming back?" he whined. Even this man's company was better than being so alone.

"I don't know. The trip here takes two hours on horseback. Just sit tight. And never, never try to contact me."

Stash watched the man ride away. His back was straight, proud. He still didn't know the young man's name.

Stefan had agreed with his Uncle Józef that he would arrive at the house on his own, as was expected. Uncle Józef did insist that he not arrive looking like he had jumped ship. Józef provided some new clothes and a couple of suitcases.

The thought of owning the crucifix troubled him. It was his, by right, but as long as he possessed it, he would feel like he belonged to Uncle Józef. For the time being, he would stay in America, but it was his decision. He wasn't being forced.

Stefan pulled the fisherman-knit sweater over his head and folded down the turtleneck collar. The heavy leather-trimmed corduroy coat matched the brown corduroy trousers that hugged his lean hips. Picking up his luggage, he started to Forest House. Even after nearly a month's time, he could still feel the stiffness in his shoulder.

The evening sun was glistening on the snow, and Stefan squinted against the brightness. He could see the house now. If he had expected it to resemble Domani z Camin in any way, he was disappointed. This was not the house of an immigrant pining for the home he had left behind.

The front lawn would be edged with a massive flower garden in the summer. A fountain and rock garden were backed up to the edge of a stone terrace that he could see running back along one side of the house.

A wide veranda ran the entire length of the front of the house and the second-floor balcony ran the same width and length above. The third floor, Stefan guessed, would be for the servants, since there didn't seem to be another building to serve as living quarters close by, only a garage. A stable was located near the edge of the woods to the right of the house.

The material for the house, he knew, had been taken from the surrounding forests. His new home was one with the forest, and the trees protected it.

Stefan knew there were hundreds of acres under cultivation for the maintenance of the animals and the people living here. Somewhere there were dairies, barns, grain silos, chicken houses. Forest House was self-sufficient. It was Józef's Polish heritage that made him insist on this. He was, first, a landowner, a man of the soil.

If the outside of Forest House had suffered in comparison with Domani z Camin, the inside didn't. A neat, uniformed maid ushered him into the large entrance foyer. In one glance, Stefan immediately doubled the number of rooms that he had thought Forest House had.

The maid showed him to the living room and then went to announce him. He looked around at the furnishings. The carpet beneath his feet was thick and silent; elaborately framed mirrors recalled the gold and white brocade of the furniture and draperies. The decor was formal and sterile. He could not imagine his Uncle Józef in this room.

"Sir, if you will come with me, please. The family is waiting in the library."

So, he would meet them all together. For the first time, he thought of meeting his wife. *Wife!* He wanted to turn and run. It was one thing to tumble the daughters of the peasant farmers on the estate when he was a teenager or accept the easy offerings of the girls who were impressed with the wealth and title of his family, but it was quite another to live with one woman, day after day, when you didn't love her—didn't even know her!

The maid opened the library. "Count Stefan Zurowski, sir."

"Stefan?" Józef was a superb actor. "Welcome!"

"Uncle Józef?" He could play the game too.

"Yes. We're so glad that you've finally arrived." He drew him to where the others were sitting. "All the family are waiting to meet you."

Stefan let his glance slide over the curious faces turned toward him. The girl was there—a child, really. The same one that he had seen hiding in the trees. She was no longer wearing the dusty green corduroys but the same frightened expression was on her face. He longed to reassure her. He wanted to protect her from whatever she feared. She was little older than Anne.

Anne's expression would have been similarly frightened before the soldier attacked her. He brought his attention back to what his uncle was saying.

"My wife, Marie."

Stefan took her hand. She was a handsome woman, but the restless expression on her face marred her looks. Her thick brown hair was caught in a fashionable coil, and her makeup was flawless. He knew who had decorated the living room.

"Your aunt Marie's mother-in-law, Mrs. Milewski, and Marie's niece and nephew, Monica and Maurice Milewski."

There was warmth in Mrs. Milewski's smile. He was reminded of Kasia.

"Very glad to meet you," Stefan said. After acknowledging Mrs. Milewski, he turned to Maurice, who stood to greet him. He had seen a man in Warsaw once like Maurice—so impeccably dressed and with the same nervous hand movements. There had been something peculiar about him, but he had forgotten what the rumors were. Maurice's handshake was brief and cold, although his smile welcomed Stefan. "And, Cousin Monica, how very charmed I'm to meet such a lovely member of the family."

Indeed, he couldn't find one criticism of her. Her movements were fluid and graceful as she extended both her shapely hands to him. As she offered her cheek to be kissed, he could see gold flecks in her green eyes. Her hair smelled of perfume.

"Cousin Stefan, we weren't prepared for such a handsome relative," Monica said. "Were we, Sophia?" She smiled at Sophia while keeping a possessive hand on Stefan's arm.

"And this, Stefan," Józef said, "is your wife, Sophia Zurowski."

Stefan walked to the chair where Sophia was sitting a little apart from the rest of the family. There was pitiful entreaty on her face.

He took her hand and pulled her gently to her feet. She was tall, but the red-gold of her hair reached only to his lips. Cupping her small pointed chin in his hand, he whispered so only she could hear. "Don't be afraid." He felt her relax.

"Uncle Józef, you have picked the most beautiful one of all to be my wife. Thank you." Stefan raised Sophia's hand to his lips and kissed it.

"I'm witnessing European gallantry," Monica sniped. "I must say that it does live up to its reputation."

"Don't be impertinent, Monica," Józef reprimanded.

Stefan laughed softly. "On the contrary, I'm afraid that I'm one of the poorest examples, but I hope that I'll never be rude." His smile and manner were devastatingly European.

Monica flushed.

"Uncle Józef, Frederic told me that a man named Jacobson came to America with you," Stefan said. "Is he still here?"

"Oh, yes, he is still with me. In fact, he's the one we have to thank for the well-kept grounds here at Forest House."

"He is a wizard with flowers," Marie said, "but he feels like he owns each one personally. He begrudges every bouquet we cut."

"Now, my dear, Stefan does not want to hear of the family feuds before he is settled in." He turned to Stefan. "Antek has taken your bags up, and dinner will be served in about an hour. So, I think that Sophia and I will have time to show you around your apartments before dinner." He turned to her. "Sophia?"

"I'm quite proud of the new wing," she said to no one in particular. Sophia preceded the two men up the wide staircase.

"I think you will be quite pleased with Sophia's choices for your suite," Józef said.

They stepped into the sitting room and closed the door.

"It went quite well, don't you think? No one suspected that we'd talked before." Józef evidently was proud of his deception.

Stefan noted the elegance of this room. It was not only tastefully furnished, but there was an air of comfort. "Sophia, your work in this room is a complete success." He wanted to say something to relieve the haunted look on her face.

"It was so much fun to do, and I'm very glad that you like it." There was just a hint of animation in her voice.

"Do you play?" He nodded toward the piano.

"Some," she admitted.

"She used to play a lot," Józef said. "But that was before Jan died. I have missed the music."

Stefan decided that there were hidden depths to this lovely girl. Somehow, her spirit had been wounded. "Perhaps I can coax her to play for me sometime. A little mazurka?"

"Perhaps," she answered softly.

He let his eyes search hers for answers. He kept his voice low as they spoke, hoping it would be comforting.

Dinner was a gay time. Manka had surpassed her usual good efforts.

The mushroom soup was thick with cream. It was followed by rafiki po krakowsky, beef roll-ups, with hot gravy. It was garnished with chopped parsley, and there were mashed potatoes, whole young carrots, and buttered asparagus with parmesan. It was a man's meal. Her efforts didn't go unnoticed.

"Manka, you are beyond price," Stefan said.

Sophia watched the cook beam with pride beneath his praise. "Ah, one who has just come from our old country can enjoy this, no?"

"You can be sure that I've had nothing to equal this since my arrival in the United States. The menus seemed to offer only something called 'hamburger' and 'hot dog'!"

They all laughed.

"We will make you good food like from the homeland!" Manka said. She went smiling back into the kitchen.

The conversation was easy and relaxed. Sophia's glance strayed to Stefan's face almost involuntarily. Often when he emphasized a remark or asked a question, he would lift an eyebrow. It gave a fascinating appearance to his already handsome face. Sophia saw that this wasn't unnoticed by Monica. She was at her charming best, and Sophia saw the intimate smiles she tried to share with Stefan.

Sophia felt she was no competition for Monica. It was all wrong. Monica should have married him.

No one noticed that Maurice was all but silent. He answered pleasantly if asked a question, but Sophia could feel his dark looks in her direction. A plan began to form in her mind. Maybe she and Stefan could reach some sort of agreement.

The coffee, nuts, and candies were served in the library while the family talked. A group of friends called for Monica, and she left. Sophia was glad her cousin had an engagement for the evening.

Marie, Sophia, and Mrs. Milewski listened as Stefan and Józef talked of Poland. Józef became a new person. He talked of people he had known, told of childhood happenings, and spoke of his mother.

Mrs. Milewski's knitting needles lay still in her lap while she dozed. Tendrils of hair had strayed around her wrinkled neck. The fire was dying down. Marie stifled a yawn.

"How thoughtless," Józef stood up. "It's getting late, and you must be tired after your journey."

Marie roused Mrs. Milewski, and they left the room.

"Good night, children." Józef said as he left the library and started down the corridor that led to his rooms in the long L-shaped wing at the rear of the house.

"Come, Sophia." Stefan smiled at her. She trembled as he placed his hand on her arm.

Sophia knew that Maurice watched them leave.

The lights in their sitting room had been dimmed. As they entered, Sophia impulsively turned to face Stefan. "I do need you desperately!"

He looked at her, his eyebrow raised very high. "I'm sure something can be arranged." He smiled.

She flushed hotly and dropped her head. "No, I didn't mean that."

With his forefinger, he lifted her chin until she was looking at him. There was kindness in his expression, understanding.

"Can we make a bargain?" Her voice quavered.

A little awkwardly, he stroked her hair with the palm of his hand.

Instinctively, she flinched. He drew his hand back. She was sorry for her action instantly. His touch was nothing like that of Maurice.

"If you don't need me desperately as a husband, my love, what can I do for you?"

She rushed on. "You need me so that you can stay in the United States, isn't this right?"

"Well," he said, "so I'm told. That precludes the fact that I do indeed want to stay." Confusion lingered in his voice.

"Oh." She felt panic rising.

"Yes, Sophia, I do need to be married to you so that I can remain in this country. And I do want to stay. What can I do for you?"

"I'm afraid of someone, and I need your protection."

"But who here would harm you?"

Whether he believed her or not, she could sense that he was taking her seriously. She guessed he was thinking of the ones he had met already.

"Must I really tell you?" She couldn't bear for him to know her shame.

"No, but how else can I help?" he asked.

Sophia nodded and then said, "Before Jan died, I was safe. I need them to think that I'm important to you and that you care what happens to me." Her brown eyes were pleading. She started to cry.

"I do care what happens to you. Very much."

"And you won't shame me before my family?"

"Shame you? How, Sophia?"

She turned her back to him.

He took hold of her shoulders and turned her to face him. "How could I shame you?"

She lowered her head.

"Sophia, look at me."

She met the gray of his eyes. She couldn't read their expression. Her words wouldn't come.

He helped her. "Are you telling me that you don't want me as a husband? You don't want to sleep with me, but you want us to keep up a pretense before your family?"

"Yes." Her answer was soft, but she didn't lower her eyes.

"Don't look so unhappy, Sophia. That isn't an impossible request. It can be so for as long as you wish it." He started for his room but then turned to her. "Sophia? I want to thank you for saving my life. I saw you hidden in the tree just before I was shot. Your face was the last thing I remembered. Lew told me how you stopped the bleeding and came for him. You were very brave."

He closed his door and she was alone.

The room was suddenly very large without him, and she walked quickly to her new bedroom. The door between their rooms was closed and would be for as long as she wanted it to be.

She had gotten what she wanted. The arrangement had been made, and he had understood so readily. Maybe he had no interest in her anyway. Józef, no doubt, had told him how odd she had been since the death of her brother. He had probably been warned that she was a little unstable.

She lay in bed and thought how easily her plan had been accomplished. As she was drifting off to sleep, she puzzled that her feeling of safety was also accompanied by a sense of loss.

Stefan had been shaken at the look on Sophia's face when she made her request. He would like to get his hands on the person who had frightened her like this. But he was a newcomer to this place. How well did he really know any of them? Even Uncle Józef? He liked this man, but he never would have branded him as a thief. Yet long ago, he did steal the crucifix. Probably none of them were what they seemed.

He did trust Sophia, though. She was innocent, as was his Anne. He would keep her safe.

CHAPTER NINE

The sun poured into her room, splashing pools of bright color on the carpet. Sophia stretched luxuriously. There was no heaviness; her spirit felt free and light. No shadow of fear hovered on the edge of her vision.

She ran a tub of water, generously adding bath salts and watched the bubbles foam and rise. She stepped out of her soft flannel gown and threw it aside. She did a pirouette around the room and giggled to herself as she slid into the warm water. Now she was really off in the head. Never had she felt like dancing nude before.

My hands, she thought, raising them from the bubbles, *will need a lot of care*. Hastily, she hid them beneath the water and sighed. Anyway, now she could stop hiding behind her rags and filth.

The jubilant spirit ebbed away, and she thought about having to leave the sanctity of her rooms. Well, she could put that off until lunchtime, anyway. She was starved, but she could forgo breakfast.

She scooted down in the tub and felt the water around her neck and ears. She would scrub her hair until her scalp tingled.

She dried herself on a large thick towel. Slipping into a warm dressing gown, she rolled her hair in a towel and fastened it securely.

There was a knock at the door.

Hesitantly, she went to answer it. "Yes? Who is it?"

"It is Helka. With your breakfast."

Sophia opened the door to the maid and looked at her in amazement. "Breakfast?"

"Miss Sophia, your husband asked Manka to fix a breakfast tray to be sent to your room this morning." Helka held the tray like it was a precious gift.

"He did?" Even to her own ears, this sounded silly. There Helka stood with the tray, so it must be so.

"Where shall I put it, miss?"

"In my bedroom, please."

Helka sat the tray on the desk and left quietly.

Sophia could not account for the tears in her eyes.

The aroma of the coffee was tantalizing. The tiny blue porcelain clock on her desk let her know it was after ten. She took the cover off the food. Scrambled eggs lay nestled beside the sausages, and there was butter and honey for Manka's fresh-baked bread. She ate every bite gratefully.

It was fun to survey herself in the full-length mirror this morning. She was glad for her good figure now. It had been hard to hide, even in Jan's old clothes. The soft, white wool slacks fit smoothly over her slim hips. Her matching white sweater was trimmed in pale green, and there were tiny green buttons at the teardrop neckline. Her breasts were shown to good advantage in the soft, clinging wool knit. She no longer looked like an unkempt urchin.

She didn't want Stefan to have reason to be ashamed of her. He wouldn't want people to feel sorry for him because of a wife who didn't think of her appearance.

The piano stood invitingly in its elegant surroundings. Sophia sat down and opened the music, a Chopin waltz.

She stretched her fingers and lightly rubbed her palms together. The keys beneath her fingers responded. The music bathed her soul. Hungrily, she let her fingers try the runs and trills that had once given wings to her heart. Her hands were unaccustomed to the exercise and would not play as quickly as her brain urged them to. She tried and then continued to work until she was totally absorbed in mastering the smooth fingering required of the waltz.

The clock chimed, and Sophia glanced up, surprised. It was only a few minutes before lunch; she would have to go down.

As she passed a mirror on her way to the door, she patted a stray curl into place and stepped out into the hall. It was quiet as she started down the corridor toward the landing, where at night the chandelier would spread its light on the fine parquet floor and the wide staircase, with its center aisle of carpeting.

A noise behind her caused her to stop and turn. It was Maurice. He must have been waiting for her to leave her room. She started to run, but he was too quick for her. He gripped her wrist. His face still looked pleasant, but his shapely lips were drawn tight.

"My dear little Sophia, how you have fooled us all. Look how you are dressed this morning!" His eyes deliberately traveled over her figure, and he toyed with the buttons at the sweater's neckline.

"Please, Maurice, leave me alone. I'm married now." Her voice was intense as she pleaded with him.

"But, my little one, you can't fool me on this. You are still as pure and untouched as the snow atop our tallest virgin timber." He kept a tight grip on her wrist.

She closed her eyes and turned her head. "Maurice, no, I'll tell my husband ..." Her voice faltered.

"You know, Sophia, that I don't really want to hurt you. I just want to touch you. I want you away from the evils of some of the men in this world. Even Stefan. Let me show you what to guard against." His voice was soft, and he seemed hypnotized and unaware of her protests. The sound of his own voice seemed to lull him into a trance.

She pressed back into the wall as far as she could go. Desperately, she pulled at her arm where he grasped it and felt a sharp pain.

"Sophia?" The voice floated up the stairs.

"I'm here!" Her voice came out in a rush, and Maurice released her wrist and clapped his hand over her mouth. She bolted from him as soon as she felt the release of the pressure on her wrist. She ran toward the corner and the landing and would have fallen halfway down the stairs except for the strong arms that caught her.

Her eyes were dry, but her body trembled. She clung to Stefan. He had been outside, and the cool, cleanness of the outdoors lingered about him.

"Are you all right? What frightened you?" The blue of the cashmere sweater he wore gave warmth to the gray of his eyes, and she took comfort from them.

She shook her head. She wanted to confide all of it to him, but the shame was unbearable.

"I'm okay now." She had stopped trembling, but she felt tears stinging her eyes.

"I must know how to help you. Soon, Sophia, when you know me better." He kept his arm around her as they started toward the dining room. "You look very nice, Sophia."

She brightened visibly at his compliment, and a little smile tugged at her mouth.

"Thank you. I didn't want my family feeling sorry that you got a 'rag doll' pawned off on you."

He laughed at her and squeezed her shoulder as he dropped his hand to her elbow. "Let's go eat. I'm starved."

"Thanks for having my breakfast sent to me."

"Don't think it's going to be a habit," he said with mock severity. "But I'm sure you don't want to skip lunch."

"No, I can't do that. You and I both could well use some extra food. Manka told me so herself," she said, laughing, and he laughed with her. It felt so good to laugh together.

The others had already gathered in the dining room. Maurice had used the back stairs and was already there, looking cool and serene. He was perfectly groomed, from the shine on his soft leather shoes to the straight, clean part in the center of his healthy hair.

"You are looking well, Sophia." His voice was polite, but there was a small undertone.

Involuntarily, she drew nearer to Stefan and stiffened.

Maurice turned to his sister with a teasing remark about how late she had been out with Stanislas Janda the night before.

"How is Stanislas, Monica?" Józef asked.

He approved of Monica seeing Dr. Janda's son. He planned to go into practice with his father in Dark Forest Village.

"Stan is fine, Uncle Józef." Monica plainly didn't consider him worth discussing at lunch today. She seemed to be in a disagreeable mood.

"And how is it that a handsome man like you, Maurice, has escaped marriage so long?" asked Stefan.

"Maurice married?" scoffed Monica. "He couldn't be bothered. All he asks of life is an extravagant clothes allowance."

Maurice laughed easily, completely undisturbed.

"Monica, you aren't being quite fair," Józef said. "Maurice earns his way here at Forest House by taking care of a lot of the paperwork. He seems to have infinite patience with details."

"Is that saying that I don't earn my way?" Monica was in the mood for an argument.

"You are here as an ornament, my dear. That has its value too." It was plain to see that Józef felt magnanimous that morning. His plans had worked out so well.

Manka served rye bread croutons with the pea soup, and there was an assortment of cold meats. Apples and cheeses were for dessert. Sophia was surprised that she had an appetite. She listened to the men talk of their morning excursion as she ate.

"And, Stefan, we must make a trip to the main logging camp before January. As a matter of fact, let's leave in a few days," Józef said.

"But what about the party?" Marie asked. "I have it planned."

"Have you sent out the invitations yet?" Józef asked.

"No," admitted Marie.

"Good. Set the party for shortly after we plan to return. You know that these trips to the main camp must be made before the heavy snows start."

"Yes," conceded Marie. "That should pose no real problem."

"Stefan, we can be ready to leave at the end of next week. I have to personally check to see if the contract schedules can be met before I sign with the government for their latest order. Soon the United States will be in the war, and these contracts are important. The contracts for the iron ore are equally important, of course, but I have a very competent man handling that right now. That trip can be put off until later."

"Well, Sophia," Monica said, "it seems that your honeymoon will be cut short. Or perhaps it never got started. I would want a trip abroad for my honeymoon."

"There is a war going on, Monica." Her uncle's tone was sharp.

"I won't have to stay here, Monica," Sophia retorted. Her fear of being left to evade Maurice's attentions made her panic.

Monica laughed. "I'd always thought you were too insipid to have red hair. Maybe you do have a temper buried somewhere."

"I wouldn't think of leaving you behind, Sophia." Stefan slipped his arm around her.

"No. No, there's no reason at all why Sophia shouldn't go," agreed Józef. "It'll be like old times. Sophia and Jan always went with me and Jacobson to inspect the logging camps."

"Stefan isn't Jan," argued Marie.

"What difference does that make?" Józef asked.

"What of Sophia's dress for the party? What of all the arrangements, the invitations?"

"Mother, there'll be plenty of time. I can pick out the material before I leave, and the dressmaker will just have to please you with the details. You don't need me. Your parties are always successful." Sophia was excited at the prospect of the outing.

"Well, if you really want to go," Marie agreed, "that should work out."

"Sophia, you can take Stefan to the village with you and show him how to dress for the North Woods!" Józef said with a laugh.

"We can go right after lunch, Father." Sophia felt more alive than she had since Jan's death. "Mother, we'll stop by the dressmakers and choose the fabric for my dress. I will specify that Wanda should make it."

"By all means," remarked her mother. "She's as good as any we have used in New York."

"Father, is there anything that we could pick up for you and Jacobson?" She felt at ease talking on this subject.

"No, thanks. Jacobson keeps all our gear in top-notch shape and ready to go at a minute's notice."

"Can you get me some red yarn, dear?" asked Mrs. Milewski.

"Sure, Grandmother." Sophia gave her a warm smile.

"Ten skeins, please."

"Of course, don't forget the books," Józef warned, a twinkle in his eye.

"Books?" questioned Stefan.

Sophia laughed. "Yes, it's just something that Jan and I always did," she explained. "We bought dozens of paperback books to take to the men at the camp. During the winter, they just about read the words off the pages of their old ones." She laughed.

Lunch was over, and Sophia and Stefan prepared to leave.

"Stefan, we observe city hours here at Forest House, so dinner will be at seven thirty," Józef said. "Father Vladek and Father Polzak will be here for dinner. And I believe Monica has invited Stanislas Janda. We used to keep city hours at Domani z Camin, and it's one of the things that I still do."

Stefan nodded his understanding.

"Mother, we'll stop at the pastry shop. I haven't had tea away from Forest House for months." Sophia had slipped into a brown coat with a cream-colored fur collar.

Józef watched them prepare to leave. Just looking at the improvement in Sophia was enough to lift his spirits. He loved this child of Marie's. He could not have loved her more if she had been of his own blood. If Jan had been more like her, he might have been tempted to make him his heir, even without being his blood relative.

But no, everything was working out fine. He still felt sorrow at the innocent boy's death, but he had never seriously considered him as an heir. He had contacted his brother in Poland even before Jan had met his accident. Stefan was better than he had hoped. He had not anticipated that his brother's son would be as satisfactory as he was promising to be.

The drive into town was enjoyable. Their conversation was light, and Sophia pointed out some landmarks for Stefan.

He was surprised that their village church was located so close to Forest House. It was closer to it than it was to the village. It was as though it was torn in its loyalty between one man and the people of the small town.

Sophia also pointed out Dr. Janda's home. He and his family had a large frame house halfway between the church and the village.

The main street was only wide enough for two cars to pass; there was pull-in parking on either side of the street for easy access to the stores. The sidewalks bustled with activity. The village of Dark Forest was well equipped with the necessary modern conveniences. The new courthouse stood proudly back from a stone-paved square. Its lines were clean and uncluttered, giving it a brisk, businesslike appearance.

The facade of the town was like any other small thriving community. But open a door, scratch the surface, and the difference sent out a warmth of welcome not to be denied. The shopkeepers were the heart of the city.

Sophia told Stefan that the shopkeepers were mostly Polish immigrants who had settled together long ago and that they were proud of their accomplishments. Everyone was proud of Józef Zurowski, she said; at one time in their lives, he had helped each of them. No one envied Józef Zurowski his wealth and position. After all, he was Polish nobility.

Sophia and Stefan's first stop was the bookstore. He laughed as he watched Sophia pick up armloads of books, not even bothering to look at the titles.

"Do they read this stuff?" He looked at one titled *Nurse Allen Falls in Love.*

"They read everything!" Again, there was her silvery laughter.

But he did see her put back a copy of nursery rhymes.

CHAPTER TEN

<hr>

T he next few days were spent in preparation for the trip to the main logging camp. Jacobson kept the equipment in top shape, but provisions had to be prepared. Manka helped Jacobson with the packaging of the foodstuffs.

Sophia watched Jacobson as he worked over the next several days. She always thought the little man grew taller as he prepared for these trips. His nose was too large for his small wrinkled face, and the thin wisps of dark hair were no longer thick enough to keep bits of pink scalp from shining through. He sang happily and teased Manka as they worked.

"Get out of my kitchen," Manka ordered with mock sternness.

"Aw, have pity on an old man, young lady," teased Jacobson. "There ain't much for a gardener to do in the wintertime."

"I'll give you some bruises to tend, if you don't stop tracking up my kitchen," she said as she brandished a heavy iron skillet at him.

The air was filled with gaiety as the foursome looked forward to the trip. Józef gave Maurice last-minute instructions on contracts and pending correspondence. He put in a few calls to tie up the remaining loose ends of business and talked with Ludlow in New York. While he had Ludlow on the phone, he invited him to come up the week of the party. It was planned for three days before Christmas.

Józef kept Maurice busy, and Sophia felt more at ease. Each morning when she practiced the piano, she locked the door leading to the hall.

Her hiking and camping clothes were packed, and she looked sorrowfully at her hands. Just as she was becoming proud of the smoothness of the healing skin and the shapely nails, off she was going into the wilds.

Determinedly, she tucked a manicure set into her bag and two extra pairs of fur-lined gloves.

They were to leave early the next morning. She had given her bridal ring to Stefan for safekeeping. When she had mentioned having Józef put it in the safe, Stefan said he would keep it until they returned. In place of the ornate heirloom, she now wore a plain wide band of gold. Her face felt warm as she remembered him kissing her hand as he placed this ring on her finger.

Stefan had packed his clothes in the canvas sea bag—the same sea bag he'd been carrying the first time she saw him coming up the road to Forest House. It seemed so long ago now.

No one but Manka was up when the party of four—Sophia, Józef, Jacobson, and Stefan—left for the first logging shack. It was not yet light, and they had all eaten enough ham and eggs to keep them until noon.

Their trip would be a series of short stops. The first stop would be at a shack only an hour's drive from Forest House. They would stop only briefly there to change vehicles. A four-wheel-drive vehicle would be their transportation to the first stop. In his dealings with the government, Jozef had secured one of the Jeep prototypes that the military was planning for their troops. Behind the shack was an old shed that housed a half-track vehicle. It would be a brief stop.

The road that headed north from Forest House ran beside the acres of tillable land. It all lay barren now, except for a field of winter wheat. The trees of the orchards could be seen only in black silhouette against the pale morning sky. In the spring, the morning air would be heavy with the sweetness of pear, cherry, and apple blossoms.

The road deteriorated quickly after it started to cut through the forest. It was an old logging road that had not been used lately. The dozers and other vehicles that had been taken up through this section of the forest had gone farther into the deep North Woods. There had been no need for them to come down here.

By the time they reached the first logging shack, it was full light. Sophia knew Jacobson needed about thirty minutes to check the tires on the front of the half-track vehicle and to check its engine. She remembered it as a special rig Józef had ordered, designed for the trips into the forest interior. It was similar to a military-type half-track, but the cab was insulated from the cold. This means of transportation had regular wheels at the front for steering and continuous tracks at the back to propel it. The purpose of this combination was to produce an automobile with cross-country capabilities. It had been especially modified so that four passengers could ride in the front cab.

As the men crawled over the engine and transferred supplies, Sophia explored around the shack. The weathered building was several yards from the edge of the woods. It was in a small clearing, and it sat sheltered against a steep hill. The hill was clear of trees, but there was an outcropping of boulders up the incline. On the very top, one large smooth boulder looked precariously balanced on a pile of smaller rocks. It could have been the remains of a fort where she and Jan might have played as children.

The thought of Jan suddenly made her think of the man that he'd said he'd seen the last time he was up here. She remembered now—he'd said the man was sneaking around the logging shack.

She saw a spot of red color and started up the hill to investigate. Maybe it was something Jan had left.

A tiny shower of pebbles was the only warning she had. Looking up again, she saw the large boulder leave its place and begin rolling at her very fast. The loose rocks landing around her feet made a quick start impossible. She stumbled and fell. The world spun around her as she was caught up in the landslide.

First, she saw the sky, and then the dirt and gravel ground into her face. Sophia couldn't control her roll down the steep incline. She stopped rolling abruptly as she hit a thick clump of weeds. The jolt to her stomach took her breath away. The sound of the huge boulder passing her ended with a crash into the side of the wooden shack. The boards splintered and pushed inward.

She sat up slowly, recovering her breath, and saw Stefan running toward her. Fear was a cold knot in her stomach and cotton dryness in her mouth. Her limbs felt paralyzed by the terror that someone had made an attempt on her life.

"Sophia, what happened?" He put his arms around her and carefully helped her to her feet. The concern on his face was comforting. Jacobson and Józef had nearly caught up to Stefan.

"I thought I saw something up among the rocks and wanted to see what it was." The reason sounded foolish. She felt like a stupid child.

"Everything is frozen, so rock slides are a little unusual this time of the year," Józef mused as he glanced up the hill and back at Sophia, who was leaning against Stefan's arm. "Are you all right?" Józef looked at her closely.

"Yes, I'm fine, nothing broken … just out of breath. And dirty. I'm glad I was wearing my old parka." She wouldn't speak of her fear.

No one laughed at her feeble attempt at humor, but Stefan teased, "Just like a girl," although his deep voice sounded relieved.

Jacobson watched as the two men made sure that indeed she had no broken bones. "Miss Sophia, you'll have to exercise your muscles," Jacobson fussed at her. "You can get stiff riding in this vehicle so long."

"The ride on these logging roads are almost enough exercise for anyone. I don't remember so many potholes and rocks." She laughed shakily.

"Sophia, if you're sure you're unharmed, we'd better get started again. It's several hours ride before we get to the next line shack, where we'll spend the night." She noticed that Józef was not looking at her but carefully studying the hill where the rock had rolled down, nearly causing her serious injury.

Stefan helped Sophia wipe the dirt off that was clinging to her parka and trousers. Back at the vehicle, she washed her face and cringed while Stefan put antiseptic on the scratches. She would have a black eye.

"You're enjoying this," she cried. "Be careful!"

"Hush, child. Hold still." There was mock sternness in his voice. "I've doctored many cuts and bruises for my sister."

Suddenly, she was angry. She had told him she couldn't be his wife, but unexpectedly, she didn't want to be anything less. "I'm not your sister!" She climbed into the cab of the half-track, ignoring his assistance. Her muscles were stiffer than she wanted to admit, and she dreaded the soreness that likely would follow.

Snow began falling, and soon there would be no trace that anyone had come this way. It was quiet, and Sophia's thoughts were muddled. Maybe she had hit her head harder than she knew. She couldn't be sure, but for an instant she had thought someone was behind that largest boulder. She hadn't looked up again until the gravel had made the path slippery under her feet, and the face was there for a split second. She got the impression of a lot of hair—maybe a beard. It could have been an animal, but a distinct impression of a human face had registered with her for a moment.

Could it have been another attempt on her life? The thought sent shivers along her neck. She was glad they weren't staying here long. There was no use telling anyone; she'd been accused of seeing things when Jan was killed. She didn't want to go through that again.

If she really had seen someone just before the boulder came toward her, then whoever was there had meant to harm her, perhaps even kill her.

She shivered uncontrollably.

When Stefan put his arm around her and drew her head to his shoulder, she didn't resist. Closing her eyes, she drew from his strength. She did need him. She knew what he thought of her; he had compared her to his sister. She hadn't known that he even had a sister, but he did mention her with affection.

Wasn't this the kind of relationship that she had asked of him? He was holding up his side of the bargain well. But she knew she was falling in love with him. It began with that kiss when he had given her the ring. Love? Yes, she may as well admit it. It had taken her a short time to fall hopelessly in love with this blond stranger who was her husband.

Their love could never mature into anything. She couldn't accept him as a husband. Maurice had made all the promised intimacy of marriage unbearable to think about. She shivered again and felt Stefan pat her arm lightly. It was the consolation one might give to a beloved sister.

Jacobson had insisted that Sophia take a couple of aspirin after her accident, and they relaxed her so much that she fell asleep.

When she awoke, it was noon, and the half-track had rumbled to a stop. This time she welcomed Stefan's offer to help her from the vehicle. They ate thick ham sandwiches and drank hot coffee from thermoses. Manka also had packed some dried fruit.

"Now, Sophia, you must walk some before we start out again," Jacobson said as he watched her gingerly try her legs.

"Come on!" Stefan took her hand, and she was forced to keep up with him.

Back in the half-track again, they continued to go north. The snow was piling up, but the vehicle had no trouble cutting a path. When the road was covered, they could follow the bright-red markings of paint that had been put on the trees lining the logging road.

They were like new arrivals. The way in front of them lay pristine, untouched. The air was pure and clean, and they could have been the first to breathe it.

By the time they reached the second logging shack where they were to spend the night, the snow had stopped. This cabin was a little larger than the first one. And like the first one, there was a shed for the half-track, backed up against the rear of the building.

"You two have a look around while Jacobson and I set up camp." Józef waved them away. "It will be light for a little while yet."

Sophia and Stefan put on snowshoes, and she slowly forced her stiff, sore muscles to move. They walked behind the cabin to the edge of a large lake.

Stefan looked across it thoughtfully. "I can see why Uncle Józef chose to live in this place. It's much like Poland. We have thousands of lakes much as it is here"

"In the summer the water looks so blue. That's where our state got its name. *Minne-sota* is an Indian name meaning 'sky-tinted water.' The Indians living here used it to describe the appearance of the Minnesota River. See the small island out there in the middle. The trees are straight and tall, very close, side by side. Many of our lakes have islands."

"Look, Sophia"—he pointed to the island— "the tall trees could be ships under full sail, painted on a blue sky. Or perhaps they could be the spires of a great cathedral."

Sophia could tell that the area known as the Great North Woods was weaving its magic on him; the North Woods often cast a spell. The tangy fragrance emanating from the evergreens was heady and exhilarating. *It has an aura of remote strangeness,* she thought. *The shadows are blacker under the crowded spruce than they are in other forests. A haunting sense of danger is created.*

The wild animals lived and fed on the bounty that lined the shores of the lakes and rivers—the birch, aspen, blueberry, crowberry, rushes—but for stalking and cover, they turned to the shadowy conifer forests. It was funny how the two types of trees kept from intermingling.

Her reverie was broken when a light shower of snow exploded around her face. Stefan had thrown a snowball at her, and there was nothing to do but return it.

Their laughter shattered the stillness of the crystal air. She caught him with a well-packed snowball and then started running slowly for the cabin. He caught up with her just before she reached the door.

"Thought you could get by with that, huh?" He jerked off the bright stocking cap she was wearing and shook a handful of snow over her head, and it slid down the back of her neck.

"Oh, no!" She ducked her head and shrugged her shoulders. Her silvery laughter was completely free and happy.

"Child, you will learn!" He growled with mock menace and put the cap back on her head, pulling it down to cover her eyes.

They took off their snowshoes and stepped into the cabin. Jacobson had a fire burning in the fireplace. Over the fire hung a black pot in which he was warming up some of Manka's beef stew. They inhaled the aroma appreciatively.

The inside of the shack was similar to the other one. There was a rough table and a plank bench on both sides. At the far end were four frames holding up wide planks that served as bunks. The fireplace was at the other end, with its hook and black pot. The basics were there for any traveler. A stack of logs was by the fireplace, seasoned and ready for use. Before moving on, they would cut enough to replace what they used. These logs would have time to season for the next person who would need them.

The hickory logs with which Jacobson started the fire filled the cabin with a warm, wonderful odor. He had cut an ash to add to the fire. Because of the oil trapped within its wood, it didn't need to season. This would subtract from the amount of wood they would need to replace. Jacobson put willow logs on the fire after they had eaten supper. These would burn slowly far into the night.

The firelight gave a golden glow to the faces of the figures gathered there. The food and fire had warmed them, and all were caught in a feeling of closeness and companionship.

Jacobson had gone to his bunk earlier. Sophia lay very still, snuggled in her sleeping bag, just listening.

Stefan wasn't sure how it happened—it may have been the safety of the darkened cabin—but he found himself talking to the others about his family. He told of the fear at Domani z Camin when they'd heard about the Red Army marching. All the world feared Hitler, but his father had had a premonition about the enemy to the east.

He released his venom as he told of finding his family; his voice broke as he told of fragile Anne. Each person listening could visualize the story this troubled Polish refugee told of his hunt for Frederic after his father's dying words had propelled him from the castle.

"What of my younger brother?" Jacobson asked. "He was with my parents when they worked at Domani z Camin. What of David Jacobson?"

"I really don't know." Stefan shook his head in the dim light. "There were only a few servants in the house. Those who weren't killed may have escaped … or they may have been marched off. Many Jews were taken to concentration camps."

The silence was painful.

Józef finally broke the stillness. "Stefan, there's something I want you to know. I didn't think it would matter, but now that I know you, I find it's important to me."

Stefan turned his head toward the sound of his uncle's voice. "Yes, Uncle Józef? What is it?"

"I didn't steal the jeweled crucifix."

Stefan said nothing as he waited for Józef to continue.

"When I decided to leave Domani z Camin so many years ago, Jacobson asked if he might come with me. I was very glad for the company. So, we just left. It wasn't until we got to America that I discovered the crucifix hidden carefully among my clothes. There was a note wrapped around it."

"Did the note tell you who put it in your things?" Stefan was surprised by the relief he felt in knowing that this man he had so recently met hadn't stolen the priceless heirloom.

"It was my mother—your grandmother, Stefan. She wrote that she hoped this would make up for the fact that I'd been born the 'second son.' I was frightened, Stefan; I can tell you. Really frightened!"

Stefan could well imagine. He knew firsthand the wrath of his father.

"The note went on to say that one of the guests at dinner that night—a young man visiting the village priest—had disappeared, and he was thought to have stolen the crucifix."

The willow logs had turned to charcoal and glowed as brightly as jewels. Stefan was reminded of the rubies set in the gold of the cross.

"Later, I got a letter from my mother. She somehow had gotten her father, who was very old at that time, to leave me a great deal of money. His lands, of course, were added to the estate of Domani z Camin. My father married my mother only to extend his lands. It was quite customary."

"Yes," agreed Stefan. "My brother, Konrad, would have married into the Jasinski family if he hadn't been killed. It would have added again to Domani z Camin lands."

"Anyway, when my grandfather died, I was sent the remainder of his fortune. I could not send the crucifix back, you see, because doing so would harm my mother. By this time, I had decided to use the jeweled crucifix. It was supposed to bring good luck to the Zurowski family, and I was part of that family, though a little removed at the time. I had an adequate fortune to live on for the rest of my life, but that was not enough. I had youth, energy, ambition. I had money of my own to invest, and there was no limit to what I could borrow on the crucifix. Maybe the cross brought me luck in my investments; I don't know." Józef stood up to stretch his legs and put another log on the fire.

"My father thought being without the crucifix brought him bad luck," Stefan said. "He blamed everything bad that happened on its loss. It twisted his mind."

"If I had it to do over, I would do the same thing," Józef said. "I got you here, Stefan. As the second son, you had nothing to look forward to anyway."

"Nothing," Stefan said flatly. "My father had not spoken to me from the time I was ten until I came back after my schooling. He told me to leave again. Father had his heir; he needed little else. Father did remarry after my mother's death. My stepmother was not aware of me at all. When my little stepsister Anne was born, I found a friend. She was the one bright spot for me at home. I loved the lands, the castle, our people, but I knew there was no future in it for me." Then his dying words again sent me away from Domani z Camin.

"Stefan, here in America the ways aren't so rigid. If you have two sons—or ten, even—they can share equally. Maybe that is the way it should be."

"At least there can be a choice," agreed Stefan.

Tears welled up in Sophia's eyes. She cried silently for both of them. Her stepfather had an estate now in his adopted land, but he had no blood family that loved him. And family was the most important thing to him. Well, she loved him, and she longed to tell him so.

And Stefan had been manipulated by his father and his uncle. Now he had a wife he didn't want.

Józef's voice in the darkness startled Sophia. "Tell me, Stefan, does Sophia remind you of Anne?"

"Sophia?" He paused briefly in thought. "I don't know. They don't look alike, of course. Anne was fragile-looking with pale-yellow hair. Her eyes were as blue as your Minnesota River. Anne was a little younger than Sophia. There was almost an unearthly quality about her delicate beauty."

"Ah, yes," his uncle said on a breath. "I know the type. They do tug at a man's heart. Our Sophia is of firmer stuff." He chuckled.

In the dark, Sophia was hoping he choked. *How dare they discuss me or compare me to this ... this Anne person!*

"Sophia is a lovely girl and will be a beautiful woman," Stefan said.

Sophia was sure that she could detect amusement in his deep, vibrant voice. *How nice of him to be so patronizing*, she thought. She lay in the darkness hating them both. All things considered, how could she feel sorry for those two? They were heartless. *I wouldn't be a bit surprised if Stefan knows I'm awake.*

Józef rose and stretched his arms wide. "Are you ready to turn in?"

"Yes, I will just rouse Sophia." He bent down to where she lay, and she had to fight to keep her breathing steady.

"Just let her sleep there, Stefan. She certainly will be as comfortable there as on those awful board cots. I'm definitely not as young as I used to be."

She heard him walk to the back of the cabin.

Now the tears flowed, hot and silent. Love for Stefan was becoming an ache inside her. She didn't want to take the place of his dead sister. She wanted to be his wife. She cursed Maurice a thousand times for his twisted mind. She decided she would fight him and dismiss the fears that he had planted in her young, impressionable mind. Then, in the next moment, she was fearful that she wouldn't be strong enough.

Dear God, she prayed silently in the darkness, *help me, help me!* She felt a little more peaceful. She would be happy and content on this trip. The time away from Forest House was a joy. Maybe after she had faced down Maurice, then she could look to her future.

But what if Stefan had no interest in her as a wife. He'd agreed all too readily to the arrangement that she had offered to him. If all men were as Maurice had made her believe, she would have had to put bars on her windows and doors when Stefan arrived. She was certain he wasn't interested in her, except as a means to stay in America.

She deliberately turned her mind to the next day. They would reach the main camp tomorrow night before supper. She looked forward eagerly to seeing the lumberjacks again. Some she had known since her first trip with her stepfather and Jan.

But in the stillness, she couldn't keep back the ghost of her fear from this morning's fright. She wanted to believe it was an accident, but she couldn't delude herself. Someone wanted her dead for some reason. Who would profit from her death? Of course, Stefan would be free of her. He shouldn't be above suspicion; he could have arranged for an accomplice. Monica wanted Stefan. Maybe they were in it together. Maurice might rather see her dead than as Stefan's true wife.

These thoughts chased around in her troubled mind until she fell wearily into a restless sleep.

CHAPTER ELEVEN

L ogging camps usually consisted of three buildings—the bunkhouse, the chuck house or common dining area, and the stables for the mules and logging sleds. This one was a family camp, so there were a few small cabins dotted around as accommodations for the married men. A large roof supported by rough logs created a protected area for the other heavy-duty machinery when it was brought back to camp. A small shed was attached to one end of the enclosure where the mechanics kept their tools to work on the large tractors.

The evening sun was casting long shadows on the white blanket of snow when they arrived. The shadows extended from the buildings, stretching out as if to welcome them.

Józef radioed ahead that they would arrive before suppertime. A curving column of gray smoke rose from the chimney of the large chuck house, wavering, spreading, and disappearing into the gray sky.

No sooner had Jacobson cut the roar of the engine than a giant of a man burst through the chuck house door and started toward them. His long strides quickly ate up the ground between them and the building. His voice boomed at them, magnified somewhat by the cold stillness of the air.

"Welcome, welcome. Come in!"

Sophia thought that anyone within a mile would come running at the sound of such a warm invitation given at that volume. There was almost a feeling of a homecoming at the sight of this big man.

Jean-Claude had been at the logging camp as long as Sophia could remember, and he never seemed to change. The black, crisp curls poking out around the wool of his stocking cap were generously sprinkled with gray. His dark blue eyes were like jewels in his tanned, weathered face. His eyes were framed with bushy black brows, and this thick black mustache was carefully trimmed above his generous mouth. The wide expanse of his thick chest and shoulders were covered by the soft flannel of his red-plaid shirt. The sleeves of this shirt were rolled up to his elbows, revealing the shirt of his long johns, which hugged his muscular arms and ended at his thick wrists in soft ribbing. He wore loose-fitting corduroys tucked into his boots.

"Don't tell me! This *must* be your Paul Bunyan I've read about!" Stefan whispered in Sophia's ear.

"Don't be silly," she said with a giggle.

Józef stepped ahead of them to meet the big lumberjack. "This is our bull of the wood, Jean-Claude. That is our term for logging superintendents," Józef explained to Stefan. "It does seem that the term fits in this case in more ways than one."

Józef's and Jean-Claude's laughter filled the air. The North Woods was the only appropriate setting for this man. He was one with the trees, the sky.

"This new husband of yours, Miss Sophia"—Jean-Claude looked at her closely— "did he give you this black eye?"

"No, no." Sophia laughed as she touched the tender area under her eye. "I tripped over some rocks and fell."

"That isn't a good story." He turned to Stefan. "It may sometime become necessary to hit her again, so she had better have a more convincing one." He laughed heartily at his own humor.

The men gathered the gear from the vehicle and headed for the chuck house. Sophia tried to walk, hoping that no one could tell how sore she really was after sitting in the half-track for the past three hours.

They were greeted warmly by the entire camp when they gathered for supper. In the winter, there wasn't a full crew, so only about one hundred remained.

Sophia had always used a small bedroom closed off from the rest of the chuck house when she stayed at camp, and Jean-Claude put her and Stefan's luggage in that room. Józef and Jacobson were taken to a small cabin that Józef used as an office when he was here, which also doubled as sleeping quarters.

Jean-Claude's wife, Josephine, smiled at Sophia and said, "Sophia, I know you'd like a warm bath before supper. That journey from Forest House to our camp is a rough one." Josephine's eyes were as blue as Jean-Claude's.

Josephine was a handsome woman, tall and strong. The tiny lines around her eyes spoke of a readiness for laughter. She handed Sophia a stack of clean towels.

The camp's electricity was furnished by generators, which made possible some of the comforts they enjoyed. The greatest luxury was the hot water. The bunkhouse was equipped with many showers, but the only tub was in the bathroom adjoining Sophia's room.

Gratefully, Sophia eased herself down into the warm water. The skin on her thigh wasn't broken, but the bruise was painful. It wasn't the only bruise that she had sustained, though, and the general soreness had worsened because of being cramped in the cab of their vehicle. A day of being able to walk and stretch would greatly improve her well-being.

She was convinced that someone had pushed that rock at her. And she was just as convinced that she wasn't going to tell anyone. Maybe the person had been trying to scare her. She couldn't bear to have everyone's eyes looking at her again, filled with pity. She'd spoken out at Jan's death, and it had been of no use.

The table was wide and long and flanked by deacon's benches. The cook was beaming and happy because of the company. The food was plain and hearty. Huge bowls of boiled potatoes, spicy baked beans in a tomato sauce, and thick slices of roast beef were placed on the table. Bright green pickles were crisp and lusciously dill. After everyone was seated, the cook served platters of hot buttermilk biscuits. Pitchers of milk and pots of coffee were within easy reach of all, along with wild blackberry jam and mounds of butter.

Sophia sat at the table, quietly enjoying the talk and laughter of those around her. Stefan was in animated conversation with Jean-Claude about forestry. It was almost like she was the outsider, the new arrival. She glanced shyly at her husband beside her. Except for the accent in his speech, he was no different from any man here. She knew the love of the land was in his blood, and the sound of rushing rivers was combined with the throb of the blood in his veins.

"Ah, Stefan, your uncle, here, was different!" Jean-Claude began as he stretched his long legs. They had finished supper and were gathered around the fireplace. Josephine was sitting by her husband's side, crocheting. She had told Sophia it was to be a new bedspread. Sophia thought of the unfinished needlework she had brought with her to work on, but she didn't want to leave the room and miss any of the men's talk.

"He actually hired one of the fern-hoppers who came into one of his camps! Didn't he, Professor?" Jean-Claude nodded to a thin, smiling man with gold-rimmed spectacles. The professor's forehead was very high, with wrinkles all the way to his widow's peak. His sideburns nearly reached to his square jaw. His lips were thin and shapely, ready to curve upward in a smile.

"He sure did!" the professor agreed. "I was a forester, just graduated from Oregon State College, and I thought that the information I had learned would be welcome at any lumber camp in the North Woods."

This brought a howl of laughter from the men.

"Well, *fern-hopper* was one of the nicer terms they gave to men like me. The lumberjacks didn't want young upstarts telling them which trees to cut and which to leave. One of the kindest things done to these forestry students was to just be thrown out of camp." The professor knocked the ashes from his pipe into the fireplace and slowly began to fill the bowl with tobacco again. "When other owners were stripping the trees indiscriminately, Józef was looking to the future."

"I didn't want to see the forest laid bare, but I'm sure some of the others didn't want that either," Józef said. "I could afford to plan ahead. Money was not as critical with me. Land I owned farther north in the Mesabi Hills was discovered to have rich iron-ore deposits in it. The ore had to be taken in fleets of specially built ore boats to smelters, so I got into the shipping business. You might say that I left the timber business in the hands of the professor and Jean-Claude for a while." Józef chuckled.

"Can you imagine what this did to me, Stefan?" Jean-Claude rolled his eyes in mock despair.

"Settled you down!" Josephine put in, her blue eyes vivid and sparkling.

"My people were les voyageurs des bois—the travelers of the woods. We French were hunters, fishermen, trappers, pursuers of wildlife—"

"You pursued the wild life, all right," Josephine said quickly.

The men roared their mirth.

"Animals, my sweet, wild animals." Jean-Claude threw up his hands in mock surrender. He rubbed his knuckle over his mustache and continued. "I was left as 'nursemaid' to a lumber camp. The professor marked the trees for cutting; my men and I cut them and stacked them by the frozen rivers in the winter. Then in spring, the thawing water would carry the logs downstream to the mills. All of Minnesota is marked with a fine thread of silver netting."

Sophia noticed that the giant Frenchman was becoming poetic. The generators had been shut down for the night, and kerosene lamps and the glow from the fireplace changed the tone of the conversation.

"This silver netting is the many, many streams and lakes that are waterways to the world. Did you know that the great Mississippi River has its source here in northern Minnesota?" Jean-Claude's question required no answer.

Józef took up the narrative. "When the locks at Sault Ste. Marie were completed, it permitted ore shipments on the Great Lakes. It had only been in use a few years when I began shipment from my mines in the Mesabi Hills."

There was a lull in the conversation before Jean-Claude asked a serious question. "How goes the war, Józef?"

"It's so hard to say, Jean-Claude," Józef answered despairingly. "The journalists here in the United States aren't taking it too seriously yet, but it's news, and they keep us informed after a fashion. I brought a stack of newspapers so you can catch up."

Jean-Claude nodded. "Good, good."

"What is current?" asked the professor.

"There is a German ship called the *Graf Spee* that was preying on Allied ships in the South Atlantic. Finally, a British squadron of three cruisers, patrolling near the mouth of the River Platte, spotted them," Józef reported.

"Did they attack?" Jean-Claude asked.

"Immediately!" Józef exclaimed. "The *Graf Spee* was damaged and forced to seek refuge in a neutral port—Montevideo Harbor."

Stefan added, "And by international law, a belligerent ship can only stay in a neutral port for a specified time."

"And then what happened?" asked the professor.

"The time isn't up yet. The world is waiting for the *Graf Spee* to come out and rejoin the battle. The British ships are just hovering." Józef's eyes gleamed at the prospect. "No doubt there will be news by the time we return to Forest House."

Everyone was quiet as each anticipated the outcome of the sea battle that was sure to happen.

Józef stood up suddenly. "As I remember, the call 'daylight in the camp' comes very early. We have covered the war, and I think that Stefan has heard more than enough Minnesota history for tonight." A yawn interrupted his chuckle.

Stefan fixed the fire for the night in the little room where they were to sleep while Sophia got ready for bed in the tiny bathroom.

"I'm sorry for the sleeping arrangements, Sophia, but I couldn't tell them I preferred to sleep in the bachelors' bunkhouse," he said. "Besides, I would not want to leave you here alone."

"Thank you." She didn't know what else to say. While he was in the bathroom, she quickly pulled off her long fleecy robe and got into the small narrow bed. The room had two such cots at opposite sides of the small room. The fireplace was in the wall between them. She tucked her feet up and wrapped them in the soft flannel of her long gown. She lay rigid and trembling, but it wasn't from the cold.

Stefan came into their room and blew out the lamp. In the darkness, she heard him unzip his pants and the clink of his belt buckle as he hung his pants over a chair. Then she heard a thudding noise, followed by his crying out.

"What is this? A baby's crib?" he growled. "This bed is too short!"

Sophia couldn't help the laugh that escaped her. It was relaxing. She heard him finally settle down, but she knew he was still awake.

"Sophia?"

"What?" She held her breath.

"When you fell when the rocks slid, did you … see anyone?"

This wasn't what she had expected to hear.

"I'm not sure. I glanced up after the small rocks began to fall and thought that I saw a bearded face and a glimpse of a red shirt. But it was all so sudden!" She had forgotten her vow not to mention what she thought she'd seen. It was a relief to share this burden with him. "Did you see someone too?"

"No. But you looked so frightened. I didn't think that your tumble down the hill could've caused the expression of terror that crossed your face. Why didn't you say something? We could have looked around."

"I was afraid to." It was easy to talk in the darkness. She felt completely at ease with him in the room now. "When my brother was killed, I thought I saw someone drop the ax on him from the tree; no one believed me. I got nothing but pitiful stares. My own mother couldn't stand to have a daughter who was off in the head." She laughed bitterly.

"Sophia, I will never laugh at you. Before I left Poland, Kasia read Psalm 68 to me: 'God setteth the solitary in families: he bringeth out those which are bound with chains …' I feel like God has set me in a new family. Tell me whenever you are afraid. You can tell me who you're afraid of." He sounded sincere.

"Maybe … later," she whispered. How could she tell him she thought someone was trying to kill her? He would want to know why and who. She didn't know the answers. Maurice had brought her great shame, but he had haunted her since childhood. Surely, he wouldn't murder her. Was he sicker than she realized? If not Maurice, then who?

"Good night, Sophia."

"Good night." She didn't think she was sleepy, but it didn't take her long to drift off.

She dreamed that she was rolling down a hill. Stefan was at the top, laughing, and Monica stood at the bottom with a wicked-looking dagger. Józef and Jacobson were there as well, laughing. An unknown figure stood beside a cabin, his shadow falling menacingly along the ground.

Stash heard the horse whinny before he was aware of anyone in the clearing. He peered from behind the Jeep in the shed and watched the man on horseback approach the old cabin. Stash quickly started for the shack.

"Hello!" Stash greeted him as a friend. His smile was a gaping hole in the bushy black beard, a startling contrast to his snow-white hair.

The rebuff was cruel. The younger man eyed Stash with calculated hatred. "You were seen in the woods. Sophia—the red-haired girl—said her brother saw you and was going to show her where you hid out." The words were like stabs from an ice pick.

"No one will believe her," whined Stash. "They'll think she's crazy." When he was upset, the red splotches on his face blazed.

"Not everyone. Her new husband seems to be good for her. And it may have been that she was fooling everyone with that crazy act."

"Why would she do that?" Stash scratched at his chin through the beard.

"It's because of her cousin. No one else in the house seems to be aware that he suffers a perversion—an unhealthy obsession with female children." The young man's lip twisted in revulsion. "The girl is afraid of him. It's obvious enough when you have seen others like him. The characteristics are all there." His laugh was frightening. "He wears a raincoat into town when the sun shines." Again, his mocking laugh.

Stash was taken aback by the hatred on the younger man's face. "I tried again to kill her." He abruptly changed the subject. He didn't like the look on the other man's face.

"Tried again? And *failed* again?" sneered the figure, still astride his horse.

"It looked like an accident. No one suspected. She was climbing up the hill outside this shack, and I pushed a huge boulder at her. She was very lucky to escape," Stash said boastfully. His wide nostrils flared.

"Don't try again," ordered the younger man. "Your luck is running out. We'll have to take our chances on what the girl knows. While they are gone to the lumber camp, I'll be able to get in to search their rooms."

As the man rode off, he thought of the ring Sophia had worn down to dinner. *Looks like Stefan Zurowski was able to escape with some of the family jewels. No need to mention that. I'll keep them for myself, for my trouble.* His superiors were only interested in obtaining the jeweled crucifix. Of course, that was only because they didn't know of the family jewels. Again, his mouth twisted in a semblance of a smile.

The maid they'd hired for the upstairs cleaned only in the mornings. Maurice would be busy eyeing the little girl who accompanied her mother to her work, so he could evade him. *It should be easy,* he thought. *The others will return on the day after tomorrow, so I'll have tonight and tomorrow to search—if I need that long.*

Sophia awoke rested. She saw that Stefan had already left the room. Outside the door, she could hear the men coming in from other parts of the camp. The aroma of coffee filled the air. She knew there would be huge stacks of flapjacks, crisp bacon, and maple syrup. She'd always eyed in wonder the amount of food these men could eat.

The morning felt wonderful! It took very little time to dress. Her thick sweater was of a burnt-gold color that caught at the matching highlights in her hair as she pulled it over her head. She tucked brown corduroys into the tops of her soft leather boots.

"Good morning, sleepyhead. Come have some breakfast." Stefan made a place for her beside him. It was easy to smile at him this morning. "Your bruised eye is much better."

For most of the next two days, the men inspected the forest and the progress of the work for the government contracts. Sophia saw them at mealtimes. Stefan dropped into his too-small bed each night with only an exhausted "Good night."

Sophia put the books she brought into the wooden bookshelves in the chuck house. She took walks and had long talks with Josephine. While they talked, she knitted. Blissfully, she relaxed.

One evening the table and benches were shoved back, and someone brought out his fiddle for an impromptu square dance. There were other wives besides Josephine and Sophia, but still there were far more men than women. If Sophia had any soreness left from her roll down the hill, she danced it out that night.

On the last day they were to spend in camp, they planned a jag deep into the forest. Jacobson stayed at camp, preparing their vehicle and gear for the return trip. Josephine, Jean-Claude, and the professor were going with them. The air was cold, and Sophia was glad for the warmth of her new fur parka.

They mounted their mules before full daylight and headed out. Stands of firs, spruces, and larches grew thicker and thicker as they went north. Where other trees would falter, members of the pine family occupied and made use of the ground.

They rode into a special stand of trees. Stefan turned in his saddle and looked around curiously. "Did you plant these? They look all the same height."

"It's a reforestation project, all right," answered the professor, "but it's a natural one, carried out by the trees themselves because of a forest fire." The professor was enthusiastic about his subject. "Some trees have what you might call built-in fire insurance. These trees here are jack pines, and the seeds within the cones pop open automatically after a burn."

"I've heard that the knob cone pine forests are the same size and age for that reason," Stefan said.

"Yeah," agreed the professor, "the knob cone is the classic example. But the knob cone differs from the jack pine because its seed can only be released from the granite-hard cone by intense heat. The jack pine cone will eventually disintegrate with time, allowing seeds to sprout."

"It does catch your attention," Stefan said as he looked at the trees.

"I can tell that you'll get along great with the professor." Jean-Claude laughed. "Just ask him a couple more questions, and he will be your friend for life!"

Their laughter floated through the trees.

They returned to the camp for lunch, and then Jacobson, Józef, Stefan, and Sophia loaded into the half-track.

The trip back to Forest House was uneventful. The clouds hung threateningly over them, but it didn't snow. They arrived midmorning of the second day after leaving camp.

As soon as they were out of the car, Monica ran to Stefan and threw her arms around his neck. "How dreadfully dull it's been while you were away," she had said and laughed. Her green eyes had sparked a shameless welcome. She kissed him as though it were the most natural thing in the world.

Stefan hadn't resisted her. He'd laughed easily. "It's hard to believe you have had any lack of admirers while we were gone."

"No lack," she'd said with a pout, "but no one important."

Monica had ignored Sophia and clung possessively to Stefan's arm as they entered the foyer.

Inside the house Marie met Józef at the door. Her face was grim. "Someone broke into the house last night!"

"No one in the village would do such a thing," Józef said. "And the tramps who come to the door ask only for food. What was taken?" But he had heard of reports of a few strangers in the area, and before Marie could answer, he asked, "Did you call the sheriff?"

"No," she answered. "Nothing was taken that I could tell, and only two rooms were touched. But they are in shambles."

"Which rooms? The library?" Józef was thinking of his safe.

Marie shook her head. "No. The upstairs right wing."

Józef's face went white. "Where Stefan and Sophia have their rooms?"

"Yes."

Only the bedrooms were in shambles. Stefan's bed had been thoroughly searched, as was evident by the mattress having been slashed into sections; the filling spilled over into the rooms. Strips of the room's paneling had been ripped from the walls. No place had been overlooked. Even pictures had been taken off of the walls and their back coverings ripped open. Clothes lay scattered on the floor with pockets turned inside out.

Sophia looked on in horror. Could Maurice have slashed Stefan's bed like that? Was it a warning to her? But if it were a warning to her, wouldn't her mattress have been slashed, too? Waves of cold revulsion washed over her. She leaned against the wall, shivering.

Sophia's room had been searched, too, but without much damage. Perhaps the intruder ran out of time. Her bureau drawers were left open, and her clothes had been pulled from her closet and lay scattered about. However, the paneling and pictures weren't damaged.

"Marie, are you sure no other rooms were entered?" Józef asked.

"Antek and I examined the other rooms on this floor, and they looked untouched," she answered. Marie extended her hand to Józef, and he held it briefly for reassurance.

Józef turned to Stefan. "Is it gone?" He had spoken very softly, but Sophia heard him.

Stefan assured him it was not. He patted the sea bag that he had carried into the house with him. He had reasoned that it was safer to have the crucifix and jewels with him until he had decided where to put them for permanent keeping.

Stefan and Józef then went to the library to find the newspapers and check on the events of the war that had taken place while they were gone. If the war escalated as expected, it would definitely affect their government contracts.

The carpenters would have to come back to the house as soon as possible. But now that Józef and the others had returned to Forest House and had seen the vandalism, Marie allowed Lois, the maid in charge of Sophia's and Stefan's rooms, to put things to right.

Sophia watched the efficient maid turn to the work in the room, the maid was grateful to be out of the line of questioning. A little girl hid behind Lois's skirts. As the child's head moved, her tight, springy curls bounced like shiny coils. Her hair was the color of sunshine, and a band of blue held the silken strands back from her round cherubic face.

Sophia smiled at her. "Is this your little girl, Lois?"

"Yes, ma'am." She smiled proudly at her child. "Mr. Maurice said it'd be all right if I brung her along with me. I only work in the mornin's. She ain't no trouble and stays right by me," the anxious mother hastened to assure Sophia.

"Oh, that's fine, Lois, fine. No problem."

"Mr. Maurice even said that he'd watch her for me sometime. Ain't that a nice thing for such a gentleman to offer." Lois blushed, obviously pleased at the attention given to her lovely child.

"Don't bother Mr. Maurice with her, Lois," Sophia's voice was sharper than she intended. She heard a chuckle and glanced up to see Maurice looking at her. His white hands were hidden deep in his pockets, and there was a pleasant grin on his handsome face.

He ambled over to her. "But you know how I watched over you when you were small." His voice was innocent, caressing. She couldn't shrug off the arm he'd placed firmly around her shoulders. "Lois, your Julie will be as safe with me as my own sweet cousin was when she was small."

"Thank you, sir." Lois smiled happily and led Julie off by the hand.

"Maurice, I won't let you do it!" Sophia gritted her teeth in anger.

"My dear, how you do carry on. You won't let me do what?" he crooned softly. "You are spineless, Sophia; you won't do anything. No one would believe you." The pleasant tone remained in his voice, but his eyes were bright and hard.

"I'll stop you, Maurice; I promise." She felt the nails of her hand bite hard into her flesh as she clenched her fists.

"You do that, sweet cousin; you do that." He smiled at her charmingly, but there was a fleck of foam on his thin lower lip.

Sophia stepped back to keep him from rubbing against her as he left the room. As the tenseness faded, she sagged into a chair and rested her head on its high back. She didn't have the strength to fight him for herself, and now she had challenged him on behalf of the child. But she couldn't let him molest the little girl. The child's life mustn't be ruined or her mind twisted because of Sophia's own fear of speaking out.

Why did they ever have to come back from the logging camp? Life had been simple and peaceful. She stiffened with resolve. There must be something she could do without having to confess to the shame she had felt over the years. Maybe Father Polzak would be able to help her. She shoved that thought aside immediately and prayed desperately in her mind. She was totally innocent, but there might not be anyone on earth, even a priest, who would believe her.

God help me. Make me strong! Make me strong.

Someone was coming up the stairs, and Sophia stood up and walked to the door. Surely Maurice wouldn't come back while the maid cleaned in the next room.

"Sophia?" Marie called her daughter's name as she approached the door.

"Mother, what is it?"

"Did I frighten you? I'm sorry. I just wanted to tell you that you have an appointment with Wanda for the final ball gown fitting this afternoon."

"Are you going into the village too?" Sophia didn't want to go alone. She knew that Józef and Stefan would be going over financial reports. She walked with her mother downstairs and neared the closed library door.

Loud voices came from the library. Sophia could hear Józef cry out his frustration.

"I feel personally cheated! The *Graf Spee's* self-destruction was cowardly," Józef roared. "Justice should have allowed the British ships to blow the German one into oblivion. They should have known an egomaniac like

Hitler would order the captain to scuttle his own ship, rather than surrender. Hitler cares nothing for individual life."

Now the only voices that came from the library were muffled. Final preparation of bids and legal contracts were being put in order before Vincent Ludlow came to take them back to New York after the party.

Marie seemed to ignore the voices from the library, and she continued talking to Sophia about the subject that interested her.

"Yes, I have a fitting too. But let's leave in about thirty minutes, and we can grab lunch in town. You get ready, and I'll tell Manka."

The clouds still hung low, heavy with promised snow, waiting for the right moment. "I hope it doesn't snow until we get home," fretted Marie as she looked at the sky. Jacobson was driving them into town.

"Wouldn't it be fun if the snow waited until the night of the party, and the people would have to come in their sleighs?" The excitement of the idea put a little color into Sophia's cheeks. And she still felt a glow from her prayer.

"Oh, Sophia, you are such a child!" They laughed together.

Sophia kept the idea alive. "The snow wouldn't scare anyone away! We've lived with it too long to let it get us down."

"I've changed my mind, Sophia. It would be a very picturesque parade. A wonderful arrival of the townspeople in their horse-drawn sleighs," Marie agreed. "It would add a touch of romance to the occasion."

Their luncheon was gay. The party was only two days away, and many of their friends stopped them to talk about it. Nearly the entire town had been invited. Józef wouldn't have it any other way.

Wanda slipped Sophia's gown over her head and expertly adjusted the folds of the skirt. Marie gasped. It was a heavy satin of pale cream with only a blush of color. The scooped neckline was edged with small roses made from the same heavy satin. A tiny pearl had been fastened to the center of each rose. The bodice produced a quiet elegance, flowing into the long skirt, where every few inches the hem was scalloped and decorated by the same pearl-centered rose.

"It's divine! Sophia, you've chosen the perfect fabric and style for you!" Marie looked closely at her daughter. "That isn't the fabric I chose earlier."

Sophia couldn't believe that Stefan had known how the fabric would change the dress. The heavy satin held a glow that made it seem to give off a light of its own.

"I'd like to claim credit for it," Sophia confessed, "but Stefan chose it. He thought this would suit me better."

"Stefan?" Marie was puzzled.

Wanda nodded approvingly. "Ah, yes, the count must love your daughter very much, madame, because he chose so carefully."

"Perhaps he does," Marie said. She looked at Sophia. "Sophia, are you all right?"

"I'm fine, Mother. This has been an exciting afternoon." She couldn't have explained. The thought that maybe Stefan did love her made her weak. She wanted him to so very badly. If only Monica would not flirt with him so outrageously. Stefan hadn't seemed to discourage her.

Sophia bristled as she remembered how Monica had greeted Stefan so openly as they returned from camp. Her face burned.

"That's better; you have some color in your cheeks now," Wanda exclaimed through a mouthful of pins. "It won't take much longer. I just need to take in the waist a little more. I think you've lost weight, dear."

Sophia wondered what the two women would think if they knew that the color in her face was due to her anger at Monica and Stefan. The contract assured that Stefan would always be her husband; it was too bad that it couldn't guarantee her a place in his heart.

CHAPTER TWELVE

～✥～

Sophia had slept late, but she knew it was snowing even before she opened the drapes in her bedroom. There was something about the hush of the morning; snow seemed to deaden the sounds of the world.

She rubbed her hand over the windowpane and peered out. A figure on a donkey was moving along the edge of the woods. It was old Lew. She wouldn't have recognized him from this distance, but there was no mistaking the familiar shape that he and Nellie made together. He must be off to check his traps a little later than usual. It appeared that he was headed toward the trail that led to the logging shack where his traps had been put beside the creek below it. But he'd be back in plenty of time to dress for their party. She had given him a special invitation and coaxed a promise from him to come. He'd always been a friend to her and Jan, and lately, he had taken such good care of Stefan when he was injured. She knew that Lew wanted to come, but he also wanted to be urged. He would be here.

She heard Lois vacuuming in Stefan's room. The temporary help hired for the party were airing and cleaning the rooms in the left wing across the wide corridor from their own wing. There would be overnight guests. Occasionally, she could hear high-pitched laughter. The festive mood of the party was infecting even the servants.

Sophia, however, wasn't excited about the party. Her heart matched the gray, heavy clouds that were spilling snow so freely this morning. Hot tears threatened behind her eyes, but she angrily fought them back. A good cry might make her feel better, but it wouldn't change the situation.

Ever since they had returned from the logging camp, Stefan had ignored her. In their sitting room, he never said a word to her. Before they went to the camp, she had played the piano for him on a few evenings. He had laughed with that deep vibrant sound that stirred her. Sometimes he would read some beautiful psalm to her from his Bible. Now he was overly polite to her at mealtimes and in front of her family. Always correct. Apparently, Monica had noticed, for she sneered at her knowingly. Her eyes seemed to say that he was tired of her already.

Stefan was attentive to Monica's advances, though Sophia couldn't recall a time when Stefan had attempted to draw Monica's attention.

Sophia wished that Stanislas was there to divert Monica's attention. He hadn't been at Forest House yesterday at all, but no doubt he would be here tonight. The occasion demanded his presence.

Sophia dressed and went down to a late breakfast. No one seemed to be in a hurry this morning, as everyone, except Monica, was still at the table. She filled her plate from the dishes on the sideboard and sat down by her grandmother.

"This is a great night for you, my dear." Mrs. Milewski patted her hand lovingly. Her little body was draped in a soft blue dress that was kind to her wrinkled, sagging skin and added depth to her faded blue eyes. She held her head erect and looked almost regal. "When I was young, it was always a great occasion to introduce the bride and groom to our people."

"Grandmother, there isn't a feudal system in the United States," Maurice explained patiently. They never were too sure what Mrs. Milewski understood. She had been able to learn the English language, but she refused to accept different customs and ways.

"This time next year, we will have a party to celebrate the birth of your son, my great-grandson." Mrs. Milewski nodded to Sophia with pride, ignoring Maurice's remarks.

Sophia flushed red and threw a quick glance at Stefan. He continued to eat his breakfast as though he had not heard.

"And what a grand celebration that will be!" Józef laughed. "The continuation of the Zurowski family here in the United States." Józef winked at Mrs. Milewski like a fellow conspirator.

"Yes, that'll be quite an accomplishment for our little Sophia." Maurice said.

"Don't mock, Maurice," retorted Josef.

"Well, as for me, I haven't looked forward to the prospect of being a grandmother," Marie said.

"No doubt not, my dear, since you've taken motherhood so lightly," Józef said. "But you may change." His glance at her looked sad. "The continuation of the great family name of Zurowski rests with Stefan and Sophia. Without an heir, all my money, all my vast enterprises have no meaning." Józef's knitted brow showed the intensity of his feelings.

"Rest assured, sir, we won't let you down," Stefan said, speaking for the first time since sitting at the table. He didn't look at Sophia, but she was intensely aware of him across the table from her. Her food caught in her throat, and she couldn't finish her breakfast.

Maurice chuckled softly as he glanced across at her.

Breakfast was finished in silence, as though each one was deep in his own thoughts.

"Maurice," Mrs. Milewski said suddenly.

"Yes, Grandmother." Maurice hung his head, waiting for her to speak further.

"Lois said that you volunteered to watch little Julie for her this afternoon. That isn't a seemly occupation for a man. I told Lois to bring her to my room. I will teach Julie to knit." Mrs. Milewski looked at Maurice steadily.

He lowered his eyes first. "But …" Maurice started but then shrugged.

Sophia looked at her grandmother in a new light. Mrs. Milewski's head was bent over her plate; she didn't meet Sophia's gaze.

Her grandmother knew! She knew about Maurice, and she was going to protect the little girl. But all these years that Maurice had tormented her own granddaughter, she couldn't have known. *Perhaps I can talk to her*, Sophia thought.

"Grandmother, may I come to your room this morning and keep you company? There are people swarming all over the house, and our own maid was anxious for me to leave my room." Sophia's voice came out in a rush before she could change her mind.

The look Maurice gave her was one of pure fear. Sophia was reminded of an animal caught in one of old Lew's traps. A few minutes later, Maurice left the table, announcing that he was going into town.

"If you are ready, my dear, let's go to my room and have a nice chat. You haven't visited me there since your new husband started taking up so much of your time," her grandmother said as she allowed Sophia to help her rise from the table.

Baskets of yarn spilled everywhere. Colorful mounds of thread gave the room a gay, festive look.

"Grandmother, you look like you've already decorated for the party!" Sophia said, laughing.

"Beautiful colors, are they not? It's an old woman's weakness. Of course, I've more yarn than I can hope to use up in the short lifetime that I have left." The old lady took comfort from the security of the abundance of yarn. "In our village there are so many poor children who need scarves."

Sophia looked at her grandmother. She wasn't at all slow-witted. She lived partly in the past because she chose to do so. She could come out when it suited her, like this morning when she gave the warning to Maurice.

Mrs. Milewski tucked her white lace handkerchief beneath the elastic of her sleeve and took up her knitting. There was a look of concentration on her round face. Her white hair was neatly caught in a knot high on her head. Sophia could see the gray web of the hairnet that kept any ends from straying.

Sophia sat down on the low footstool beside her grandmother's rocker. "What are you working on now?"

Her grandmother held up the fine work that was about half finished. She looked at Sophia with a twinkle in her faded blue eyes. "This is for your baby, my great-grandson!" She laid a hand on the shiny softness of her granddaughter's hair so near her knee.

"But what if there is no son, no children?" Sophia said softly. "What if there are none?"

The old lady laughed softly. "Don't be impatient, dear. You are young and healthy."

"And scared," Sophia added bitterly.

"Afraid of having babies?" Her grandmother looked at her in sympathy. "It's no easy thing, Sophia, but the rewards are so great."

"Scared of being a wife!" The cry tore from Sophia in anguish. She stood up with her back to the old lady. "I'm twenty years old and repulsed at the thought of being in bed with my own husband! But still I love him so much it hurts."

Sophia sat back down on the low stool and buried her head on her grandmother's knees.

"I see," the old woman patted the weeping girl's shoulder. She was silent a long time. Then she asked, "Maurice?"

Sophia nodded her head and sobbed uncontrollably.

The old lady sighed pitifully. "I thought you had escaped! You always had Jan near you." She took a deep breath before trying to explain. "Your real father knew about Maurice shortly after he and Monica came to live with us, and since he was a doctor, he understood. Maurice was sent away. There were treatments, many sessions. Your mother never knew of her nephew's illness; she just thought Maurice was away, attending school. She wouldn't have allowed your father to bring his nephew into the house, had she known. Maurice's parents were killed in an accident. When Maurice was brought home for the funerals, he never returned to Switzerland. Your own father took Maurice and Monica in to live with him."

Sophia had stopped sobbing and was listening to Mrs. Milewski, but she kept thinking this story didn't mean much to her now.

"When your father died and Marie later married Józef Zurowski, I was pleased. Józef wanted us all to come here to live. Maurice was so much better by then, and we would have no near neighbors. I thought the illness had been conquered."

"Maurice was always so clever, so able to fool everyone."

"Yes, Sophia, even his old grandmother, it seems, who knew about him. When I saw his unusual interest in the maid's little girl, I thought his sickness was starting again. I didn't know that it had never really been arrested."

"He was always there, waiting, touching." Sophia shivered as she remembered.

"But it's over, Sophia. I will take care of it."

"My life is ruined," Sophia said simply.

"Have you told Stefan?"

"No." She drew back in horror at the thought.

"He would understand your fear. I see great wisdom in your husband. He is a man who has suffered much. Are you going to add to it? A man with a coward for a wife?"

"Coward?" she repeated. "I've kept all this to myself since I was a little girl."

"My dear, that shows a great deal of pride but not much courage, I'm afraid."

"But what can I do?"

"Face the situation. I'll take care of Maurice. The rest is up to you. I would've helped sooner if I had known. Forgive me; I can't tell you how sorry I am." The pain in her eyes was more than Sophia could bear.

"Don't blame yourself, Grandmother; you didn't know." Sophia hugged the plump, round shoulders.

"No. I didn't know." Then a gleam of mischief came into her eyes. "If I remember correctly, and I am quite sure that I do"—a smile played around Mrs. Milewski's lips— "one night spent with the man you love can chase away a lot of unpleasant memories."

"Grandmother!"

"Don't be shocked, my dear. It's God's wedding gift. You know it says in Genesis, 'And God blessed them and said to them, Be fruitful and multiply.' It's just the way of life. Your mother, I fear, hasn't been a very good example of the loving wife. But fortunately, that is something your heart can teach you."

"But, Monica?" Sophia hated herself for bringing up her cousin's name.

Mrs. Milewski laughed. "Just a touch of envy, Sophia. Monica is in love with Monica, very much like her aunt Marie. But when she falls in love, she will learn."

Sophia left her grandmother's room. Her heart was singing and free. Her outlook on the ball tonight had changed from one of gray doom to sparkling anticipation. She ran lightly up the stairs to her room.

She turned the corner at the landing, humming happily to herself. The door from the left wing opened, and Maurice stepped out into her path. She gasped. He had appeared so suddenly.

"If it isn't our sweet, little cousin."

"I thought you'd gone into town," she said.

He came closer, his face very near to her own. He put his hand on her shoulder.

"It's no use, Maurice. You don't frighten me any longer."

He dropped his hand from her shoulder. Her eyes stared at him in disgust, and she hoped he couldn't hear her heart pounding.

"You've talked to Grandmother already," he said, his lips forming a pout.

She looked at him in repulsion. His face had changed. The assured, handsome face was now that of a petulant, spoiled boy.

"It's not fair, you know, for Grandmother to ruin my fun. I just want to touch you, Sophia. I just want to touch you. I want you to love me." Tears rolled down his face.

There was no pity in her for him. When she thought of the anguish and terror he had put her through, she wanted to hurt him.

"Grandmother will take care of you," she threatened. "She will tell Josef, and you will be sent away again. This time forever!"

"No, I won't go. I'm not sick." His lower lip pushed out ever further in rebellion.

"That is for them to decide." She abruptly turned and left him in the corridor alone,

Sophia leaned heavily on the door that was now closed between her and Maurice. She held her breath and could hear him sniveling and mumbling to himself.

The room was empty. Sophia sat down at the piano. For an hour, the flowing music bathed her soul and soothed the pain and loss. She had been cheated of a normal childhood, but she still had an entire life ahead of her.

She glanced out the window when she heard the car. From her window, she couldn't see who approached the house from the lane, but it was probably Jacobson. He had gone into town to pick up their dresses.

Excitement caught her as she thought of wearing the satin dress tonight. She was glad that Stefan had chosen a different fabric for her dress than her mother had originally picked out for her.

She splashed cool water on her face and carefully patted it dry with a towel. She brushed her hair into place and left their rooms.

The staircase that led from the second floor spiraled gracefully into the large entrance foyer. To the right of the foyer was the living room— gold, mirrored, and elegant. The large formal dining hall, not the small dining room where the family usually ate, opened wide double doors into a ballroom spacious enough for the grand party. The ballroom itself was as large as the living and dining rooms combined.

Furniture was being rearranged in preparation for the gala evening. The ballroom had tall potted plants near seating areas, which brought out the color of the green leaves in the green-and-gold floral-print wall covering.

Florists were still bringing flowers in for every room in the house. An enormous gold chandelier, dripping with crystals, hung from the ceiling above the gleaming smoothness of the polished floor. The end wall was a single mirror, as though to record the scene for future viewing.

A glassed-in porch led to the outside terrace. Sliding doors were tightly fastened and heavily draped against the winter weather, but in summer it was an inviting place for a breath of fresh air between dances. For this evening, this alcove was where the orchestra would be situated. The music stands were already in place in front of the small black folding chairs.

Their luncheon consisted of cold meats, cheeses, and fruits. Manka wouldn't hear of having the party food catered and insisted on doing it in their own kitchen. Marie objected, but Józef upheld Manka's decision. So, the kitchen was bustling, with no time for doing anything as mundane as fixing a heavy lunch. There would also be a light dinner served earlier than usual.

Vincent Ludlow had arrived late last night, and Sophia listened as Marie and Monica shared reminiscences with him of their latest visit to New York. The excitement for the evening's ball was building.

"I know you have a special tailor on Savile Row who does your bespoke suits; but, Vince, I looked all over New York and ended up back here at Wanda's Dress Shoppe for my gown." Marie laughingly teased her guest.

"Dark Forest does have many things going for it." Vincent Ludlow lifted his wineglass. "Perhaps its greatest assets are the lovely ladies of the Zurowski family."

Monica lifted her glass. "I'll drink to that. But some day I'm going to talk Uncle Józef into letting me live in New York."

"Perhaps Vincent can find you a job there," suggested Józef, "and you won't need my consent." He smiled with good humor.

"Uncle, dear, I'll wait for your approval and allowance." Monica smiled charmingly and obediently.

"Helka, we'll have our coffee in the library," Marie directed the serving girl, heavily laden with the silver tray. "I think it's the only place we'll be out of the way."

Maurice hadn't come down at all, and Monica disappeared after lunch— the hairdresser had come to Forest House, and Monica wanted her hair done first.

Marie left the library as soon as possible, but Sophia remained, listening contentedly to the men.

"Vincent, is the government going to agree to the two-week extension we need to supply the iron ore?" Józef was sitting behind his desk tapping his fingers lightly on the contract in question.

"Yes, their deadline wasn't that crucial. But the deadlines soon will be. The United States is going to enter this war. Mark my words! There's no doubt about that. The question is when."

The frown that crossed Mrs. Milewski's features made her look ancient. Sophia knew that she had suffered through invasions in Poland and lived with the news of Poland since she had been in this country.

Józef picked up a fat manila folder. "And these additional contracts are what you base your suppositions on?"

"That and other things. There are still many journalists who are calling this a 'phony' war, but too many countries are becoming involved. And

Hitler must be stopped. There is already an act coming up for vote to supply our allies with all the needed weapons and equipment."

"Yes, I read that," Józef said.

"The *Baltic Queen* got back from her second trip to Poland," reported Ludlow. "It arrived the day before I left New York."

"The supplies got through all right?" asked Józef

"Yes. The food you sent was distributed through the Red Cross, and nothing was questioned."

Ludlow's reports were crisp and businesslike, but Sophia could tell that Józef and Stefan felt the news in a personal way.

"Did you learn if anyone was able to find Frederic and give him my letter?" Stefan asked. "I want to know if Frederic and Kasia are safe. I wanted them to know I had arrived safely."

"Yes, Stefan, your letter got through. And you got a reply." The lawyer opened his black briefcase on the edge of the table beside his chair and pulled out a long white envelope.

"Do you mind?" Stefan asked as he walked away from the rest of them and stood by the window to read his letter.

The talk was low and general, with nothing catching Sophia's attention while Stefan read Frederic's letter. She watched his face. She saw his eyebrow lift expressively as he read. A look of bewilderment crossed his face, and he rubbed his chin thoughtfully.

"If you gentlemen will excuse me, I need to rest for tonight," Mrs. Milewski said.

The two men rose. The old lady patted Sophia's shoulder reassuringly as she left the room.

Stefan walked back. Józef, Ludlow, and Sophia looked up at him expectantly.

"The reply from Frederic is a little disconcerting. But I'm not surprised." Sophia watched his face as he continued. "When I first arrived here, I was introduced to Father Vladek. And something kept tugging at my memory. He was just arrived from Poland; came over with me on the *Baltic Queen* I was told. I was in sick bay the entire trip and didn't see him. I finally remembered Frederic telling me and Kasia that a priest was murdered just before I left Danzig. I don't know why it bothered me, but it did."

"Did you think that our Father Vladek was acquainted with the other priest and should be told?" Józef asked.

"No," Stefan answered. "This priest was killed near my rendezvous point for boarding the *Baltic Queen*. I thought perhaps that the priest that you were expecting was murdered and someone took his place."

"But that would mean that the man we call Father Vladek is an impostor, maybe a murderer!" Józef said.

"Yes. I had asked Frederic in my letter if the priest down at the waterfront had been identified. And his letter said"—he raised the thin sheets of paper in his hand— "that the body was identified as Father Vladek, on special assignment on his way to the United States."

"Did the man just want to find a way to come to the States?" Vincent Ludlow asked, clearly shaken. "Or do you suppose he's after something?"

Josef told Vincent of the crucifix that Stefan had brought with him on the trip from Poland. Vincent passed his hand over his eyes as though to erase the trouble he could foresee in their future.

Sophia remembered the look of greed she had seen on Father Vladek's face as he had looked at the Zurowski wedding ring on her hand on the night of the dinner. He would go to great lengths for what he wanted—she was sure of that now.

"There have been rumors that an elite group of Nazis are operating a smuggling ring," Vincent said. "They are called the Nazi Art Committee. A friend of mine in a high position in the CIA said rare art objects have been reported on the underground market for sale. They are raising money for the 'Fatherland.'" Vincent ran a well-manicured hand over the silver streak in his hair. "They haven't been able to catch anyone or prove anything yet."

"The Zurowski jeweled crucifix is such a secret treasure that only someone from the area surrounding Domani z Camin would know of it. It was shown on private occasions," Józef said.

"But well worth a great deal of effort to steal, Uncle Józef," Stefan said.

"It's priceless," Józef said in a husky voice.

"Mr. Ludlow, your friend in New York—could you reach him by phone?" Stefan asked.

"I suppose so. It's two days before Christmas, but he lives in New York and will be in town with his family. Why do you ask?"

"Why don't you call your friend? He can contact the proper authorities closest to our town in Dark Forest. Positive identification of Vladek must be made by someone in authority."

"That makes good sense, Stefan," Józef agreed. "You do that, Vincent. Although I'm sure that the most important thing we can do right now is not to tip our hands to the phony Father Vladek. He'll be here tonight. Since only the four of us know, it shouldn't be hard to hide it from him. You know," Józef snarled, "I never did like that man!"

They left Vincent Ludlow alone in the library to make his phone calls.

From her bedroom window, Sophia watched it snow. There had been near-blizzard conditions all day, but now the wind had died down. Snow was piled and drifted, but the people would come tonight. Nothing could keep them away.

Sophia pushed back the troubling thoughts that clamored for attention in her mind. All she wanted to do now was to look forward to the ball. She was free of Maurice. She was free to dream of her handsome husband, of their future together. Maybe she could break down the ice barrier that had frozen between them since their trip to the North Woods logging camp.

CHAPTER THIRTEEN

Dinner was Manka's special suflet z kartofli, a light potato soufflé sprinkled with parsley and bread crumbs and topped with melted butter. The pike had been cut into pieces and fried to a delicate brown in the fresh, rich butter and served with a French wine. Sautéed mushrooms had been added to the green peas. Gooseberry compote was served with coffee at the table.

Everyone seemed to feel the excitement of the evening because the talk and laughter flowed freely around the table. Nothing that had happened could dampen their spirits. Even Maurice seemed to be enjoying himself; no trace of trouble showed on his too-handsome face. His hair was perfectly in order, with the center part arrow-straight; his grooming was immaculate.

Before Jan's death, Józef had hosted wonderful parties at Forest House, but never before had there been a party in which Sophia was given any sort of recognition, not even a birthday party. Jan had never wanted a birthday party, and she always went along with him. Now she wanted to savor every minute of this party. The people would begin arriving in three hours, but she wanted to linger over her bath and then dress very carefully. The hairdresser was to come to her room soon after dinner.

She pinned her hair up high to keep it dry. The tub stood waiting, filled very near the brim, with light pink suds bubbling on top. She stepped in gingerly. Not a drop of water splashed out, and she settled down to soak in the scented water, with the liquid warmth around her neck, very near her chin.

Soothed and relaxed from her bath, she put on the exquisitely made undergarments that Wanda designed for her to wear with her dress. They were light as breath and edged in soft lace. The dressing gown she put on was made similar to a monk's robe with a hood, but it was of clinging green cashmere, held together in the front by a braided silk cord.

It was going to be a long night, and she lay down on her side on the chaise longue, her hand resting under her cheek, to give herself over to the joy of anticipation. Her matching green bedroom slippers were beside the chair, and she pulled her feet up into the warmth of the dressing gown.

She hadn't expected to sleep, but the sound of a door closing awakened her. It was the door to their sitting room. She could hear the swish sounds of footfalls on carpet as someone neared her bedroom door.

"Sophia?" Stefan knocked at her door." Are you awake?"

"Yes." She walked over to the door, listening intently.

"May I come in?" Stefan's voice was firm yet questioning.

She opened the door for him and stood back as he entered. The door closed quietly behind him, and the look he gave her was one of compassion. Sophia let her eyes rest on his face for a moment before she dropped her head. She had been dreaming of him, reliving the moment when she had rushed down the stairs and lay against his chest. She was feeling again the strength of his arms around her.

"Sophia, I just came from your grandmother. She wanted to have a talk with me." There was sadness and anger in his gray eyes.

"No!" Sophia cried. "She had no right!" She turned her back to him. Hugging her own body, she doubled over as though in pain and rocked back and forth, trying to find comfort.

Stefan put his arms around her and drew her to him. He laid his face against the bright softness of her hair. He held her tight, and she clung to his arm that encircled her shoulders, crying softly. Gradually, the crying stopped, and he turned her to face him.

"I had to know sometime, Sophia. I couldn't bear to think that you hated me so much that you cringed every time that I touched you."

"But, Stefan, I don't want you to pity me. I'm ashamed that I never had the courage to say something. But I was innocent, and I didn't think that anyone would believe me."

"Sophia, there is no one who would doubt your innocence. It shines in your eyes, in the way you smile. I think I loved you from the time I saw you hiding beneath the spruce as I walked up the road to Forest House." Stefan cupped his strong hand under her chin. "If, at some time in the past, Maurice raped you"—he didn't flinch as he said it— "it's over now; he can't hurt you again. We've told Józef. Maurice is to be sent away tomorrow."

"No, Stefan, Maurice never went that far. He didn't ..." She faltered and couldn't say the word *rape*. "His sickness fed on my fear. He was always around, hiding, touching."

"Don't think of it again. It's over." He held her as she hid her face against his shirt. "I'm glad it's over for you, Sophia."

She loved her name as he spoke it.

"It was hard for me to face the fact of your abuse after"—he swallowed hard— "Anne."

Sophia went rigid and pulled away from him, and he dropped his arms. "I lost my sister—"

"And I won't be her replacement," Sophia snapped, suddenly angry. "You say you love me, pat me on the head, and say that you are sorry for what Maurice made me go through!"

"Sophia, you misunderstand," Stefan began.

"Oh, do I really? Not one word about 'loving me' until you heard of my trouble; not one thought of me until you could compare me with your *Anne*. No wonder it was so easy for you to comply with my request to keep the door between our bedrooms closed. It must have been a great relief to you. You had no interest in me as a wife!"

"Sophia, I suggest you stop." Stefan's gray eyes flashed black.

"No!" she cried, reckless in her anger. "You were nice to me at first. Sure! You were sorry about your sister. Then when we came back from the logging camp you dropped all pretense. Not a word to me until today! Playing up to Monica!" She cried out in pain as he gripped her shoulders hard.

"You little spitfire! If I'd had any doubt of your innocence, you've erased it. You don't know how desirable you are. After our trip to the camp, I didn't know if I could trust myself around you. And now I find that I no longer have to treat you so delicately." His eyes now teased her. "You love me."

"I didn't say that," she countered angrily.

"You will." He seemed maddeningly sure of himself.

She stood helpless as he slowly untied the belt at her waist. There was little triumph in the fact that his hands were trembling. The dressing gown fell open, and he slipped his arms inside. Her flesh burned beneath the thin garment where his arms touched. She felt his lips on her bare shoulder, traveling slowly up the softness of her neck. She had no control over her body's response to him. New feelings that she didn't know even existed now left her weak, clinging to him for support.

"Still think I have you confused with my sister?" His voice was husky with emotion. She nodded weakly, unable to speak. "You may have a lot to learn, my innocent little wife, but I think I'll find you a willing pupil." There was laughter in his eyes. He turned abruptly and walked out. She heard the slam of the sitting room door as he left.

Sophia threw herself on her bed, clutching the green dressing gown around her trembling body. She wasn't shaking from fear, but never had she felt so alone. It was as though she were the last person in the world. She pulled the cover over her until the trembling stopped. She had to get through the night. Stefan would be at her side, touching her arm, smiling at all the guests, receiving their congratulations. But they would all look at her and know. Her husband didn't really want her!

There was a knock at the sitting room door, and Sophia was surprised at the quickening of her heart. *Stefan's come back!* She couldn't bear to have him see how shaken she was.

"Madame?" the voice inquired.

Sophia quickly got up from the bed and opened her bedroom door.

"Madame? It's time for me to do your hair." The hairdresser stood in her white uniform, looking anxious. "I'm afraid I'm a little behind schedule."

"That's all right, Becky; so am I." *That's truly the state of my affairs now,* Sophia thought sadly. "Come in, and let's get started." Sophia sat at her vanity table, and Becky reached for the comb and brush in the large pockets of her nylon uniform. She started brushing Sophia's hair with quick, nervous movements.

"Such lovely hair, madame! It just seems to cooperate with all my plans." The tiredness seemed to drain from the little woman's shoulders, and she straightened. With deft fingers, she used the tools of her trade pulled from the deep pockets of her rustling uniform. In very little time, Sophia's hair was finished. Soft curls played about her temples and delicate bangs feathered over her brow. Becky sighed with pleasure as she placed the ivory satin headpiece on the red-gold of Sophia's hair. Tiny seed pearls gave it the appearance of an elegant tiara.

"Now, if you wish, I'll help you with your dress, and then I can repair any damage that might be done to your hair while dressing." Becky was eyeing the shimmering satin creation.

Soon afterward, Sophia stood before the long mirror, gazing at her transformation. There was no trace left of the frightened child that she had been so recently. She was different from the tip of the pearl-covered headpiece to the toes of the satin shoes peeking out at the hem of her dress.

With lavish praise and a few quick touches to Sophia's hair, Becky left the room.

Sophia had heard Stefan return, and the sound of his movement sent little ripples of unease along her spine. She walked around, touching things, picking up a book, glancing at a magazine—she couldn't sit down for fear of crushing her skirt. The incident in her bedroom only an hour ago would not leave her mind.

The door opened abruptly, and Stefan entered with a package in his hand. He put it into his pocket.

Sophia started at his appearance.

"Did I startle you?" A look of pain crossed his face.

Stefan was splendid in his evening clothes. A midnight-blue coat gave color to his gray eyes, and the gold medallion, magnificent against the dazzling white of his shirt front, was the sign of Polish nobility. It enhanced the gold highlights in his straight fair hair.

"Sophia, I'm sorry for this afternoon. But you pushed me too far." His face was grave.

"I love you, Stefan," she said simply.

A smile transformed his face. He brought her hand to his lips. "You've told me at a devil of a time, woman," he growled. "I can't touch you for fear of crushing your dress." Then he looked at her seriously. "You do know the implications of what you say, don't you?"

"Yes, I love you. I want you as my husband in every way." She flushed hotly but kept her eyes steady in his gaze. It was almost like an unconditional surrender to an enemy.

"And you aren't afraid?" He held both her hands against his cheek.

"A little," she confessed.

"Sophia, there's nothing to fear. If only we didn't have to go downstairs ..." He held her gently and pressed his lips to her forehead.

"But we must!" She stepped back, horrified at the thought.

"Just teasing, love." He let his lips briefly touch hers as he continued to hold both her hands. "By the way, you do look ravishing. You are as beautiful in that dress as I imagined you would be. And I've something else for you." For the second time, he slipped the Zurowski wedding ring on her finger, but this time his eyes held a definite promise.

He took the package from his pocket and opened it. Sophia gasped as the light caught the gleaming rubies and sapphires mounted in an ornate setting. The smooth ivory of her neck and the simplicity of the satin dress showed off the necklace to its best advantage.

His hands were gentle on her bare shoulders as he fastened the necklace. They stood reflected in the mirror—a regal couple who would look at home in the court of any king.

"It's time to go." He opened the door, and she stepped out into the hall. He followed her and offered his arm, and they walked slowly toward the landing at the head of the spiral staircase.

As the people who had gathered caught sight of them, a hush fell upon the entire house.

"The Count and Countess Stefan Peter Werten Zurowski."

Sophia heard the pride that rang loud and clear in every word of Józef Zurowski's introduction.

The orchestra began playing the Polish national anthem as Stefan led his young bride into the center of the ballroom.

When the anthem finished, the orchestra began a waltz, and as Stefan led Sophia into movement with the music, the mirror in the ballroom reflected the swirl and grace of many dancing couples.

"So, you turned out to be Cinderella," Monica sniped at Sophia as they waltzed past each other. Monica's long, green silk swirled around her slender figure. The brilliance of the chandelier caught the glitter of envy in her hard-green eyes.

Sophia smiled as she heard Stanislas say, "Don't be catty, Monica. It's unbecoming."

Sophia and Stefan were swept up and surrounded with the good wishes of their friends. Everyone had come to give best wishes to the nephew of Józef Zurowski.

Only the most adventurous stayed to continue the party in spite of the weather, and many left shortly after paying respects to the couple and sampling the delights offered at the Zurowski table. The spread was enormous—cold cuts of meat, bakery rolls, tea cakes, and fruit. An unending variety of tempting morsels covered small squares or rounds of bread. These kanapki were arranged invitingly on wide silver trays.

Antek directed his help in serving champagne. Józef also had instructed Antek to bring up old Polish honey wines from their own cellar, made here at Forest House, for those who preferred it.

Many families had come on sleighs drawn by a horse or mule, and Jacobson saw that their conveyances were ready when they wanted to leave. The man's great nose grew red from his trips out into the cold.

It was very late, and only about twenty-five young couples and those who planned to spend the night at Forest House remained. Maurice, as part of the hosting family, danced with many partners and was observed being very gallant and proper.

Dr. Janda stood with his wife, Janke, who watched him devotedly as he talked with Vincent Ludlow. Her own chestnut hair was lightened by the passing years. Her face was kind with a capacity for patience and endurance. She had been a perfect wife for the doctor. Stanislas Janda stood next to his mother's chair, his hand relaxing on the back of it.

Vincent Ludlow had tried to keep an eye on Father Vladek during the evening. Sophia had overheard him telling Stefan and Józef that his friend, Jim Brady, had assured him over the phone that he was notifying the CIA in the largest city close to Dark Forest. "He told me that a German agent was spotted in New York about three months ago and then dropped out of sight," he'd said.

Jacobson watched the last of the guests leave who had come in their sleighs and wagons. He smiled as he remembered that it always had been like this when they first came to Forest House.

He closed the stable door and trudged back toward the lighted house. The wind was picking up, and it had begun to snow hard again. More people might have to spend the night at Forest House than had planned. *Manka would love that*, he thought as he grinned to himself.

A dark shape appeared against the white of the snow, moving slowly in the direction of the house, parallel to Jacobson's path. Jacobson stopped and watched it for a while. It looked like a horse. He followed it, and when it got within the yellow pool of light from the veranda, he saw it was a donkey—Lew's old donkey, Nellie. The animal came up to the veranda and stopped.

During the party, Sophia and Stefan both had asked Jacobson if he had seen Lew. They were hurt that he had stayed away.

"I was sure that I'd talked him into coming," Sophia had told him.

Jacobson walked onto the veranda and stomped the snow from his feet. He took off his stocking cap and shook the snow from it. The curtain of snow was becoming thicker. Once inside the house, he caught Józef's eye.

Józef motioned Jacobson into the library and closed the door behind them. "What is it?"

"I don't know, but Nellie, Lew's donkey, just showed up at the front of the house, and the saddle is empty. I plan to put the animal in the stable and give her some oats."

"No sign of Lew?"

"None. And where you see one of them, you always see both. Besides, on a night like tonight, the animal wouldn't wander off."

The library door opened, and Sophia entered, followed by Stefan.

"Jacobson, I looked out the terrace door and saw Lew's donkey. Where is he?" Sophia asked, looking around expectantly.

"We don't know, dear," Józef answered for Jacobson.

"I was sure he'd be here tonight," she said. "I saw him leave about midmorning to run his traps. I thought he'd be back in plenty of time to be here tonight."

"You saw him where?" Józef asked quickly.

"He was on the path along the woods—the one that leads to the first logging shack. He has traps up there along the creek."

"I remember he always traps on that creek," agreed Jacobson.

Sophia put her hand to her throat as she sat down in a nearby chair. "You don't suppose something has happened to him? That's where Jan saw a stranger over a year ago, and then, when we were there, I thought I saw someone up by the rock before the slide started." The memories ran together and flooded over her.

"And you didn't say anything?" Józef asked.

Stefan put a protecting hand on Sophia's shoulder.

"No," she answered reluctantly. "I was afraid no one would believe me. No one believed me when I saw someone before Jan's death."

"I did have a man check the area, Sophia, and no one was found," Józef explained gently. "Then later, Lew told me he'd seen strange tracks up by the creek, and again I had it checked out."

"But if Lew is out there tonight on foot, we must find him. He will freeze to death in a very short time," Jacobson said, remembering the sting from the wind.

Józef nodded. "I'll have Manka fix hot coffee and sandwiches for us to take. We'll leave here in about twenty minutes." He walked quickly out of the library with Jacobson on his heels.

Sophia stood close to Stefan with her face turned up to his. "Please be careful. You're not familiar with the woods here yet, and in a blizzard, it's so easy to get lost."

"Don't worry about me. You won't be able to lose me so easily now."

She slipped her arms around his neck invitingly as he bent his head toward hers. His lips melted into her own, but she felt the hard leanness of his body pressed against her own for only a moment.

"You wait for me here while I go up and change," he said. "I won't be long."

She watched Stefan as he disappeared through the doorway. She truly had felt like a countess tonight or perhaps a fairy-tale princess, but harsh reality had intruded like the clock striking midnight.

Poor Lew. She knew that he was hurt and in trouble. Never would he allow Nellie to leave his side otherwise, especially in this storm.

Józef and Jacobson came back into the library, dressed for the snowstorm. Jacobson carried the knapsack of thermoses and wrapped sandwiches. Vincent Ludlow came back into the library to wait with the men until they left.

"Is Father Vladek still out there?" Józef nodded toward the rooms where the party was still going on.

"Father Polzak excused himself hours ago to go to his room, and Father Vladek followed him just minutes later," Ludlow reported.

Józef drew his heavy brows together. "I didn't know they were staying at Forest House tonight."

"Father Vladek asked Marie for an invitation for the night because of Father Polzak. She graciously asked them both to stay," Ludlow informed him.

Józef took out his pocket watch and looked toward the door.

"I told Stefan twenty minutes. Jacobson, go ahead to the stable and put Nellie in and get our horses ready. We will be there shortly."

Jacobson nodded and left the library. Józef walked over to the window and pulled back the curtain. "This surely is a blizzard. Bad night for man or beast."

The door opened, and Stefan came into the room. His face was grim. "It's gone, Uncle Józef!"

"What's gone, Stefan?" The man's thoughts had been on Lew.

"The jeweled crucifix," he said, exhaling loudly. He still didn't believe it. "And the rest of the jewels."

Józef stared as if he'd misunderstood. "Are you sure?"

"Quite sure. I left a light burning in my room, but it was dark when I opened my door. I immediately thought of the crucifix. My sea bag had been carefully repacked as it had been, but when I checked the hiding place at the bottom, it was empty. I searched the entire room; they are nowhere to be found."

Again, the door opened, and Mrs. Milewski stood in the entrance. Her eyes were full of tears, and her lips were trembling.

"Józef," she said, her voice breaking.

"What is the matter, matka?" He took the old woman's hand and gently led her to the sofa.

"Maurice is gone!" she cried softly.

"Gone? Perhaps he went to his room or to the kitchen. He's probably somewhere in the house."

"No. I've looked everywhere and have had the servants looking. He's disappeared." She covered her face with her hands, and her shoulders shook silently.

"Don't worry, matka; we will find him," Józef said.

"He *must* be found," she murmured as she raised her head to face Józef. Her eyes were filled with anxiety. "I think we frightened him into running."

"It may be more than that," Józef said grimly. "Some valuables are missing." He turned to Ludlow, saying, "Call the sheriff and highway patrol. Give them a description of Maurice's car." Then he turned to Stefan. "We can't wait any longer. We have a long ride in this blizzard. We can only hope to find Lew at the shack."

Sophia felt the wool of Stefan's jacket against her face as he quickly embraced her before he left.

The party had dwindled to a few couples, most of them Monica's friends, so Sophia knew she wouldn't be missed now. All she wanted to do was go to her room and wait quietly for the men to return. She would pray for Lew's safety.

She helped her grandmother to her room and tried to comfort the worried old lady. She had seemed to shrink and was unable to carry the worry of her runaway grandson. She leaned gratefully on Sophia's arm.

All will turn out well, Sophia told herself. *They'll find Lew at the logging shack with nothing worse than a sprained ankle. Some hot coffee and food will revive him, and he'll be hopping mad at his own clumsiness.* She smiled to herself at the thought. *Maurice will be found with the crucifix and jewels. I've no doubt he took them, probably out of spite.*

Sophia felt the smooth fabric of her dress on her skin as she let it slide off her shoulders and onto the floor. The satin dress would hang on a padded hanger in her closet, holding memories for her forever. She was wearing it when she first told Stefan she loved him. She hugged herself in the darkness and smiled. She put on a soft white nightgown and slipped between the warm sheets.

The promise she'd read in Stefan's eyes before he left had caused a tingle of electric excitement to run through her body. The words he had whispered, with his lips close to her ear, were, "I will be back tonight. Wait for me."

She lay waiting as she listened to the wind howl around Forest House.

CHAPTER FOURTEEN

$$\text{⟞⟑⟞}$$

Jacobson saw a gust of wind whip up a tiny funnel of snow into a miniature twister in the beam of his high-powered flashlight. He hunched his shoulders against the cold and tightened his grip on the bridle of his horse. Securing the reins of the third horse at the hitching post outside the stable, he went back to slide the heavy wooden door shut.

The little man was puzzled. Maurice's horse was missing. *Can't imagine that one wanting to be out on a night like this*, he thought. *Maybe someone from the party asked to borrow it to go home.* It was the best horse in the stable—strong, with the endurance of a mule.

He looked toward the house and saw a golden glow through the white of the snow and then two blurred shapes. They disappeared into the garage. A few minutes later, they appeared at the door again and started toward the stable, where he was waiting.

"Jacobson, all set?" Józef shouted to be heard in the wind.

"Yeah. Maurice's horse is gone. Did someone borrow it to go home?" Jacobson shouted back.

"I don't know. But Maurice is missing too, and so is his car. He couldn't have left with his car *and* his horse!" Józef was now close to Jacobson and lowered his voice. "The jeweled crucifix has been stolen. Maurice may have it."

"He won't get far on a night like this," prophesied the little man.

"No, he must have known that. Probably hid his horse so we wouldn't know which way he'd gone," Józef reasoned. "But then, it's hard to know what he was thinking."

"Ludlow is calling the police and highway patrol," Stefan added. "They may have him back at Forest House by the time we return."

Józef mounted his horse. "The most urgent thing right now is to find Lew. And the only thing we can do is check the trail all the way to the first logging shack. That's going to take several rough hours."

Józef picked up the coil of rope thrown over his saddle horn and tied the end to the buckle of his saddle bag. He handed the coil of rope to Jacobson and then let out enough length of rope to allow his mount to be three feet in front of Jacobson's. Jacobson looped the rope securely onto his saddle and passed it to Stefan. Then he walked his horse in place behind Józef's.

Józef turned in his saddle and yelled to Stefan, "All set?" Stefan motioned with his hand, and Józef urged his horse forward toward the trail. The attached rope would assure them of not becoming lost from one another.

Earlier, they could have taken the shortcut; there was no question of doing that now. It was too dangerous. The horses could easily miss the trail and stumble, breaking a leg. It might not have been possible to even reach the logging road cut into the woods, had it not been that the trail leading to it was at the edge of the forest. They could ride near to the trees and use them as markers, as well as a windbreak.

The wind and further accumulation of snow obliterated any tracks that Nellie had made on smoother ground near to Forest House. About halfway to the logging shack, they stopped to rest their horses and warm themselves with the hot coffee.

Jacobson took his flashlight and searched the trail a few feet farther ahead. It was no use. Their tracks were swept away nearly as fast as they made them, as were any that Nellie might have made.

They remounted and started again, this time with Jacobson breaking the trail and Józef at the rear. It was easier going among the trees, but the wind managed to blast through the clearings, needling snow into their faces. Their wool caps were pulled down around their ears, and their knit scarves were folded up, leaving only their eyes exposed to the cold.

In their younger days at the logging camps, Jacobson and Józef had been out in weather such as this, but that had been several years ago. Tonight, they were forced out in search of a friend, a man known to them for many years.

"Our horses are becoming tired, and we're making less progress than before," Stefan said. He noticed Józef was unsteady in his saddle. "We'll have to spend the night at the logging shack; we could never make the trip back tonight."

Jacobson held up his hand, and they halted. Stefan dismounted and walked to the man on the horse in front of him.

Jacobson bent toward Stefan. "The creek where Lew set the traps is only a few yards off to the right." He pointed into the darkness.

"Give me the light, and I'll check. You stay with Józef."

Jacobson didn't protest.

Stefan led Jacobson's horse back beside Józef and unfastened the rope that had kept them all together. He tied one end of the rope around the tree closest to the edge of the logging road and kept the other in his gloved hand.

The beam from the flashlight was strong, but it uncovered nothing. He found the chain that kept one trap in place near the edge of the water, but the trap was covered with snow. The metal links were a black line coming from a low branch of a tree and disappearing into nothingness near the snow-covered ground.

Stefan searched as far as the rope would reach in all directions into the woods. It was hopeless. The blinding whiteness did not allow him to see beyond his next step. He spent several minutes uncovering a mound that looked like a man might be hidden underneath only to find a frozen deer carcass.

He decided it would have to wait until morning. Lew might very well be beyond any help, and the two older men, especially Józef, also would be if they didn't get to the cabin soon. Stefan hated himself for not discouraging Józef from coming out in this blizzard; in reality, however, he knew there was nothing he could have done to stop his uncle. He pulled the rope taut and followed it back to where it had been tied. He could see the men and horses only as black shapes outlined by white, but they had not moved.

As they neared the cabin, a flicker of color showed through the window, like a weak lighthouse beacon in a sea of white. They pulled up, all three abreast.

"Lew must have decided to hole up in the cabin." Stefan looked at the two men beside him.

"No. If he were just staying here to last out this storm, he would have Nellie right in there with him." Józef could hardly talk for shaking.

"I'll go up and look through the window before we go in," Stefan suggested. He was thinking of the German spy Ludlow had been so sure was after the jeweled crucifix. Perhaps Maurice had beat him to it, but the spy had to be somewhere. Stefan didn't want to rush into anything without knowing. Someone was in the cabin, and there was a fire. That was almost an invitation.

He pressed close to the window and cupped his hands around the sides of his face. The fire in the fireplace had burned down low; a little while later, and they wouldn't have been able to see it from the outside at all.

A kerosene lamp on the rough plank floor spread a dim glow in a small circle around it. Beside the lamp, sprawled on his stomach, was a man. He wore a red shirt, and there was a dark stain over the back of it. From Stefan's view through the window, this man didn't look at all familiar. Sophia's accident flashed through his mind; she'd said she thought she had seen a red shirt. The man's head was uncovered, revealing thick white hair.

Stefan was stunned. He had expected to find Lew, but instead had discovered a man who clearly had met with violence. From the awkward position of the torso and limbs, he was sure the man was dead—and must have been for some time, as the fire had burned down to a small flicker.

Deliberately, Stefan turned his back on the scene in the shack and made his way back to where Jacobson and Józef were waiting for him.

Józef was hugging himself very tightly and was bent over, with his head nearly against the horse's mane. Stefan could see that it was an effort for him to straighten. He watched Jacobson lean over and steady him with a light grip on his arm.

Stefan told them of seeing the man in the cabin and added that he was fairly certain that the assailant was gone. Stefan led his horse and Józef's toward the shack, as Jacobson rode alongside, keeping Józef steady in the saddle.

Entering the cabin cautiously, they peered into the shadowy corners to see if it was indeed free of other occupants. Stefan helped Józef into a chair, picked up the kerosene lamp, and turned up the wick. The beam from the lamp caught the dead man full on, showing the ugly features of his still face.

Death had robbed the man of the warmth of life, leaving his face a caricature of horror in black and white. The pallor of his skin contrasted grossly with his thick white hair and dark beard. His sightless eyes were wide, completing the expression of shock on his twisted features.

There was a sharp intake of breath from Józef. Stefan glanced at him, but Józef was looking at Jacobson.

"No, it can't be." His voice registered stunned disbelief. "Do you remember this man?"

Jacobson nodded. "There can be no mistake—the same thick, ugly features. He just looks older." There was finality in Jacobson's agreement.

"Who is he?" Stefan asked, looking from Józef to Jacobson.

"Stash Contoski. It was long ago, yet it might have been yesterday." Józef shook his head sadly. "At the dinner at Domani z Camin, the night the jeweled crucifix was stolen, this man was there. He was the nephew of our village priest, visiting from Kraków. His disappearance the next morning was enough to brand him as a thief. Now, so many years later, he turns up again when the crucifix is missing."

"Well, once again he does not have it." Stefan had finished going through the man's pockets and the coat hanging from the wooden peg by the door. A pitifully small bundle of clothes was beside the man's hand. It was obvious that he was packed, ready for flight.

"It seems that he really was a loser." Józef uttered the words that were like the man's epitaph.

Stefan wrapped his scarf more tightly around his neck and lower part of his face. "You both stay in here. I'll put the horses in the shed with the half-track. I thought I remembered seeing stalls behind the vehicle." He picked up the flashlight and headed for the door. "There was an old canvas in the back of the vehicle. I'll bring it in to wrap up this man."

The wind caught the wide door, and it banged fiercely against the side of the shed. The horses whinnied in fright, but Stefan had a firm grip on the reins. He quickly unsaddled the animals and put them in the shelter, divided off from the vehicle. He rolled up the saddle blankets to take inside with him. They would probably need them.

He pushed aside the canvas cover from the back of the half-track to get the tarpaulin that was stowed there.

He heard a moan.

He flashed the light back toward the horses, but their heads were hanging low, and they were making no movement.

The sound came again, and this time he flashed the light into the vehicle. The roll of tarpaulin was there, and beside it lay Lew. His eyelids quivered in the brightness of the flashlight. There was blood on the hand that lay motionless, extended toward Stefan.

The roll of tarpaulin was held together by a canvas strap, so Stefan adjusted it to sling over his shoulder, supported by his back. He wrapped Lew carefully in the saddle blankets and carried him back into the cabin.

Jacobson had built up the fire and had hung a kettle of snow over it to melt.

While Stefan wrapped up the corpse and put it onto the back of the half-track in the shed, Jacobson tended to Lew's wounds.

The same knife that killed Stash had missed its intended mark on Lew. The puncture had missed his heart, but he had lost a lot of blood.

Weakly, the man raised his hand and tried to talk. His hand fell, helpless, and consciousness slipped from him again.

Jacobson washed the wound carefully and used the bundle of clean clothes belonging to the dead man to tear into strips of bandages. They pulled the rough plank table to one side of the fireplace to use as a bed for him.

Stefan gave Józef the last of the hot coffee from the thermos and looked toward the back of the small cabin to see if there was anything they could use. Supper had been early, and no one had eaten much at the party.

One corner of a battered cardboard box was sticking from beneath the edge of one of the plank-board cots, and Stefan pulled it over to the light. There were a few tins of food. Evidently, the dead man kept his supplies together, possibly so he could hide them at a minute's notice if anyone came to the cabin. There wasn't much—two tins of beef broth, two large tins of beans, a little coffee in the bottom of a can, and half a loaf of stale bread. A box of salt had gotten wet and was a hard, useless lump.

Stefan nudged the box toward Jacobson with his booted foot. "Think you can do anything with that? It doesn't look promising, but we'll all need some food inside us to help keep us warm. The wind sure whistles through the cracks in these walls."

"Yeah," agreed Jacobson. "If that man we found has been living here, he sure has been roughing it."

"But he no doubt thought it was worth it if he was in on the planning to get the crucifix." Stefan felt no sympathy for this man who had so nearly caused harm to Sophia.

"He saw the cross," Jacobson assured Stefan. "He knew that it was worth a great deal of hardship. It just seems that he was not as good a judge of men. His partner must have turned on him."

Józef had pulled his chair closer to the fire. "Stefan, now that we have found this man and Lew, I'm beginning to doubt that Maurice took the crucifix." Józef closed his eyes momentarily, as if in relief. "He probably took off in fear of being sent away tomorrow. Somehow, the dead man must have taken it, or the man posing as Vladek took it and came up here."

"Sure," Stefan said. "Vladek brought it up here for this man Stash to identify. You say he had seen before. This elite group of Hitler's would leave nothing to guesswork. I have an idea that if one of their agents brought back an unauthenticated work of art—in this case, the jeweled crucifix—he wouldn't be received warmly."

Józef nodded. "I think that you're on the right track, Stefan. And when Vladek didn't need Stash, he simply got rid of him. There was no need to dispose of the body because the chances of anyone coming up here before Vladek got safely back to Germany were a million to one. And there wasn't much time either."

"Lew must have seen Vladek or Stash, and one of them tried to silence him," added Jacobson.

"That would have been Vladek." Stefan had suddenly remembered something. "When I was still at Frederic's house in Danzig and the real Father Vladek was murdered, the killer used a knife. So, the same man must have attacked all three men." Stefan paused in thought before he continued. "What I can't understand is why this man, Stash, a native of Poland, would inform German agents of the Third Reich of a Polish treasure."

"I can guess." Jacobson's mouth twisted bitterly. "Stash's mother was from Germany, and after the scandal caused by the belief that their son had stolen the jeweled crucifix, they moved back to where her people still lived—in Berlin. After Stash disappeared, he eventually wound up with his parents in their new home." He paused for effect. "Their new choice of home was not a good one because Stash's mother was also Jewish." The silence was heavy. "I think Stash's treason was a desperate attempt to escape death for himself and his family—or possibly worse."

Lew moaned on his makeshift bed, and Stefan went over to him. When Lew moved his lips, Stefan bent low to catch his whispers.

"Don't know who got me. Was looking in the window. Saw a man on the floor and"—Lew paused to catch a weak breath— "then something struck me from behind. Later when I came to, Nellie was beside me. I pulled myself up by the window ledge and sent Nellie home. I managed to crawl into the shed and up into the back of the half-track. I was afraid to go into the house in case the guy who hit me was still here. Did she come down?"

"Yes. When Nellie came to Forest House without you, Sophia remembered seeing you head up the trail to this shack," Stefan told him.

Lew smiled. "Sophia's a smart girl."

Stefan smiled back at him. "She is some girl, for sure." He thought of her warm, yielding body against him before he left. He had told her he would return tonight, and now that was impossible. He pushed these thoughts from his mind. "It's all right now. You're going to be all right. We know who stabbed you."

Lew nodded, evidently satisfied with Stefan's words.

Jacobson put a cup of the warm beef broth into Stefan's hand. Stefan slipped his arm beneath Lew's shoulders to support him while he put the broth to his mouth. Lew drank thirstily. Stefan settled the old man once more and tucked the saddle blankets around him.

They had found some chipped blue-enamel bowls, a battered coffeepot, and a few bent spoons on a board that had been nailed up for a shelf. Jacobson used one of the bowls to dip their supper into the other bowls.

Jacobson had indeed done something with the things that Stefan had found in the box. Into the remainder of the beef broth, he had put the beans from the two large tins and added a little melted snow. He had cut up the thick ham from the two remaining sandwiches Manka had made and put it into the pot with a small chunk of the hard salt. When this bean soup began to bubble, he thickened it with the stale bread. He toasted Manka's thick homemade bread from the sandwiches by holding the slices over the fire on a stick.

"Jacobson, does Manka know you can cook like this?" asked Stefan, as he rolled his eyes in appreciation.

The grin on Jacobson's face threatened to split his cheeks.

Józef chuckled. "The fact that Jacobson has always been the best stew-builder in all of our logging camps is a well-kept secret from Manka. If she knew what he could do, she would probably go into a huff and never come out."

The hot food had strengthened Józef, and Stefan relaxed when he saw the strain ease from his uncle's face.

It looked like they would be able to leave in the morning. They could take the half-track back. That would be faster, and they would be sheltered from the cold. The horses could be tied on behind the vehicle.

Jacobson had said there was a scoop attachment for a tractor at Forest House. This could be used to clear the road from the big house to the main highway, so they could keep the half-track hidden. The spy should not be alerted that the men had been out during the night.

It was still snowing, but the wind had calmed. Jacobson knew that the driveways would need to be cleared with a scoop on a tractor, so that those who had not left the party at Forest House early now would be able to get to their homes.

Stefan brought in the bedrolls that Jacobson had put on their horses, and he placed them before the fire. It was too cold to sleep on the narrow bunks at the back of the shack.

Jacobson banked the fire with willow logs. Stefan brought in additional logs that he had found stacked beside the shed.

Stefan turned up the collar of his coat and settled down to watch the fire dance and glow around the logs.

"Where do you think Vladek is now?" Stefan speculated aloud.

"I've been wondering that myself," Józef said. "The logical thing would have been to run."

"But he couldn't have gotten very far in this storm," Jacobson pointed out. "No doubt he was here and back at Forest House before the worst of the blizzard was upon us."

"That's right. Ludlow was watching him and said he retired very early. He probably went to your room during the party, Stefan, and found the cross and the rest of the jewels. Then, later, after Father Polzak was asleep, Vladek came up here on Maurice's horse. After Stash identified the crucifix, Vladek killed him. He no longer had any use for him."

"Lew must have just missed seeing Vladek leave the cabin when he looked in the window. Vladek probably saw Nellie's tracks and slipped around and found Lew," reasoned Stefan. "What puzzles me, though, is why Lew was still up here in the woods when he had told Sophia he planned to attend the party."

"That may have been my fault," admitted Józef. "He may have seen Vladek's tracks. So many strange circumstances happened around here in the past year that I told Lew if he ever saw any tracks in the woods to check them out. Right before Jan was killed, Lew reported seeing tracks of a man down by the creek. We checked it, and we did have the sheriff investigate. Later, Sophia insisted that she had seen someone cause Jan's death."

He looked toward Stefan in the dim light. "I had this investigated too, but there was no evidence of anyone being at fault. Sophia suffered not only the loss of her brother, but she also had to endure the skeptical glances of those around her. Even her mother was unkind." His words were heavy with the apology. "Then, on top of all that, I've learned that Maurice has been terrorizing her since she was a child. Honestly, Stefan, I didn't know that. I guess she was too ashamed to confide in me. I failed her."

Stefan was so angry that he didn't trust his voice. Sweet, scared Sophia, who had stiffened when he stood too near and had jumped if he touched her. In the darkness, he clenched his fists. He wanted to hold her; make her feel safe. But he remembered a spark of her awakening, and he knew they had a future.

Jacobson's voice finally broke the silence. "You know, I've been thinking. I wouldn't be surprised if Vladek is at Forest House right now. He has no way of knowing the theft of the crucifix has been discovered. He had already come here and was back near Forest House before we left. He could have used the shortcut through the woods at that time. He didn't want to show his face because he wanted everyone to think he was asleep. He probably doesn't even know that we aren't in our beds at Forest House. With Maurice's horse missing, he may have a route of escape planned."

"That's right!" Józef exclaimed. "Forest House is so full of guests who were forced to spend the night that I suspect no one is sure of who is there."

"If we can get back before it's completely light, we should be able to keep him from knowing we haven't been there all the time. Everyone will sleep late after enjoying themselves at the party." Stefan was glad that all who had gathered in the library before they left had agreed to keep their leaving a secret.

"Yes, that's the only reasonable thing. In this blizzard there is nowhere else for him to go. He's trapped in Forest House, but he feels safe in his priest's robe. We three, Sophia, and Ludlow are the only ones who know of the crucifix, so he won't be alerted. Our guests are safe as long as he isn't suspicious."

It was still dark when Jacobson drove the half-track out of the shed. Lew was feverish, but Stefan managed to get some of the hot broth into him before they ventured back out into the cold. The others quickly gulped the reheated coffee from the night before and grabbed the small amount of gear from the shack. The saddles had been thrown into the back with the body of the man. The horses were tied to the back of the vehicle.

Stephan was lost in his own thoughts as they rumbled back toward Forest House. It took about an hour. Jacobson parked the vehicle behind the stable, out of sight. He stabled and fed the horses.

The dead man would stay in the back of the half-track for the time being.

"There's not a light in the kitchen, so that means that Manka isn't even up. We made it back in time," Józef said.

"What about Lew?" asked Stefan.

"There's a daybed in my room. We will take him there and have Dr. Janda look at him as soon as he is awake. He can be trusted."

The snow that continued to fall hid the men from view of the windows as they approached the house. Stefan carried Lew into a back entrance that led directly into Józef's suite of rooms.

Józef unlocked the outside entrance to his bedroom door with a key on a ring in his pocket and stepped back to let Stefan enter with the injured man.

Stefan gently laid Lew on the daybed and looked around the room. A pang of sympathy stirred. He felt a loneliness for family and homeland here that Józef had kept separate from the rest of the house. His mourning was not for public display. He had made a choice many years ago. It was like the death of a terminally ill beloved son. It was better this way, but one could not help wishing things could have been different.

A bright red shield with a magnificent white eagle had been Poland's national emblem since the early 1200s. A copy of such a shield held a place of honor over the head of Józef's bed. A huge canvas held memories of Domani z Camin in muted oils. The view in the painting looked toward the castle, past the round tower and through the gate. One wing of the house gleamed pink with the setting sun. The courtyard showed servants working and children at play. Also visible were other buildings serving the castle household. It was summer in the painting and masses of bright flowers added warmth to the gray stone walls.

Another picture was of a woman. She was young, and her hair was the color of honey. She wore a polonaise—an elaborate blue overdress with short sleeves, a fitted waist, and a blue draped cutaway overskirt. There was a look of daring in her blue-gray eyes. Stefan knew, instinctively, that this was Cecylia Zurowski, his grandmother and Józef's mother—a woman who loved her second son so much that she made certain he got what had rightfully belonged to her firstborn. She had stolen the jeweled crucifix for him and had maneuvered her own father into bestowing money on him that also should have gone to the rightful heir of Domani z Camin.

Stefan could not condone what this woman—his own grandmother— had done, but he was overwhelmed by the love she had shown Józef. In biblical times, another mother had once deceived her own husband to place her favorite son, Jacob, in a position to receive his older brother, Esau's, birthright.

There had been no mother's love for Stefan at all.

He stood by the door, watching Józef talk to Lew. A few minutes later, he and Józef went out together. It was going to be a hard day, but they must act natural so that no one would suspect that they had spent the night anywhere other than Forest House.

CHAPTER FIFTEEN

A strange feeling settled over Sophia as she opened her eyes. She felt sluggish and tired; then she remembered the terrifying questions that had piled on them at the end of the gala evening. The few people in the library had seemed an island far removed from the merrymaking of the rest of the house.

She got out of bed and padded barefoot across the soft carpet to the window. She pulled back one side of the heavy blue drape to look toward the stable and beyond, to where the trail began. Snow fell only lightly now. The sky likely would be clear by late this afternoon. Sighing, she let the curtain drop back into place.

What a night it had been. After leaving her grandmother's room, she had shown their maids the extra beds to make up for the many guests; it seemed to have taken hours. The Jandas were in Stefan's room. She had assured them, when they protested, that they weren't putting him out at all. Stanislas was bunking with Vincent Ludlow. She could tell that the suggestion hadn't appealed to either one of them, but even Forest House found it hard to sleep so many extra people.

She yawned deeply and rubbed the back of her neck to massage her tired muscles. The emotional upheaval had taken its toll.

In the morning light, the declaration she had made to Stefan seemed unreal. It was just a fantasy acted out in the romantic setting of their dimly lit sitting room. The actors in regal costume, as reflected in the mirror, didn't seem real in the morning's light.

She hurriedly bathed and dressed in the most cheerful thing she owned—a long-skirted dress of red and white that was gathered at her small waist with a wide, soft leather belt. She used a matching red scarf to hold back her red-gold curls and slipped her slim feet into soft red-leather slippers.

Manka had help from the kitchen staff and the maids, but with so many to fix breakfast for, someone was needed to direct traffic. Monica wouldn't be up until afternoon, and Marie would sleep late too. Sophia knew it was up to her.

As she went through the house toward the dining room, she felt repulsed by the flower arrangements in every room. They had added to last night's celebration, but now they reminded Sophia of a funeral.

The large dining hall had been completely cleared of the evidence of last night's party, and a red and green Christmas centerpiece was in the middle of the snowy white tablecloth. Tall red tapers stood in silver candleholders on either side of the holiday bouquet. The food stood covered and ready on the sideboards for the guests, whenever they wanted to help themselves. Sophia spoke to a couple of early risers who were tackling the blueberry muffins and hot tea.

Her destination was the breakfast room, and as she neared it, she heard voices. She quickened her step, anxious to ask of Lew, but she stopped as she reached the door.

Józef and Marie sat at either end of the small table, and Father Polzak and Father Vladek sat on one side. The chair beside Stefan on the other side was vacant.

"Good morning, darling." Marie smiled at her daughter.

Sophia couldn't help the surprise that registered on her face. "You're up early, Mother."

"Yes, dear, I couldn't sleep for worrying about Maurice."

"No one knows yet where he went?" she asked.

Stefan had risen from his chair and come toward her. She noticed dark smudges beneath his gray eyes.

"Good morning, sleepyhead." He kissed her casually. "You were resting so peacefully when I came down that I didn't have the heart to wake you." His eyes were on hers as he spoke, willing her to agree with him. He seated her at the place beside him.

Father Vladek gave a quick glance at Sophia's face and then went back to his breakfast coffee.

Manka hadn't served them any food. It was Christmas Eve, and the family fasted and kept vigil until the first evening star signaled the time for the Polish wiligia supper. For the past month, the family had observed certain fast days in preparation for the coming of Christmas Day. Breakfast was prepared that day only for the benefit of the overnight guests.

"You say the lad was upset over a family matter and ran off without telling anyone?" Vladek asked.

"I know that he's too old for such a trick," Józef said, "but we have spoiled him, I'm afraid."

"Darling, you've been good to him." Marie's tone was serious.

Sophia couldn't account for her mother's change of attitude. She knew that Marie hadn't been told of Maurice's sickness and that she had assumed that he had unaccountably become sullen, as Monica so readily did. Sophia guessed that Marie thought it her duty to be concerned over her nephew.

"How are the roads this morning?" Sophia asked as she turned to Stefan.

His eyes on hers were filled with warm expression. So, everything had not been a dream.

"Jacobson put the scoop on a tractor this morning, and he and the sheriff are clearing the road to the highway," Stefan answered.

"That is good," said Father Vladek.

"What's the hurry, Father? Don't you like our hospitality?" Marie teased.

It was Father Polzak who answered. "Mrs. Zurowski, we must get to the church. We must prepare for midnight Mass. You have not forgotten, have you?" The old priest's face beamed with pleasure.

"Oh, no, Father Polzak, no one could forget," Marie hastily assured him.

"Did you say that the sheriff is helping Jacobson?" Vladek asked. "Could they use any other assistance?"

"Thank you, Father, but the tractor is doing all the work. Jacobson is pointing out the edges of the road while the sheriff drives," Józef said.

Ludlow came into the room. He had finished his breakfast in the large dining hall, but he did accept another cup of coffee. "I stepped out on the terrace, and it looks as if the road-clearing operation is progressing very fast. The snow has stopped." He settled in a chair beside Sophia. A coolness clung to him from being outside; the white streaks in his hair could have been ribbons of frozen snow.

"It has stopped snowing, then?" Vladek asked.

Ludlow nodded. "Yes. But I heard on the radio that this was the worst blizzard in this part of Minnesota in the past ten years. The snow removal crews are working on the main highways now, but they won't be passable until late this afternoon."

"I think I'll take a walk down to where the men are working with the tractor." Vladek said. He set his cup gently into its delicate saucer and stood up.

"That's a good idea," Stefan said, rising from his chair. "I could use a walk too." The two men donned their heavy coats and went outside.

Józef smiled reassuringly at his stepdaughter. "Sophia, as soon as Dr. Janda comes down, will you let me know?" He and Ludlow stood to leave the room. "We'll be in the library. Excuse us, Father Polzak. Marie."

As Józef left the room, he heard Father Polzak asking Sophia how she and her new husband were getting along. Marie must have sensed Sophia's hesitation, and she began warmly praising Stefan to Father Polzak. He couldn't account for the change he'd sensed in Marie, but it was a welcome one.

Vincent Ludlow wasted no time on preamble as he sat down across from Józef, who sat behind his heavy oak desk. Józef was wide awake and alert, but he felt tense.

"I had a call from my friend, Jim Brady, early this morning. He got into our airport a few hours after I called him yesterday, and he's been with the CIA agents in Dark Forest ever since."

"I didn't know we had such agents in Dark Forest," Józef stated simply. He was beyond surprise, however; nothing could ever surprise him again.

"Józef, you underestimate your importance to this country, especially so with the war beginning to escalate. The man with vast resources of raw materials, steel mills, shipping ..." Ludlow stood up as though to defend his case.

Józef stopped his speech with a wave of his hand. None of that mattered to him now. "All right, so we have agents in Dark Forest."

Ludlow looked a little sheepish at his own outburst. "Yes, Jim is with the agents and your lawyers in town."

"Why the lawyers?" asked Józef.

"They have files, pictures on each of your family members. There is always a possibility of one of them being involved. The agents—"

"What are the plans for stopping Vladek," Józef interrupted, "if he is, indeed, the German agent?" Józef was impatient for proof. The long night had taken its toll, and he was worried about Lew, Maurice, and the crucifix.

"Vladek is the man. The agents were able to establish his identity by taking fingerprints at the church. The only clear copy of fingerprints there belonged to Father Polzak and an enemy agent they identified as Bruno

Krump. They also had a photograph that your lawyers recognized. There's no doubt." Ludlow clapped his hands together softly as if closing his case.

"Skip the details and get to the essentials," Józef said tersely. "When will he be picked up? And what about the Zurowski jeweled crucifix?"

"They'll be waiting for him where Forest House's drive meets the main highway. The agents will be disguised as part of the snow removal crew. He'll be taken away, and the story that'll be given to everyone is that Father Vladek left because he had an opportunity to serve the church with work among the refugee camps in Europe. No one will question that. The sheriff will take the body of the man you found in the cabin. His body will be buried by the county as a vagrant."

"And what about the crucifix?" Józef pressed.

"If the agents find it on Krump, it'll be returned to Stefan, and no mention of it will ever be put into any files," Ludlow answered. "Józef, the agents will be glad not to mention the family treasure; it would make their job even harder if it were known that such a fabulous object was at Forest House. It would be an open invitation."

"I hope they can take Krump without anyone else being hurt or killed." Józef thought of the body in the back of the half-track and of Lew lying feverish from an attempt on his life.

"The men are professionals," Ludlow assured him.

"So is Krump," Józef said pointedly. "So is Krump."

When Stefan and Vladek returned from their walk, Father Polzak insisted—much to Vladek's dismay—that they should wait until all the other people were gone before they left. The old priest said he felt a responsibility for the safety of the members of his parish.

Polzak thought again that Father Vladek didn't seem particularly cut out to be a shepherd of a flock; perhaps he would do better teaching in a school. There was a restlessness in the younger man and a suppressed impatience that Father Polzak glimpsed beneath the calm exterior he presented to those around him. *It's more than calm*, the old priest thought. *It's cold, unbending.*

As close friends, the Jandas were staying on at Forest House for the wigilia feast. It was also an excuse that allowed Dr. Janda to tend to Lew.

Józef and Stefan both insisted that no one else outside the family should be put in danger, so Stefan would drive the priests to the church in the Jeep. The only plausible excuse that could be given was that roads still were dangerous.

The scoop had scraped and piled the snow high on each side of the road, but the surface it left was solidly packed. The Jeep skidded sharply to the right into a snowbank before the deep-grooved tires caught hold, and Stefan was able to center the Jeep between the banks of snow.

There were no cars in sight as they neared the turn-off at the main highway. Only one lane had been cleared. A bright-yellow snow plow had stopped alongside the road. Behind it sat a truck with the highway department's insignia painted on its door. The highway crew stood beside the vehicles. The crew waved their hands.

"Those boys don't have an easy job today," Father Polzak sympathized.

"And it's Christmas Eve too," Józef said.

No one else commented.

Stefan kept driving steadily toward the stone gates.

"It seems an odd place for them to rest," Vladek said.

"It's as good a place as any," Stefan said easily.

They were nearing the turn-off, and apparently Vladek's inner alarm sounded. No evidence was in sight, but he may have had a gut feeling or seen an incongruous expression on the face of one of the snow removal crew. Like an animal, he suddenly was aware of a trap.

"Oh, no, you don't!" yelled Vladek. With one hand resting on the side of the Jeep, he vaulted over the side and ran for the safety of the woods, some one hundred yards from the road.

Stefan quickly stopped the Jeep and turned off the motor. The agents had started running toward them, but they wouldn't be able to reach the fleeing German spy in time. Stefan knew that Vladek had roamed the woods during his short stay in Dark Forest, and no doubt he had a getaway route planned. Vladek had used Maurice's horse to return to Forest House, but he hadn't put it back into the barn when he returned. So, he'd made emergency escape plans.

"You won't get away, Krump!" Stefan shouted after the man. He was out of the Jeep, running after the enemy agent.

Krump was an excellent specimen of a man and was in top condition, but neither man could run fast because of the deep snow; some of the drifts were waist-high. Still, Stefan might not have been able to catch him if not for the long robe Krump wore as his priest's disguise. The robe caught around Krump's boot, and he went down in a drift. Stefan was upon him, his knee thrust hard into the man's stomach, before Krump could raise his gun. Krump's upper body doubled forward with a groan, and Stefan pushed Krump's right hand, which was gripping the gun, deep into the snow. Making a hard-gloved fist, Stefan hit Krump with a solid right, square to his left jaw. Krump eased back into the snow, his eyes closed, awake to nothing going on around him.

Quickly, Stefan searched the unconscious man and found what he was looking for. The crucifix and jewelry were together in a leather pouch attached beneath the man's flowing cloak. He could hear the agents from the truck nearly upon them and without turning, he shoved the leather pouch inside his shirt. He felt the bag slide down and rest safely where his shirt was tucked into his pants, held by a strong wide belt. His woolen jacket was loose, so no one would notice any extra thickness at his waist.

The agents carried the unconscious man to their borrowed truck and started for town. As Stefan got back into the Jeep, he looked back toward the spot where he had caught up with Krump. The long chase had made a straight mark through the smooth blanket of snow. The area where they had fought and the agents had trampled made the rest of the design; the sign of the cross was clearly cut into the virgin whiteness of the covered ground.

Józef was silent for the rest of the ride into town. Even when they stopped at the church and let out the shaken Father Polzak, Józef said nothing.

"A German spy," Polzak said again in disbelief. "How horrible. I'm just glad he wasn't a real priest. He was such a cold man, so unsympathetic."

"Father Polzak, the Nazis are all cold and unsympathetic," Stefan said gently. He could tell that the old man was truly in shock.

"I'm glad that no one is to know that the man was an impostor, though. Such a disgrace to put on a holy robe and deceive the people. But I should've known!"

"Father Polzak, no one will know. And don't blame yourself. This man was well trained. Besides, he is evil," Stefan consoled the priest.

"But don't you see, my son?" The priest shook his head sadly. "I felt this evil and didn't cry out against it. A man of God should recognize evil in every form. It is our calling!"

"Don't blame yourself, Father Polzak," Józef said, echoing Stefan's words. "This man was here only a short time. I've no doubt that you would have exposed him, given a little more time."

"Yes! Yes," he agreed. "You are right, of course. I would've cried out against him as soon as I was sure!" Stefan thought the old priest straightened at this declaration. "I'll see you tonight." He turned and walked up the path into the wide carved doors of his church.

Stefan didn't want to speculate on Father Polzak's fate if he'd confronted the phony priest about his attitude.

They were wanted in town to help fill out some final papers on the German's identity and known contacts in the area. As they drove into Dark Forest to meet the agents, Stefan briefly told Józef about taking the jeweled crucifix from the unconscious man.

The meeting would take place in the county highway department office. The cover would be maintained, although the weather conditions and the holiday would ensure that few people would be out. Certainly, a highway crew would not be an unusual part of the scenery.

Józef agreed with Stefan that it was best not to mention the finding of the crucifix. The man was wanted for murder, not theft, and the agents were going to leave out any mention of the jeweled crucifix from their reports anyway. And the objet d'art and jewels did belong to Stefan Zurowski.

The man Vladek/Krump was conscious and sitting in a chair when Stefan and Józef got to the office of the highway department. His eyes, like splinters of ice, directed hatred at Stefan.

Stefan's mouth twisted in a cruel smile of acknowledgment.

"What about undoing my hands and letting me smoke," Krump said to the agents. It was a request, but the coldness of his voice made it a command.

"I think we all feel safe enough to do that," sneered the closest man.

"Just for five minutes," ordered Jim Brady, the man in charge. Jim was an ordinary-looking man. His face could be seen in a crowd and never again recalled. Of medium height, his shoulders were narrow, and his manner deceptively mild. His baby-blue eyes looked innocently back at the world from his round, pleasant face.

Krump rubbed his wrists carefully and then reached his hand to the inside of his coat and brought out a package of cigarettes. The package was unopened. Slowly, he pulled the thin gold band from around the package and pulled out a smooth white cigarette.

Stefan watched the man, and something tugged at his memory. He couldn't bring it to the surface.

Krump held the cigarette lengthwise between the fingers of both hands and rubbed the smoothness of the cigarette paper. In one quick movement, the man broke the small cylinder with a snap, and Stefan saw a small white capsule disappear into the man's mouth.

Vladek doesn't smoke! That's what had been trying to surface in Stefan's mind. He jumped at Krump, and they both went backward in the chair.

Stefan tried to pry the man's mouth open, but Vladek/Krump had clamped his mouth tight.

Instantly, the agents took over, but it was too late. Krump's teeth had broken into the capsule, and the poison was already beginning to take effect.

Krump lay still, a triumphant grin twisting his thin lips. A look of surprise and pain ravaged his face, and then his eyes stared sightlessly at the ceiling.

"We should've expected this," Józef stormed vehemently. "Hitler orders suicide rather than capture. Don't you remember the scuttling of the *Graf Spee*?" He looked angrily at the faces around him.

"Well, this simplifies my work," Brady said. "I can take the next flight out and still be home for Christmas."

Agents already had been assigned in Dark Forest to keep watch over Józef Zurowski, so no new orders or men were needed. Officially, there was no jeweled crucifix in existence, so it stood to reason that it could not be reported missing.

Stefan and Józef walked back to the Jeep and headed home.

CHAPTER SIXTEEN

―――――――――――❦―――――――――――

Sophia listened to Lois hum happily to herself as she worked. All the house staff—Manka, Lois, Helka, and Antek—quickly got the household running smoothly again after the ball, with everything in its proper place. The extra rooms had been cleaned, and the freshly laundered linen was folded and put into the large scented closet.

Marie insisted that Lois and Helka each take a flower arrangement as Jacobson prepared to take them home. They were spending the holidays with their families in Dark Forest. To Manka and Antek, Forest House was home. And Jacobson had been at Forest House as long as Józef.

Lois helped Julie into her warm, woolly coat as the little girl danced with excitement. There would be a Christmas tree at her grandmother's house in Dark Forest. The tree would sit grandly on a table, and there would be presents.

Sophia smiled as she watched the little girl.

"Merry Christmas, Julie." Sophia hugged her quickly and handed her a beautifully wrapped package.

"Oh, thank you!" Julie's round eyes were shining. "May I open it?"

Sophia laughed. "Wait until tonight after your supper."

Jacobson closed the door behind him as he went outside, shutting out the sound of the little girl's laughter. Sophia thought the house seemed so empty. Stanislas and Monica had volunteered to cut the Christmas tree that would be decorated tonight, and Stefan and Józef weren't back from town.

Any house would seem lonely to her, she admitted to herself, if Stefan wasn't in it. There was a ragged catch in the deep breath she took. *Dear God, keep him safe.*

Lew was going to be fine. They had told everyone that it had been an accident. He had hit his head on a low branch, fallen off Nellie, and cut his shoulder badly on a jagged rock. He would be kept in bed for a couple weeks. No one had reason to question it. Dr. Janda was the only one who had to be told the truth. He was an old man, and as a doctor, he would probably die with a great many more secrets than this one.

Sophia hunted for things to do to keep her mind off Stefan and Józef taking Vladek to the authorities. She had tried to help Manka in the kitchen, but she was not welcome. Manka had prepared for the wigilia supper days in advance. She had made all the traditional foods, beverages, and decorations, or others had made them under her close supervision. The dance had required extra preparation, and she had several last-minute things to do. No, she had nothing that Sophia could help her with.

Mrs. Milewski always set the table for the wigilia supper, and Sophia and Monica had always helped her. Sophia headed for the dining hall. She heard Mrs. Janda's shy voice offering to help just as she reached the door. She sat down and watched.

A thin layer of hay was put on top of the long, polished dining table, and then a white tablecloth carefully was laid on top. Wigilia is the traditional vigil supper. The feast commemorating the birth of the God child, and she knew the thin layer of hay was to help remember that the Holy Child was born in a manger. Small sheaves of grain, tied up with colored ribbons, were placed in the corners of the room. As Mrs. Milewski put each sheaf into its corner, she knelt briefly, crossed herself, and said a silent prayer for a good harvest in the next season.

Sophia went to the linen closet and brought out a stack of snowy white napkins with a silver Z embroidered in the corner. The silver napkin rings were initialed as well. Mrs. Milewski and Mrs. Janda reverently handled the silver and china that would be used at the wigilia supper. The crystal goblets were brought from the glass front cabinet; each was etched with the letter Z.

A small delicately carved manger scene was added to the centerpiece. Mary and Joseph looked over the baby Jesus, and the shepherds stood at one side with two little lambs. The three wise men knelt at the other side, offering gifts; one wise man laid down his crown. A star stood directly over where the child lay, by means of a small stiff wire connected to the roof of the stable.

Sophia knew that Józef had made this Nativity scene himself many years ago because there had been one like it at Domani z Camin.

"The table looks beautiful," Marie exclaimed as she came into the room. She walked around, fingering things as though to add the finishing touches. "Mrs. Janda, your husband asked to be near his patient, so I had your things moved to a guest room on this floor. You may want to rest before dinner," she explained.

"Oh, yes, thank you very much. I would like to rest." She turned to Mrs. Milewski. "Thank you so much for allowing me to help with the table." Her shy smile was warm as she quoted from the book of Luke: "And she brought forth her firstborn son, and wrapped him in swaddling clothes, and laid him in a manger; because there was no room for them in the inn."

"It's good to have someone to talk to who really remembers how it used to be in the old country," Mrs. Milewski said fondly.

"I'll show you the room, Mrs. Janda," Marie said kindly.

Sophia watched her mother's back as she led the way to the guest room. Maybe it was her worry over Maurice or just the mellowing that came with the Christmas holidays, but Marie definitely was a little more considerate. She had always been a gracious hostess, but her heart wasn't always in it.

"The men should be getting back soon, shouldn't they?" Mrs. Milewski asked, surveying the table. She wiped her hands, palms down, on her lace apron. "They only went to the church."

"You know how it is in winter, Grandmother. They may have had to stop and help someone out of a ditch." Sophia laughed nervously. The excuse was close enough to a lie as to make her uncomfortable. "I'm sure they'll be back soon. They know that the evening star is the dinner bell on Christmas Eve!"

Mrs. Milewski laughed. "You sound almost like a child, Sophia. Oh, it will be good when there are children again at Forest House at Christmastime!" The old woman hummed to herself as she put away the extra silver.

"I guess that I'll get ready for supper and watch for our evening star." Sophia hugged her grandmother lightly. She left the dining hall and started for her room. Restlessness was pressing in upon her.

As she started up the spiral staircase, she looked at the antique Ives wagon spring clock on a massive wall shelf. It had been a favorite of hers since she first came to Forest House as a child. Now only the lateness of the afternoon registered as she looked at the clock.

Somewhere in the back of the house, she heard laughter. It was Monica and Stanislas, returning with the tree. She ran quickly up the stairs. Stefan would return; nothing short of a national emergency would keep Józef from

Christmas Eve at Forest House with his family. She pushed the worry from her mind. It was all routine for the CIA agents; nothing would go wrong.

After bathing she put on the dress that she had ordered Wanda to make especially for tonight. It was of holly-green velvet with wide turned-back cuffs of white satin. The white satin was recalled again in trim that edged the modestly scooped neckline. She brushed her red-gold curls until they shone. Her only jewelry was the Zurowski wedding ring.

She went to the piano and gathered the sheets of music that would be needed for the carol singing after supper. Leaving a light burning in their sitting room, she closed the door behind her and started downstairs. As she reached the foot of the stairs, the front door opened and Stefan and Józef came in. She hadn't heard their Jeep arrive.

"You look beautiful, my dear." Józef smiled as he looked at her. Stefan stood behind Józef. His eyes underscored the words that Józef uttered.

Sophia laid a hand on her stomach as she felt an unaccustomed flutter.

"Has there been any news of Maurice?" Józef asked. A frown creased his forehead as he drew his brows together.

"No, Father, nothing. Mother again called the highway patrol a few minutes ago, and they said that they were just now getting enough help from other counties to clear the main roads leading into Dark Forest. We shouldn't expect to hear anything before tomorrow." Sophia hadn't moved from the stairs.

"What they mean is that he was probably long gone before they even put out the all-points bulletin for him." Józef rubbed the creases in his forehead wearily. "Well, he'll be picked up soon. I guess there's no great hurry. But he won't be home for the wigilia supper."

Sophia looked at her stepfather sadly. She wished that she could feel sorrow over Maurice's disappearance, but she felt only relief. Maybe it would be best if he were never found. Maybe he could get away and start a new life. No, that wouldn't be the answer. He was unbalanced; he couldn't be helped by just running away.

"It's getting a little late, children. I must go to my room and get changed." Józef smiled at them as he walked toward the corridor that led to his rooms in the back wing of the house.

Sophia noticed that the music sheets in her hand were shaking, and she held them against her skirt. Stefan walked to the stairs and stood in front of her.

"You're trembling. Are you cold?" Stefan asked.

"No, Stefan, I was afraid for you. Did the agents get Vladek?"

"Yes. Everything is all right now."

"I'm so glad." She let out the breath she had been holding.

Sophia felt his eyes moving over her. Instinctively, her hand flew to her neck.

"No." Sparks danced in Stefan's eyes. "No," he repeated, more gently this time, as he removed her protecting hand. "I can't get enough of just looking at you." He growled softly, but he smiled at her tenderly. For a few seconds, he buried his face in the soft curve of her neck and then put his lips against her ear.

Then he bounded up the steps, two at a time, toward his room, whistling gaily as he went.

The mirror by the piano in the living room reflected the heightened color in her cheeks. She had expected to see the print of his lips branded into her neck.

When Sophia went downstairs, Mrs. Milewski was standing by the window, watching for the evening star. Antek announced dinner as soon as its light appeared.

Everyone gathered in the dining hall, waiting to break and exchange the oplatek. These thin, unleavened wafers were stamped with the figures of the Christ child, the Virgin Mary, or the holy angels.

Reverently, Józef picked up a wafer. He held it in his big hand and looked at it. "When my mother was alive, she sent me a wafer every year after I left Poland. It was like I was still part of the family and was, perhaps, just visiting a foreign country. I was able to partake of the bread of love like I was there."

Józef led them in exchanging good wishes as they partook of the wafers. Marie rested her hand on her husband's arm and a tear ran down her cheek. Józef patted her hand.

The table had been set for thirteen, but only twelve were to be seated. This extra place was kept in expectation of the coming God child. A candle burned brightly in the window to guide any stranger who might be passing into their midst. This stranger might be the God child in the form of a human man. Józef read this Polish custom to them in the form of a poem from a small leather volume.

"When I was a little girl," Mrs. Janda's said, "we worked the words 'Guest in the home is God in the home' on a small tapestry sampler. The custom of leaving the extra place comes from this ancient Polish adage."

"There was one hanging at Domani z Camin," Stefan remembered.

"Yes," agreed Józef. "My mother told me she had made it when she was a girl."

At this time of year, Manka and Antek ate with the family.

So, with the family, including Manka, Antek, Jacobson, and the Jandas, twelve sat down to supper.

Mrs. Milewski had asked to help Manka and Antek serve the meal. The traditional almond soup began the supper, but fish was the basic ingredient for the eleven-course Christmas Eve dinner. The appetizer was pickled herring served with individual salads, followed by clear barszcs and mushroom uszka. There was pike filet baked with cream and baked sauerkraut and mushrooms. The pike in aspic was nestled beside white mounds of cauliflower with a crumb and butter topping. The fresh, fried salmon came with tender potatoes with tomato sauce.

Darkness came with the night as the dinner progressed. Prune compote preceded poppy seed cake, followed by nut pudding. Pastries, nuts, and candies were brought in with the coffee.

One of Sophia's presents to Stefan was a copy of the *Adventures of Paul Bunyan*, a first edition published by the Heritage Press. She was rewarded by a wide grin of boyish delight.

When she opened his gift to her, she was stunned—pearls. They were the most lustrous, beautifully matched pearls she had ever seen. Everyone exclaimed over their magnificence as Stefan carefully fastened the strand about her neck. His fingers were as light as moth wings on her skin, but they felt like tiny tongues of flame.

Sophia saw the look that passed between Stefan and Józef; she saw Stefan's slight nod. These pearls must have been brought from Poland, so Josef had seen his mother wear them. They seemed even more precious.

She also received an exquisite music box from Monica and a white scarf from Józef and Marie. The scarf was soft white cashmere trimmed with white ermine.

It was time to go to midnight Mass. Jacobson was staying at the house with Lew. Although the old man was improving, someone had to stay with Dr. Janda's patient.

Jacobson had hitched up the horses. Stefan, Sophia, Monica, and Stanislas were going to the church in a bright red sleigh. The Jandas' car would follow, with Józef, Marie, Mrs. Milewski, Manka, and Antek in the Zurowski car.

Sophia changed her green suede slippers for shiny black fur-lined boots. Her full-length mink coat reflected the rich brown of her eyes. She worked her small hands into her black kid gloves and thrust them both deep into her mink muff. With a slight flourish, she draped her new scarf around her head.

She turned to face Stefan. "I'm ready!"

He had been watching her with a smile on his lips. "Did you ever slip out at midnight on Christmas Eve and listen at the stable?" he whispered in a conspiratorial tone.

"Yes." She laughed softly. "Once Jan and I slipped out. We weren't allowed to go to Mass because he had the chicken pox."

"Did you hear the animals talk at midnight on Christmas Eve?" asked Stefan with a twinkle in his gray eyes.

"We promised not to tell." Sophia put her finger across her lips.

"I'm devastated. You're the most innocent of hearts that I've known. I thought surely you would've heard the domestic animals assume human voices on this holy night!" His voice was warm with laughter, but his eyes were serious.

Stanislas and Monica came gaily into the hall, and the young people went out together to the sleigh. Heavy lap rugs were tucked in around them, and the horses trotted easily down the lane toward the turn-off that led to the church. In the distance, the sound of the church bells wafted toward them on the clear night air. The moon and stars bathed the world in light, revealing an animated scene from a Christmas card.

The church was inspiring, with the traditional Nativity scene and the candles burning. The Christmas carols were sung by the congregation with lusty, thankful voices. It was the time of prayer, and Sophia knelt beside Stefan in the dimness of the church.

There was another time that she had knelt in this same church on a special occasion. It was the time of her proxy marriage to Stefan. He was no more than a name then. Vincent Ludlow had stood in Stefan's place, as coldly legal as the forms she had signed.

Now, beside her, Stefan was warm and vital. She reached for his hand in the darkness, and it was there, ready to take hers into his own. She relived the vows in her mind that she had taken. They were one in spirit; she knew that Stefan was in her mind, saying the vows with her.

The large white Paschal candle was lit. Sophia knew that it represented the light of Christ coming into the world to dispel darkness and death.

The music from the organ hit a crescendo and lifted her spirit. There was a gentle pressure on her hand. This was their real marriage; she would count their anniversaries with each passing Christmas Eve.

After the service, Sophia watched Stanislas join his parents. The roads were still risky, and he wanted to drive them home.

Stefan helped Sophia and Monica out of the sleigh in front of the house, and he drove on to the stable to unharness the horses.

"Good night, Monica, and Merry Christmas," Sophia said to her cousin.

"Good night, Sophia. Merry Christmas to you," Monica returned affectionately.

They parted, and Sophia climbed the stairs slowly. She walked through their sitting room and into her bedroom and went to the window facing the stable. She leaned her face against the icy coldness of the window glass. After a while, she saw the stable door open and saw Stefan making his way to the house. The moon bleached his hair silver in its light. She dropped the curtain and clutched her coat around her. She couldn't move.

The door to the sitting room closed softly, and he was behind her. He slipped her coat from her unresisting arms and tossed it onto the floor. She was still facing the window, and his arms went around her, holding her gently to him as he softly kissed her bare neck.

She reacted with a violent trembling and stood erect, away from him. He turned her to look at her face. It was completely colorless in the moonlight; her eyes were black and wide with terror.

She held up a small hand helplessly, as though to ward him off. "I ... can't," she said.

He looked at her. His face was terrible in the eerie light. "I've been patient, Sophia, but I won't force you. A man shouldn't have to force his wife. But don't blow hot and cold with me, or I might not be responsible for my actions." His words were harsh.

She stood silent before him. There was no defense she could offer.

"I thought you realized that your cousin was sick. I thought you had accepted it. Your kisses were an indication of it." His voice was heavy with questioning. "But I once told you that the door between our rooms would be open when you opened it. I'll be good to my word." There was a bitterness in his tone that seemed directed to himself as much as to her. "I'm a Zurowski, and we are honorable."

He walked to the door between their rooms. He walked through and closed it firmly behind him.

Sophia crumpled to the floor; she could no longer find the strength to stand.

It was over. He had shoved her away when she couldn't overcome her fear. She wanted to be his wife so desperately. Would he help her?

No. No, she cried silently. It was something she had to work out herself. She could kill Maurice for the anguish, the fear he had instilled in her.

She knelt by her bedside. *God, help me!*

She slowly pulled herself upright. When her knees would support her, she let loose of the bed and unzipped her dress. She let the green velvet pool around her feet. Deliberately, she stripped off all her clothes before she reached for her nightgown. Then, in a moment of resolve, she wadded the nightgown into a ball and threw it across the room.

She listened. She had heard Stefan getting into bed, but now there was no sound. Maybe he had gone to sleep.

No, there wasn't any backing out. She couldn't stand his anger. Anything was better than that.

Noiselessly, she walked across the floor; she felt the cold air on her bare skin and the brush of the carpet under her feet. All the shivering wasn't due to the cold.

The doorknob felt unyielding beneath her hand. She closed her eyes and turned it. She opened the door and closed it behind her. She heard no sound from the wide bed. No movement.

"Stefan …" She was beside his bed. She stood in the moonlight, and it washed over her white body.

"Stefan?" she called again.

"Are you sure, Sophia?"

"I love you. I'm sure," she managed to say through the chatter of her teeth.

"Regardless …?" asked Stefan, his voice hardening a little.

"Yes." Her lips were stiff as she answered, but she was resigned.

"Oh, Sophia, what did that man do to you!" His voice registered the anguish he felt.

She began to cry. Uncontrollable sobs shook her.

"You're freezing." He sounded angry. He pulled back the cover and drew her into bed. She got in beside him, an obedient child seeking punishment to find the comfort of security. She didn't resist as he drew her into the curve of his own body, her back resting against his chest.

"Please, Sophia, what did Maurice do?" Stefan asked.

"I don't know when it really started. Maurice was always there, half undressed, exposing himself, reaching for me, laughing when I'd run away. It felt wrong. I'd be sick to my stomach, vomiting through my tears. I couldn't tell anyone."

"Oh, Sophia, you weren't to blame," said Stefan.

"I did think it was my fault. I always thought I was somewhere that I shouldn't have been. If I told on Maurice, I would be the one who was wrong. No one would believe me. Someway, he always managed to stay hidden from the others. No one but me ever saw him."

Sophia was drawing comfort from Stefan's arm around her. She knew she could tell him more. "The weekend Jan and I turned eighteen, he went off with some of the guys from town. No one was in the stable, and I was saddling my horse when Maurice attacked me. He was on top of me, pulling at my clothes, mumbling that he'd show me what he could really do. We heard the Jeep drive up to the stable and then Jacobson talking to the dogs. Maurice hit me hard on the side of my face and told me it was my fault. I told everyone that I had fallen from the hayloft."

"It's okay, Sophia. All that is over," said Stefan. He rocked her gently. With the burden of her guilt lifting, she relaxed and fell asleep.

Sometime during the early morning, she turned to Stefan and found him waiting for her. He kissed her face hungrily and then covered her parted lips with his own. She pressed against the hardness of his body, no longer afraid but searching.

Afterward, they lay still, not wanting to move. He finally rolled to one side and propped himself up on his elbow and looked into her face. He kissed her soft, full lips.

Dawn's light came in through the window. "You are so beautiful. I can't believe you are really mine. Oh, Sophia, life is now perfect." His breath was long. He cradled her close in his arms, protecting, rocking her gently, until again she surrendered to him.

CHAPTER SEVENTEEN

C hristmas morning sent bright, experimental rays of light into the bedroom where they lay.

In wonder, Sophia rubbed her hand over the firmness of her breast, down the flatness of her stomach, to the gentle curve of her thigh. It was a wonderful present that Stefan had given her this Christmas—not just relieving her of her fears but giving her a sense of her own worth. He had unlocked her mind, made it free to reach out and touch new thoughts and new experiences.

Her arm was folded beneath her head as she watched the sleeping man at her side. He loved her! She only now knew how much he really did love her. The way he made love to her spoke of how hard it had been for him to consider her wishes. She felt selfish and humbled.

Cautiously, she touched the scar of the bullet injury on his bare shoulder. There was still a dark discoloration around the pucker of the small round wound. She pressed her lips softly on it. She remembered the first time she had seen his face. As now, it was still, his eyes closed. She let her hand stray to his wide chest and touched the small gold saint's medallion on the thin chain around his neck. She stretched her hand, palm down, and laid it lightly on his abdomen; the hard muscles beneath his skin were firm and defined. She looked again at his face. A smile played at the corner of his lips, but his eyes remained closed.

"You're not asleep!" she accused.

He opened his eyes; his smile deepened. "If you'd known I wasn't, I would've missed your early morning examination!"

He grabbed her hand as she started to jerk it back, and he pulled her on top of him. He made love to her with fierce passion, and she, at last, was free to respond.

Christmas Day was a quiet time of being with family or perhaps having friends drop in. It was lunchtime before the family gathered all together. There were potato croquettes, fried golden brown, and served with tender pink slices of ham. The asparagus was seasoned with butter and added a bright color to the meal. The aroma from Manka's whole wheat bread was better than a dinner bell. Sophia found that she was ravenous.

The chocolate torte was one of her favorites; Manka had filled it with sweetened whipped cream and shredded Brazil nuts.

They were served their coffee in the living room, so that they could enjoy the Christmas tree. Sophia sat on the sofa beside Stefan. She was aware of the warmth where his arm touched hers. The contentment was enveloping. If she could have, she might have purred.

Józef smiled at her. "You look radiant today, my dear."

"Thank you, Father. This has been a wonderful holiday season." She hoped she wasn't blushing.

"Yes," he agreed, "if only we would hear something about Maurice."

"Oh, don't bother about Maurice," Monica broke in. "My little brother has done something I've always wanted to do. He has run away from here!"

"Do you really hate us all so much, Monica?" Józef asked sadly.

Quickly, Monica sank before Józef's chair. Her eyes were pools of emerald water. "Oh, no, Uncle Józef. I don't hate you at all." She stood up abruptly and faced the members of her family. "I don't hate any of you." She flung up her hand helplessly. "But there's nothing here for me. If I had known that Maurice was leaving, I might've gone with him."

"But, Monica," Józef said, "what of Stanislas?"

"Stanislas is nothing but a good friend," she answered gently. "He never can be anything else. His heart is here in the town of Dark Forest; his only ambition is to take his father's place."

"Is this so terrible?" Józef asked.

"No, not for him. But I don't want such a life. I'm only alive when I'm in New York or some big city where the pulse of the throngs of people excite me!"

"Monica, I won't pretend to understand," Józef admitted. "But you have a right to your own life. I'll contact Vincent Ludlow when Christmas holidays are over at Candlemas and ask him to help you get settled in New York. I'll give you an allowance and my blessing."

Tears rolled down her face as she joyfully hugged her uncle's neck. "Thank you, Uncle Józef, thank you!"

"My dear, I don't think that I'm doing you a favor. And when you want to come home to Forest House, you are always welcome." He patted her shoulder awkwardly.

"Sir?" Antek stood in the doorway. His inscrutable face was unreadable.

"Yes, Antek, what is it?" Józef asked.

"The telephone, sir. The highway patrol's office calling."

"Maurice!" The urgent whisper came from Mrs. Milewski.

Józef walked quickly from the living room, across the wide entrance foyer, and into the library. He closed the door behind him. Everyone accepted second cups of coffee while they waited nervously for Józef to finish the call.

Mrs. Milewski chose a yellow bon-bon and sat staring at the cheerful confection in her hand.

Józef seemed to have aged as he walked slowly back into the room. Marie crossed the room and slipped her hand through his arm. He patted her hand absently.

"They've found Maurice," he announced.

"Thank goodness." Mrs. Milewski let out a loud sigh of relief.

"He's dead."

"Oh, no!" The color drained from Mrs. Milewski's face, leaving a death mask. Sophia hurried to her grandmother's side and drew her head to her shoulder. The old woman lay very still, whimpering like a wounded animal.

Monica looked stricken. "But what happened?"

"His car had slid off into a ditch. The coroner said he hit his head in the accident, but the cause of death was exposure. He froze to death," he said in disbelief. "There were no signs of a struggle where he might have tried to get out, so he must have died without regaining consciousness."

"Then he was spared the agony of knowing," Marie said.

Józef nodded, thankful, at least, for that.

Monica knelt with her head on a chair and sobbed.

"They want one of us to identify the body." He suddenly looked old, unable for the task.

"Uncle Józef, I will go," volunteered Stefan.

"Thank you, Stefan." The relief on Józef's face was pitiful to see.

"Stefan, I want to go with you." Sophia stood and walked to his side.

"Are you sure?" He didn't touch her.

She nodded.

They drove down the road, away from Forest House toward the highway turn-off that led to Dark Forest. Sophia sat sideways in the seat with her knees pulled up. She was huddled in the seat like a child. When she raised her head toward Stefan, her face was wet.

"I can mourn for Maurice now. I couldn't have yesterday." Tears spilled slowly down her cheeks. "Now that I know love, I can realize the extent of his illness. He was sick, Stefan, very sick."

"Yes, darling, he was." He briefly rested his wide hand against her damp face.

"I love you, Stefan." Her eyes shone through her tears.

"I love you, Sophia Zurowski."

The coroner's office was closed because it was Christmas Day, but a stooped worried-looking man met them at the door with a huge ring of keys in his hand.

He shook hands with Stefan. "I'm Dr. Bascomb. May I offer my sympathy for such a tragedy during these holidays."

Stefan thanked the man, and they followed him down a dimly lit corridor until he stopped before a metal door. He fished for the right key on his ring, unlocked the door with a snap, and pushed it open. The black letters on the door read MORGUE.

Maurice's body was unmarked except for an innocent-looking bruise at his temple. He looked strangely at peace. The procedure was over quickly, and they left the building with the doctor, who locked the doors behind them.

They drove back in silence. Sophia sat very near Stefan, drawing courage from his strength.

"It's best this way," were the only words she said on the trip home.

"Yes, darling, I believe it is," he answered her quietly.

Arrangements were made for the funeral, and Monica went to New York directly after the service. Józef had told her he could see no reason to wait until after Candlemas.

Near the middle of January, Lew was able to go back to his home. He fought against the fuss that had been made over him, but he did allow Sophia and Stefan to take him to his cabin.

They had gone the day before and cleaned it for him. It was fun for them both. Jacobson had concocted one of his special stews, and it was bubbling on Lew's wood stove when they arrived. Lew had protested the extravagance when he saw the bouquet of Shasta daisies that Sophia had bought at the florist for his homecoming.

"If God had wanted us to have flowers in the winter, he would've made them grow outdoors!" he complained, but he eyed them appreciatively. "And I guess you want to be invited to lunch?" He wriggled his nose at the steam escaping from the kettle.

"Of course!" Jacobson helped himself to four bowls and dipped the stew into them. The four sat at the table, talking to each other around the flower arrangement. Lew wouldn't allow Sophia to remove it.

The days passed in peaceful fashion. Stefan spent many hours shut in with Józef, going over ledgers, contracts, and procedures for the vast holdings. Forest House was a haven for Józef; his real business was carried out in various places. Soon, Stefan would see it all firsthand.

As often was the case now, they sat together in the library with their after-dinner coffee. A closeness had developed among those who remained at Forest House after Maurice's death and Monica's leaving. Marie had changed dramatically. She had mellowed; she wanted to love her husband and be a mother to her daughter. They had spent many mornings at the dressmaker's, working on a wardrobe for Sophia—Marie earlier had checked Sophia's wardrobe and pronounced it inadequate. Sophia humored her.

"Darling, you see what this means, don't you?" Stefan turned to Sophia from where he sat across from Józef's desk. He and Józef had been talking about a trip.

"That we get a honeymoon after all?" she teased.

He laughed. "Well, you could call it that."

"Sophia," her stepfather said, "Stefan has learned everything he can from facts and figures. Now he has to travel to the mines, the mills, the shipyards, and the other lumber camps. He must meet the supervisors, the managers, and see for himself what is going on."

Józef pulled a map from his desk. Sophia came over to the desk and sat on Stefan's knee, slipping her arm around his neck.

"First, you go to South America to look into the possibility of reopening an abandoned copper mine next to our active one." He took another sheet from his desk drawer marked ITINERARY. "Then you can work your way back to the States. Of course, most of our holdings are in the North and Midwest."

Their plans were made and the luggage packed, and they left Dark Forest at the end of February. Sophia was dressed in a smart gray suit accented with red, her mink draped casually across her arm. She had matured and ripened into a beautiful woman—assured, poised. She was ready to meet more of the world if Stefan were beside her. She reached for his hand; it was there, open, to receive her small gloved one.

It was summer in South America. Days, Stefan spent at the copper mine with the workers and managers; nights were for themselves.

Occasionally, they took a day off to wade barefoot along the beaches and to make love on the warm sand. Stefan became bronzed, and his fair hair bleached lighter by the sun.

The sight of him made an ache in Sophia's throat and tears in her eyes. She loved him desperately, and never so much as when his suntanned body covered her own.

He told her the story of the runaway priest from the Knights of the Teutonic Order and the jeweled crucifix. She held him close as he talked of his youth—shunned by a father who had hated him as a child and who had betrayed him as a man.

"Sophia," he murmured against her skin, "finding your love was truly like coming home."

Sophia's heart swelled with joy and protecting love. He needed her too.

The months were wonderful—sheer heaven—but neither of them was sorry when the time neared to return to Forest House.

It was April, and Sophia heard the same explosion of spring in the North Woods that called the birds back from as far away as the Gulf of Mexico and the West Indies. But her desire to return was triggered by looking at the calendar rather than instinct.

In a deciduous forest, the trees greened slowly under the gradual warming of the spring sun. The North Woods was different. It was a sudden happening.

She could remember the waters suddenly being let loose from their icy prison and bubbling happily to wake up the rest of the land. Trees and bushes instantly flushed green in answer to this signal. Spring winds rippled the lakes with silver flashes, causing spills and overflows to urge the streams to race faster. Spring swooped down on the land, accompanied by millions of beautiful birds, diving and settling into the marshes. One morning, a bugle was blown, and spring awakened.

Sophia wanted to walk through the woods and seek out the flowers: the blue lupine, purple fireweed, and colorful yellow poppies, contrasting with the dark, rich soil. The heath bushes boasted thousands of tiny red-and-white bells.

Moose would thrust their muzzles into the mirrored surfaces of the ponds to drink deeply before going to the marshes to browse the tender leaves of the aspen tree. The beavers would go after the aspen too, but they would fell them for construction of new dams. The she-bears would lead their clumsy cubs out to begin lessons.

Sophia smiled to herself as she remembered seeing a cub slap haphazardly at trout. These scenes came to her as she gazed at the calendar. No, Stefan must not miss this.

They arrived at the airport a day earlier than expected and hired a cab to take them to Forest House. They wanted to surprise Józef.

As they drove up the road to the house, they saw Lew riding Nellie on the trail along the woods. They waved from the window.

It was good to be home. The welcome was warm, though a little overwhelming. Marie had changed even more. The lines in her face were softened; there was a look of contentment in her eyes.

Sophia sat by her bedroom window, looking out. Stefan had changed clothes quickly and had gone out to the fields to talk to the men who were plowing. He stood by the edge of the newly plowed field. His hands hung loosely at his side as he studied the turned acres. She could see the contrast of the rolled-up white shirtsleeves against the brown of his arms from her window. She watched as he stooped down and picked up some of the soil and rubbed it lightly together in his hand. Then he turned his hand over and let it fall back to the earth.

Sophia remembered when Stefan had quoted the first two verses of Psalm 19 to her during their travels: "The heavens declare the glory of God; and the firmament sheweth his handywork. Day unto day uttereth speech, and night unto night sheweth knowledge." She repeated these words aloud.

The child within her body—hers and Stefan's—fluttered with the first sign of life. Another Zurowski responding to the call of the land. She lay her hand lovingly over her abdomen and smiled.

The evening passed quickly, and now just the family sat around the table: Józef, Marie, her grandmother, and she and Stefan.

Stefan glanced at Sophia, and she nodded in encouragement. He cleared his throat, preparing to make his announcement, and he smiled at Sophia. "Around the time of the next harvest, Sophia will give birth to the first of the next generation of Zurowskis."

"Oh, Sophia, Stefan. How wonderful! Marie, we must have an announcement party!" said Józef. Sophia saw a tear slide down his face. "We'll have to bring the carpenters back to build a nursery!"

Sophia and Stefan received congratulations from the rest of the family gathered there. Stefan held Sophia's hand.

"Also, we've decided not to keep the jeweled crucifix. We have all the good fortune that we need right here," he said. Sophia felt his hand tighten around hers. "Now, more than ever, Poland will need compensation for the devastation perpetrated by the descendants of the ancestors of the Order of the Teutonic Knights."

Sophia knew that Stefan felt in his heart that the blessings and good fortune believed to be embodied in the jeweled crucifix should be endowed to his wounded homeland. In the future, he would return to his homeland and rebuild his ancestral inheritance. But this was, for now, his home.

EPILOGUE

S ophia lay on her bed, watching her two-year-old son sleep—the next generation of Zurowskis and the pride of his father and his grandfather. His red-gold curls and gray eyes, so like his father's, and his bubbling personality had captured the entire household.

"Are you resting?" asked Stefan as he entered her room.

"Yes, I am, but I feel fine. Konrad finally wore himself out."

"Wore you both out! He's a handful; that's for sure. Just wait until you have the next little one to chase," he said. "You should let the nanny do more for Konrad."

"The doctor said this new baby should be born at festival time," Sophia said.

"Another harvest?" he asked.

"Another blessing," Sophia countered.

ABOUT THE AUTHOR

C. S. Arnold lives on a farm in Tennessee with her husband, a few black cows, a chocolate Lab, a Lhasa-Poo, and several ponds full of fish. She has two sons, a daughter-in-law, and three grandchildren.

She's had several short, short stories published in Christian periodicals. In 2018 she published a children's book, *The Patchwork Princess: The Adventures of Ra-me, the Traveling Troubadour—Book 1.*

In 2019 she published *Blaze the Dragon: The Adventures of Ra-me, the Traveling Troubadour—Book 2, and Mudcat the Pirate, The Adventures of Ra-me, the Traveling Troubadour—Book 3.*

Printed in the United States
By Bookmasters